# TWENTY YEARS, TWENTY BOOKS
## THE ACCLAIM CONTINUES FOR MARCIA MULLER AND HER SHARON McCONE NOVELS

Marcia Muller has been called the Mother of the Modern Female Sleuth. Over two decades ago she introduced Sharon McCone, a female detective who was street-smart, emotionally complex, and a brilliant shamus. Muller broke new ground. Other writers soon followed. . . . But Muller has stayed the front-runner with a heroine who continues to evolve, plots that surprise, and writing that dazzles. As the *San Diego Union* observed, "The years have been good to both the creator and her creation: though widely imitated, they have not been surpassed." Now the first recipient of the Ridley Award and the 1999 recipient of the first *Romantic Times* Lifetime Achievement in Suspense Award, Muller has written twenty Sharon McCone mysteries. Both author and detective are just entering their prime . . .

## PRAISE FOR
## A WALK THROUGH THE FIRE

"Incandescent characters and descriptions of Kauai. . . . Muller is 'must' reading for all mystery fans. Start with this one, then go back and enjoy the others."

—*Cleveland Plain Dealer*

# AND PRAISE FOR MARCIA MULLER AND HER CHARACTER SHARON McCONE

# Sharon McCone Mysteries by Marcia Muller

# MARCIA MULLER

# A WALK THROUGH THE FIRE

**WARNER BOOKS**

A Time Warner Company

WARNER BOOKS EDITION

*Cover design by Diane Luger*
*Cover illustration by Tony Greco*
*Hand lettering by David Gatti*

Warner Books, Inc.
1271 Avenue of the Americas
New York, NY 10020

Visit our Web site at
www.twbookmark.com

 A Time Warner Company

Printed in the United States of America

Originally published in hardcover by The Mysterious Press.
First Paperback Printing: July 2000

10 9 8 7 6 5 4 3 2 1

For Sharon DeLano
with thanks for loaning Sharon McCone her given name
and for thirty-seven years of friendship.

Many thanks to

Susan Nakata, Caroline Spencer, and all the great folks
at the Hawaii State Public Library System,
for their invaluable assistance.

Major Louis L. Souza and Bayard Doane,
Honolulu Police Department, for their insights into
law enforcement in the Islands.

Pamela Beere Briggs and Bill McDonald, for technical
assistance on filmmaking and many enjoyable hours on
location for *Women of Mystery*.

Peggy Bakker and Melissa Ward: this is getting to be a
habit, but you help me more than you know!

Bill: first reader, fixer of convoluted phrases,
and staunchest supporter.

The author apologizes to the people of Kauai for
somewhat altering the landscape of their beautiful island. Any resemblance of the characters in this novel
to actual persons, living or dead, is purely coinci-
dental—and most likely impossible.

# A WALK THROUGH THE FIRE

Forged by fire and cradled by water, the Hawaiian Islands are a study in extreme contrast. A place where opposites attract—and repel.

Impenetrable forest gives way to sun-washed beaches. Flat cane fields back up to rugged cliffs. Breezes play and hurricanes rage. White sand mingles with blood-red dirt. Honolulu, a high-rise metropolis, lies only a short distance from the rural past.

The ancient Hawaiians believed that their gods often walked in human guise, just as their humans often embodied godlike qualities. Standing by the sea on a moon-silvered night, you can share their belief. There's always a sensation that something not quite of this earth watches from a point just out of sight. From there, beneath the swaying branches of the ironwood tree. Or there, beyond the next row of wind-rippled cane. Or there, on the narrow ledge of the towering pali—one of the mountains formed by fire from the earth's core.

The ancients had a saying, "Ahi wela maka'u," meaning "Somewhere between fire love and fire terror," that ambiguous area of the emotions where you are drawn to *either extreme. I understand this saying all too well, because that place has always existed within me. If anything, it has grown since I last visited Hawaii.*

*During my time there I walked through every degree of that fire.*

# APRIL 1

·

San Francisco

## 11:50 A.M.

"I feel like a goddamn fool."

"What?" I hadn't been paying proper attention to what Hy was saying over the phone because I was trying to decipher the hand signals my nephew and computer expert, Mick Savage, was flashing at me from my office door. I waved him off.

"A goddamn fool." Hy Ripinsky's tone was injured; my lover and best friend knew me better than anyone, and had radar for those rare occasions when I didn't listen to him.

"Why?"

"Because I should've known better than to trust Virgil. What kind of name for a contractor is that, anyway—Virgil? The jerk called me at my ranch and asked if I could come over here to the coast so he could dig a hole."

"A hole."

"Yeah, by the foundation of the old house." Hy was currently at the property we jointly owned in Mendocino County, where we were trying to get construction of a house under way and where the unseasonably rainy weather was doing its best to thwart our efforts.

"And?"

Mick reappeared in the doorway, somewhat wild-eyed, his blond hair standing up in stiff points that defied gravity. Again I waved him away.

Hy said, "What d'you think? Virgil never showed. Plus it started storming like a bastard fifteen minutes ago, so now I'm stuck here and I can't find any matches to light a fire."

"Stuck there? Don't tell me you flew."

"Borrowed that Cessna we're thinking of buying."

"*You're* thinking of buying." The Cessna, in my opinion, was a piece of junk.

He ignored the comment. "So now I'm stuck here. No way I'm flying in this storm, and— What the hell did you do with the matches?"

"What did *I* do with them?" I realized I sounded sharp, but it had been an awful morning for me, too.

"McCone, you made the fire last time we were here. Think."

That was true, and I couldn't blame him for being irritated. The stone cottage on the cliff's edge above Bootleggers Cove must be cold, damp, and miserable.

"Did you check the kindling basket?"

"First place I looked."

Mick reappeared, rolling his eyes in alarm.

"What about that blue bowl on the kitchen counter?"

"Nope."

"Well . . ." My nephew was hopping around now, as if he badly needed to pee. "Try the dirty-clothes hamper."

"Why the hell—"

"Because the jeans I was wearing that last time're in there. The matches're probably in their pocket."

"And women think men are strange creatures."

"Just look. I've got to go now." I cradled the receiver and said to Mick, "What, for God's sake?"

"Come on. Hurry!" He turned and rushed from the room. I heaved a sigh, got up, and followed him onto the iron catwalk that fronted McCone Investigations' suite of offices, high above the concrete floor of Pier 24½.

Three of my five staff members stood around the desk in Mick's office when he and I came in, staring at the brand-new computer—something he called a Wintel— that he'd coaxed me into spending a small fortune for. Ted, my slender, bespectacled office manager, fingered his goatee nervously and kept at a distance. Craig Morland, in sweats and running shoes looking nothing at all like a former buttoned-down FBI field agent, had his arms folded across his chest; his expression suggested that he feared the machine might attack him.

Charlotte Keim, on the other hand, was very much on the attack. She advanced aggressively toward the desk, her petite features set in stern lines. "You varmint!" she said to the computer, her Texas accent more pronounced than usual. "When I get through with you, you're gonna be roadkill!"

At that instant a sickening thump came from under the desk. "Hell and damnation!" Rae Kelleher's voice shouted. She backed out of the kneehole, rubbing the crown of her curly red-gold head, a smudge of dirt across her freckled nose.

"I *told* you it was plugged in," Mick said to her.

A cold sense of foreboding washed over me. "What's going on here?"

"Uh . . ." Mick looked down at his shoes.

*"What?"*

"I . . . don't know. I mean, I must've done something wrong."

"Why?"

"Well, you asked me to print out the report on the McPhail case. And I tried to. But it's . . . like gone."

*"Like* gone?"

"It's gone."

There were no hard copies of the report on a major industrial espionage investigation, due to be delivered to the client that afternoon.

"So's everything else," Mick added in a small voice, still hanging his head. It seemed to me that his shoulders were shaking slightly. Well, if he wasn't already crying, I would—in the well-remembered words of my father— give him something to cry about.

"Mick," I said, "you are supposed to be a computer genius. You got suspended from high school for breaking into the board of education's confidential files. You smashed the security code at Bank of America and very nearly got yourself arrested. Last week—against my explicit instructions—you obtained federal information that even Craig couldn't call in markers for. So how in hell could you lose all your files?"

He shrugged.

"I don't believe this!"

"See for yourself." He motioned at the machine.

I went over to the desk, narrowing my eyes against the unholy light, which I—one of the top two or three technophobes in San Francisco—am convinced is evidence that computers are a creation of the devil.

A message was displayed there. White letters on the blue background: "April Fool! I've already ordered the pizzas!"

I blinked. Relief welled up, and I staggered back, laughing and letting Ted catch me. Belatedly I'd remembered my promise that if Mick could trick me this April Fools' Day, I'd treat the entire office to pizza.

## 1:33 P.M.

"Shar," Ted said through the intercom, "Glenna Stanleigh's on line two."

"Calling from Hawaii?" Glenna Stanleigh was a documentary filmmaker who had offices on the ground floor of the pier. For the past two weeks she and her crew had been shooting a film on the island of Kauai.

I depressed the button. "Hey, Glenna. What's happening?"

"Nothing good." Her Australian-accented voice was strained. "Sharon, d'you think you could come over here? As soon as possible?"

"To Kauai? Why?"

"I want to hire you. My backer on this film agrees it would be a good move, so I can pay your usual rate and cover all expenses. And there's plenty of room in this lovely house I've got on loan. You could bring Hy along, make it a vacation of sorts."

I hesitated, thrown off stride by the unexpected request, as well as by Glenna's tone. Even at the worst of times she displayed a sunny disposition that could be off-putting to us curmudgeonly types, but now she sounded miserable.

I said, "You'd better tell me what's wrong."

"Can't. Not now. Somebody might overhear."

"When, then?"

"When you get here. Please, Sharon."

An undercurrent of panic in her voice made me sit up straighter. "Glenna, I can't drop everything and fly over there without knowing why. Besides, I'm not licensed in Hawaii. I'm not sure I could arrange it so I could work there. I could refer you to an agency in Honolulu—"

"No! I need somebody I can trust. It could be . . . well, a life-and-death situation."

"Are you serious?"

"Never more so. I think somebody's trying to kill me—or kill someone else on my crew."

"What! Why d'you think that?"

"Something happened this morning. I really can't go into it now. And there've been other incidents. Please, Sharon, I don't know what I'll do if you won't help me."

I was silent, considering. On the other end of the line I heard Glenna breathing hard, as if she was about to hyperventilate. "Just a minute." I reached for my calendar, paged through it, noting appointments that could be rescheduled and work that could be shifted to staff members. My personal caseload was light this month, and recently Rae had shown that she could handle the day-to-day operations of the agency as well as I could, if not better. Besides, Hy and I had been talking about getting away to someplace warm and sunny.

"Give me a couple of hours," I told Glenna. "I'll see what I can do."

"Ripinsky, it's me. Did you find the matches?"

"Right where you said they'd be."

"Good. Listen, Glenna Stanleigh called. She wants me to fly over to Kauai as soon as possible."

"Oh? Trouble?"

"Big trouble, according to her. She claims somebody's trying to kill her or one of her crew members."

"Claims? You don't believe her?"

"I don't know what to believe. She sounds panicky, wouldn't go into details on the phone. Anyway, I think it's worth checking out. She's got a house on loan, and she suggested you come along, as sort of a vacation."

"Hmmm. Tempting, but you know what'll happen. I'll get sucked into this thing as well, and that'll be the end of the vacation."

"Would that be so bad? We've worked well together in the past."

"That we have. You're not licensed in Hawaii, though."

"Yes, but I've been thinking: Your company has a

Honolulu office. I could probably work under RKI's umbrella."

"Most likely you could. I can set it up. And I might as well go along; I haven't met any of our people in the Islands yet. You want to make the travel arrangements, or should I?"

"I will. How soon can you get down here?"

"Storm's letting up some. I'll fly down later, meet you at your house this evening."

"What about the Cessna?"

"It's on long-term loan."

"Well, don't take any chances with this weather."

"Not to worry, McCone. I've flown reckless in my time, but that was before I had you to come home to."


## 3:42 P.M.

"Hawaii?" Rae said. "When d'you leave?"

"There's a flight at eight-forty tomorrow morning. Hy and I will be on it if you'll agree to take over here."

We were seated in a booth at Miranda's, our favorite waterfront diner, enjoying a midafternoon break. Rain streaked the already salt-grimed windows and turned San Francisco Bay to a gray blur. Inside, the diner was warm and cozy, redolent of freshly brewed coffee and fried food.

Rae didn't reply. Instead she stared at the window, a frown creasing her forehead.

I added, "I'm sure this trip won't last long enough to interfere with your wedding plans." Rae and my former brother-in-law, country music star Ricky Savage, were to be married in May.

"Better not, since you're to be my best person." The frown deepened.

I began to feel uneasy. Ricky's marriage to my sister Charlene had hardly been one to instill confidence in his regard for the sanctity of that institution, and ever since he and Rae had announced their engagement I'd had my fingers crossed against him doing something to shatter her happiness.

She sensed what I was thinking and made a hand motion to dismiss the idea. "Don't mind me. I'm grumpy today. The thing is, we'll be lucky if we're married by September."

"Why?"

"This new album of his is taking a long time to pull together. He and the band're down in Arizona at the studio this week, and their sessions haven't been going well. By the time he gets back, there won't be time to plan a May wedding—even a small one like we want."

"So you'll be a June bride instead."

She scowled. "No way! I refuse to become a stereotype at this point in life. And July is out—that's when I married my first husband. And August is when Ricky married your sister."

I shook my head at the complexities contemporary society breeds. Rae and Ricky had any number of anniversaries they didn't want to be reminded of, plus the difficulties of dealing diplomatically with Charlene, the six children he'd had with her, and her new husband. Of course, complexities are more easily surmounted when one, like Ricky, is reputed to have earned upwards of forty million dollars the previous year . . .

"You know," I said, "I may be sabotaging my own request, but why are you still working? You could be in Arizona with Ricky."

"Not while he's recording. Those sessions are too intense. And when he's in L.A. on his record company's business his time is taken up in meetings. The fact that he's gone so much is why I need to work. I'm not the sort of person who can do nothing."

"What about this book you're writing that you won't tell any of us about?"

"I've kind of put that on hold. It was supposed to be glitzy and sexy, but what there is of it's turned into . . . I don't know what. Till I do know, I can't work on it." She laughed, shaking her head ruefully. "Funny, back when I didn't have any money I used to dream about what I'd do if I was rich—mainly shop till I dropped. Then, when I got together with Ricky, I discovered I don't like to shop. I'd much rather order what I need from a catalog, and anyway, those old thrifty habits die hard."

"You could take up a hobby."

"Like what?"

"Well, tennis or golf or—"

The look she gave me was one of pure astonishment.

"No, I guess not."

"*Definitely* not. So I work. Investigation is the only thing I've ever been good at, and when you put me in charge last winter I found I've got a real talent for management. I've got no problem with taking over the agency while you're gone. In fact, you may come home to a streamlined operation."

## 6:11 P.M.

"Swimsuit. T-shirts. Shorts. Couple of dress-up outfits. Wonder if I should take my Magnum? Hassle, filling out the declaration forms for the airline—"

"Jesus, McCone, when did you start talking to yourself?"

I turned, saw Hy standing in the bedroom doorway, and felt a rush of pleasure. With this tall, lean, hawk-nosed man I shared a life, the cottage on the coast, a love of flying, and—upon occasion—certain risky ventures. He was loving, generous, sentimental, and strong. He could at times be enigmatic, mercurial, bullheaded, and downright dangerous. Right now he was just plain wet and weary.

"So how was your flight?" I asked.

He crossed the room and flopped down on the bed next to the clothes I'd piled there, running long fingers through touseled dark blond hair and smoothing his luxu-riant mustache. "Grim. You're right about the Cessna—it's a piece of crap. Altimeter went out on me, magnetic compass was whirling around like a mouse in a Mixmas-ter, and coming into Oakland the radio started up like a banshee wail. So when *did* you start talking to yourself?"

"I always have, when I'm home alone and neither of the cats is around to talk at. Anyway, I'm glad you finally agree with me about the Cessna." Hy's old Citabria had been totaled a month before in an incident for which I still felt partially responsible. We'd been trying to replace it, but hadn't found a used plane we both liked.

"You know," he said, "after tonight I'm leaning more toward that Warrior we test-flew last weekend. I'd forgotten how much I like a low wing."

"Low wing's fine with me, but that Warrior's got its drawbacks." I sent a lacy bra sailing toward the pile on the bed.

He caught it, looked it over speculatively. "Pretty sexy. I thought this was supposed to be a working trip. What's wrong with the Warrior?"

"I don't like the rudders. And the interior's kind of grungy. There's no reason we can't work in a little romance over there."

"A little—or a lot—suits me fine. I know what you mean about the interior. It'd take over ten grand to bring it up to snuff. But what's wrong with the rudders?"

"Too stiff for my liking. Catch!"

"You *are* thinking of romance. Yeah, you do have to kind of animal the controls around. And it really could do with a prop overhaul, maybe a fire-wall forward treatment, too."

"So what're we looking at beyond the purchase price?"

"Thirty, forty grand. You know what, maybe we should be considering a new plane. When you factor in the expense of making a used one right, there's not a hell of a lot of difference."

"There's a difference. And new planes depreciate very rapidly. Should I take my gun along?"

"Nope. I checked with our Honolulu office, and it's

okay for you to work under our umbrella, but they tell me carry permits there are as rare as hens' molars. If I registered the plane to RKI, they could insure it under the company policy and take the depreciation in exchange. That would defray some of the expense."

"So talk to your partners. The expression's 'hens' *teeth*.'"

"I could've sworn it was 'molars.' I'll do that when we get back."

"Good. And it *is* teeth."

"Guess you're right."

"I'm always right."

" 'Most always. C'mere, McCone. Why wait for Hawaii for the romance?"

# APRIL 2

•

Kauai

## 4:00 P.M.

"So what this adds up to is that somebody's willing to go to extreme measures to stop you from making the film."

I was perched on the edge of the backseat of the old red Datsun, my elbows propped on the bucket seats that Glenna Stanleigh and Hy occupied. The car, on loan to her along with the house, wasn't air-conditioned, and moisture coated my body beneath the too-heavy jeans and tee that had seemed flimsy in San Francisco that morning. I slid my right hand off Hy's seat back and pulled the cotton fabric away from my torso, then lifted the hair off my damp neck.

"It would seem so." Glenna took her big, expressive gray eyes off the one-lane bridge we were crossing and glanced at me in the rearview mirror, her distress plain. Then she returned her gaze to the line of vehicles waiting at the other end, raising a hand in thanks when we passed.

We'd been driving north from Kauai's Lihue Airport for nearly forty-five minutes. Although I'd made many trips to Hawaii, I'd never before visited the Garden Is-

land, the state's oldest and fourth largest in size, some
seventy miles northwest of Honolulu. At first we'd
passed resort complexes and shopping centers, new housing developments and cane fields. At Princeville, once a
sugar plantation, an expensive-looking planned community spread for miles on the north shore; then the road
narrowed and wound through hill and valley, forest and
farmland, taking us back a century or more.

A river lay to our right now, placid and brown, with
trees whose branches trailed in the water lining the opposite bank. To our left a flat plain spread toward distant
cloud-shrouded peaks; dirt roads cut across it among wet-
lands and what I recognized as taro patches. Glenna
braked abruptly to let across a pair of weather-beaten
fishermen who had parked their equally weather-beaten
sedan on the shoulder, and I nearly slid forward between
the seats.

"Sorry about that," she muttered.

I pushed back onto the seat, anchoring my feet more
securely on the floorboard. All around them was a litter
of soda pop cans and crumpled take-out wrappers, and
the seat on either side of me was piled with clothing, a
still camera, notebooks, and clipboards. It reminded me
of Glenna's office at Pier 24½. She could function in
chaos that would sink the average person and, if anything, seemed proud of it.

"Okay, let's go over what you've told me." I held up
my hand and began ticking items off as I spoke. "We've
got a sound guy who broke his ankle when he fell into a
leaf- and branch-covered hole that he swears wasn't there
the day before. A tape recorder that disappeared from a

room at the bed-and-breakfast where some of your crew are staying. A vandalized rental car. A hit-and-run accident involving one of the vans. And a stolen camera."

"An Arri SR3 that the rental house in Honolulu is going to charge me a bloody fortune for. We had to come up with a huge cash deposit before they'd let us have another."

"That camera wasn't yours?"

She shook her head, the ponytail into which she'd tied her long light brown curls brushing my forearm. "It's much cheaper to rent than to own. A package like the one we're using here—meaning the camera and various lenses—would be way out of my price range. I really feel bad about the first camera being stolen, since the owner of the rental house is an old school chum of Peter's."

"That's Peter Wellbright, your partner in the venture?"

"And the man whose father, Elson Wellbright, wrote the manuscript the film is based on."

There was an odd, guarded tone in Glenna's voice. I glanced at Hy; he shrugged and looked out the side window at a pair of kayakers on the river. Although he hadn't involved himself in the conversation—after all, as he would say, this was my case—I knew he was making careful mental notes.

"All right," I said, "I can see how what happened to your sound man might be taken as an attempt on his life. The accident with the van, too. But what about this idea that somebody's trying to kill you? Where did that come from?"

She slowed for a town that was coming up. "I suppose I might've been making too much of it."

"Let me be the judge of that."

We were passing small businesses, a mission-style church, a couple of shopping centers, a school. Hanalei, population around 500. Glenna seemed preoccupied with the traffic and pedestrians, even though there was very little compared to what we'd encountered near the airport and in the resort area at Kapaa. She waited till the road narrowed and the trees closed in over it before replying.

"Here's what happened. It was yesterday morning, around five. I've taken to rising early, walking along the beach to where it's blocked by an ancient lava fall. The path that takes you there winds through thick vegetation—ironwood and papaya trees, mostly. It looks wild, but the Wellbrights employ a staff of gardeners who keep the property in good shape. Yesterday . . ." At the first of two one-lane wooden bridges that formed a dogleg over another river, she slowed to let a pickup cross from the other side.

"Yesterday," she repeated as we began rumbling across, "I was walking along the path when I heard rustling and cracking in the underbrush. Thought little of it. The Wellbrights've got at least five dogs that have the run of the place. But next there was a sighing sound and—wham! A small papaya tree came down nearly on top of me. Just missed, but I got badly scratched up by the branches." She held up her arm, which was webbed with bloody lines.

I looked to my right, saw a sand beach and turquoise sea through wind-whipped trees. "Was it blowing this hard yesterday morning?"

"Not at all. It was still."

"So for the tree to fall—"

"Someone had to've pushed it. When Peter went to investigate, he found signs of digging around the roots."

"But you didn't see anybody?"

"No."

"Hear anything, other than the sound the tree made?"

"No." She hesitated. "D'you think I overreacted?"

"Not given the other incidents you've described."

"Thank God. For a while after you called back and said you and Hy would be coming, I was afraid I'd created a tempest in a teapot. It's just that this film is really important to me. The subject is legends and myths told from the viewpoint of a missionary descendant who deeply cared for the Hawaiian people and their heritage. This state is troubled both racially and politically; the Hawaiians feel they've gotten the short end of the stick, and they have. Peter and I hope that my interpretation of Elson Wellbright's work will give other groups more understanding and empathy."

If there was a common theme among the diverse subjects of Glenna's documentaries, it was in her intent. She firmly believed that contemporary society's many ills stemmed from people's inability to get inside the minds and hearts of those who were different from them, and her films were made with the hope of involving viewers to the extent that they would put their fears and prejudices aside, if only momentarily. Her work was serious yet entertaining, and she'd completed a surprising number of projects for someone only twenty-six. Her career had begun with a short on the Vietnamese refugee community that had won a Student Academy Award in the documentary category while she was still in college at UCLA. I knew her well enough to recognize that a steely resolve and ambition lay beneath her pretty, perky exterior.

As if aware of what I was thinking, she went on, "Of course, the film's also important to me from a commercial standpoint, and with Peter's backing I don't have to skimp. He's given me a budget of three-quarters of a million dollars, and then there're things such as the loan of the house. If it turns out as well as I think it will, I could get a major TV sale to a network like HBO."

"Well," I said, "then we'll just have to ensure that nothing more happens to interfere with your progress. I noticed when we were talking about the tree incident that you hesitated when I asked if you'd seen or heard anything. Why?"

". . . You're going to think this fanciful."

"Try me."

"I felt something. A presence."

"A presence."

"I can't put it any other way. Could've been human, could've been something else entirely."

"I don't understand."

"You will. After you've been on this island a few days, you will."

The town of Waipuna, some ten minutes along the road, was really more of a hamlet: pastel houses, many of them on stilts, lining dirt lanes that meandered off toward the palis or the sea; pizza parlor and deli; small shopping center; video rentals, T-shirts, surf shop, organic foods, chiropractic. The mission-style church was weathered and in poor repair, not of guidebook quality. The other buildings were mainly one-story, of board or shingle, with rippled iron roofs. Banana trees and coco palms and flowers of stunning hue grew everywhere. The blossoms spilled over railings and latticework and gave off a wonderful sweetness.

"'Waipuna' means 'spring water,'" Glenna told us, jockeying the car into a narrow space in front of the small cinder-block supermarket. "The land around here was taro patches planted by the ancient Hawaiians. What you're smelling is mainly ginger that grows wild around the springs." She motioned at what I'd taken to be a roadside drainage ditch, where plants bearing white and red flowers grew.

Hy got out of the car and took my hand to pull me from the backseat. I stepped out into the hot parking lot, glad of a chance to stretch. The supermarket had plate-glass windows plastered with signs advertising specials on everything from beer to ahi tuna. To one side of the store stood a prefab shed with a banner proclaiming it the headquarters of Ace Tanner's Helicopter Tours and Flight Instruction.

Glenna saw me looking at it. "His real name's Russell Tanner," she said. "He's famous, in a way. A lot of photographers and film companies, including me, use him to get to places that're otherwise inaccessible. The road ends a few miles beyond the Wellbright property, and there's no way to go farther unless you hike, take a boat, or fly in."

Hy was eyeing the shed with great interest. He possessed a helicopter rating, although, as far as I knew, it wasn't current.

I said, "If you're thinking of flying one of those things—"

"You've got an unreasonable prejudice against them."

"—I won't go along."

"Want to bet?" He grinned wickedly.

When I looked around, Glenna had grabbed a cart and was pushing it toward the store. "Come on," she called. "You'll have plenty of time to get to know Russ later. He might even be at the party at Pali House tonight."

I hurried after her. "What party?"

"Oh, I forgot. Celia Wellbright, Peter's mother and the grande dame of the Wellbright clan, is giving a cocktail party at eight, in honor of the arrival of my security team."

"Security team?"

"That's what Peter and I decided to call you. I also let it out that Hy's a partner in RKI. They're well known in the Islands, and I'm hoping that his presence will discourage whoever's been doing these things. Anyway, Celia took it as an excuse to throw a party—any excuse for a party. So let's go buy some gin and tonic. I've a feeling we'll need a tall cool one before we traipse up the pali."

Of course Hy disappeared on us, and when we came out of the market we found him by the shed, in conversation with a tall man in aviator's sunglasses and a camouflage jumpsuit. His face was deeply tanned, with high cheekbones, a straight nose, and full lips—a handsome combination of East and West. His jet-black hair hung nearly to his broad shoulders. I glanced at Glenna, and she said, "Russ Tanner."

At the sound of his name, the man turned and called, "Hey, Sweet Pea, you got something in that bag for me?"

She took out a bottle of beer and made as if to throw it to him. He waved his arms, fending her off, and turned back to Hy. "So the guy says to me, 'But how do I *know* you can put this thing down there?' And I say to him, 'Man, I can put this thing down on the head of a pin without disturbin' any of the dancin' angels.' That shut him up. He's probably still tryin' to figure it out."

"You get a lot of passengers like that?"

"Fair amount. Can't leave it to the pilot, got to prove how much they don't know. What d'you expect from shirts?"

"Shirts?"

"What I call 'em. They wear those knitted shirts with little emblems sewn on 'em. Probably order 'em from some preppy catalog, like Bean. Shirts, shorts, boat shoes. Glasses—usually graduated bifocals. Blow-dried hair. You know the kind. They're why I prefer my film people, like Sweet Pea here. Film people, they're all nuts."

Hy glanced at me, smiling faintly. That was a sentiment I'd often expressed about helicopter pilots.

"So who's this?" Tanner asked, motioning to me and taking off his sunglasses. His eyes were a striking shade of blue.

Glenna introduced us, adding, "Sharon's a private investigator. And a pilot."

Tanner looked me over, his eyes lively with curiosity. "You as good a pilot as this guy?" He jerked a thumb at Hy.

I said, "Less experienced, more by-the-book."

Hy said, "She's better."

"Ever fly a chopper?"

"No."

"Come on over to my helipad while you're here. I'll give you a free lesson."

"Uh, thanks."

Hy was now stifling a grin.

Glenna said, "Will you be at the party tonight, Russ?"

"At Pali House? Forget it. I may be a distant relative, but I haven't set foot in the place for years. Tonight I'll be holding down my regular stool at the Shack, and if you folks've got any brains, you'll join me."

The phone in the office rang. He glanced its way, then winked at me and said, "You take me up on that free lesson, pretty lady." As he hurried to pick up, he called to Hy, "As for you, man, we'll get you current, and then we'll have us some *fun!*"


My first sight of Glenna's borrowed house nearly took my breath away. Not that it was opulent; if anything, its appearance was unpretentious: white, one-story, raised a foot or so above the ground, with a red shingle roof that sloped on all four sides and a wraparound porch, or lanai, as they're called in the Islands. Magenta plumeria twined up the support posts and cascaded over the rain gutters, and the lanai was surrounded by flowering shrubs to which I couldn't put a name.

The house was set well back from the road on a rise above a lawn nearly the size of a football field, a lawn screened by a thick stand of palm and papaya and bamboo and banana trees. As we drove in on the gravel track, I spotted chickens pecking at the grass and again smelled the sweet scent of ginger. Glenna pulled the car up beside a detached garage, and I glimpsed a patch of sea, waves breaking on a reef.

When I got out and turned to survey the lawn, my gaze was pulled upward to a backdrop of ancient wrinkled palis that dwarfed everything else and seemed close enough to touch. A flock of egrets flew in formation past the peaks, where black rock stood out in sharp contrast to the deep green vegetation clinging to the crevasses. Purple-veined clouds draped the palis, poised to release a torrent. In spite of the place's natural loveliness, the air was charged with a sense of potential violence that immediately made me edgy.

Glenna didn't seem to feel it. "Spectacular, isn't it?" she said. "It's called Malihini House—'Malihini' is the Hawaiian word for 'newcomer to the Islands.'"

"Quite spectacular," I agreed, glancing at Hy. His face was still, wary.

"And quite a change from the city," she added. "No sounds but the sea and the silence."

An unearthly screech came from behind us.

Hy said, "What the hell?"

"Well, it would be silent, if it wasn't for *him*." Glenna pointed at the lawn, where a rooster was strutting purposefully toward the hens, crowing his lungs out.

"I thought they only did that at dawn," I said.

They both stared incredulously at me.

"City girl," Hy said.

"They don't?"

"God, no."

"Roosters," Glenna told me, "chickens in general, are very stupid birds. They don't know dawn from dinnertime. This one is especially stupid; I've even heard him crowing in the middle of the night."

"Is he a pet?" I asked.

"What? No, of course not. They run wild all over the island. Why would you think that?"

"Well, if he's not a pet, how d'you know it's the same one that's crowing?"

She frowned. "Now that you mention it, I don't know as it's the same one."

"Then you can't claim that this guy's exceptionally stupid."

"Well, no, but look at him."

The bird did appear intellectually challenged.

Hy said, "I can't believe we're standing here in this heat having this conversation. Open the trunk, Glenna, and show me where to stow our bags."

## 6:55 P.M.

I was shaking the wrinkles out of a long black-and-gold cotton dress that Glenna had assured me would be perfect for the Wellbright party when Hy appeared in the doorway of our bedroom, his index finger pressed to his lips. I frowned and watched him cross to the bathroom. A few seconds later he called, "McCone, I can't find where you packed my razor."

Packed his razor? He was a master packer, never needed any help from me.

"Will you come in here and see if you can find it?"

Very puzzled now, I went over there and peered around the doorjamb. Hy was at the far end of the narrow space, flattened against the wall between the twin sinks and the linen closet. He held his finger to his lips again and motioned for me to join him. When I did, he put his arms around me and whispered in my ear. "Did you hear that clicking sound when you crossed the bedroom?"

"Just the motion sensors Glenna warned us about. She's right—they're really annoying."

"I think they're more than motion sensors."

"They look pretty standard to me."

"Look, yes. Function, no. I checked the security command center by the front door. The indicator lights aren't registering that the sensors're on—meaning they're hooked into some other system. Somebody's monitoring us, could even be making audio- or videotapes. We're out of range here—one of the few places in the house—but if you back up and stand by the door, you'll hear that click again."

I backed up and heard the telltale noise from the sensor mounted in the corner of the bedroom. Quickly I moved back to Hy.

"This is awful! What're we going to do about it?" I heard the anxiety in my voice, told myself this was an unreasonable response to the situation. But two months ago my life had been invaded, my privacy violated, my very identity threatened. Now even the slightest incursion into my space held a nightmarish, nearly life-threatening quality.

Hy sensed what I was feeling, drew me close. "Tonight we can't do anything. We'll just have to watch what we do and say in the areas those things cover."

"God. Can't we disable them?" In spite of his reassuring touch, I felt my fingers begin to tingle—only one of a variety of physiological responses to stress I'd experienced in the past month, which an SFPD psychologist had assured me would go away in time.

"I don't know enough about this particular type of system to try, but tomorrow first thing I'll call our Honolulu office, see if they can help. If necessary, I'll have one of our people come over here."

"Who would want to keep tabs on what goes on here? And why?"

"The situation won't be clear till we meet everybody involved. Particularly this Peter Wellbright. You noticed how Glenna acted when you first mentioned him."

"Yes, as if she wanted to say more about him, yet wasn't sure she should. Well, we'll meet him soon. He lives next door, she tells me, down the path through those papaya trees, and he's coming over before we go to the party."

"Which reminds me—we'd better get ready."

The reason for Glenna's strange reaction to my mention of Peter Wellbright became apparent when Hy and I joined them on the lanai. She was barely able to keep her eyes or hands off him.

Wellbright was a tall, slender man with horn-rimmed glasses and fine brown hair, whose dress and mannerisms suggested Ivy League colleges and exclusive men's clubs. In spite of being around forty, he moved with an adolescent awkwardness; I could imagine him on a tennis court, playing badly. Although he clearly didn't mind Glenna's attentions, his body language was far more reserved.

When she'd first spoken of Peter before leaving for Kauai, Glenna had referred to him only as her partner and backer. They'd met through a mutual friend, a Silicon Valley entrepreneur who dabbled in the arts. Glenna had been looking for someone to finance a documentary on the Islands; the friend knew of Elson Wellbright's unpublished manuscript and suggested Peter let her look at it. But when she expressed interest in using it as the basis for her script, Peter told her he would have to consult with his family after he made his move back to Kauai. Surprisingly, in light of the fact she had little money and supplemented her income with teaching jobs at two university extensions, Glenna had gone ahead and paid a scriptwriter to begin work without any assurance of permission to use the manuscript and with no certainty of financial backing.

When Peter returned to Kauai and broached the subject to his family, they were adamantly against the project. Their resistance surprised and angered him, and he became determined to make the film, so he called Glenna, asking her to fly over and firm up an agreement. That was a month ago, and it was clear to me that in the intervening weeks their relationship had altered markedly. Something—the seductiveness of this climate, the intimacy of working together, or mere proximity—had brought them together romantically. As she made the introductions, Glenna glowed.

Wellbright fixed us gin and tonics from makings on a patio table, saying, "We'll be fashionably late to Mother's, hopefully with a buzz on."

I asked, "Is that a good idea, seeing as it's the first time Hy and I will meet her?"

He smiled as he handed around the glasses. "It's the only way to arrive at one of her parties. And don't worry, she'll be so smashed that she won't remember she hasn't known you all your lives."

There was an awkward silence. What do you say when someone you've just met comes out and tells you his mother's a drunk?

"Look," Peter said easily, sitting down next to Glenna, "it's no secret about my mother. I'm trying to prepare you. Parties at Pali House have a way of becoming . . . colorful, to say the least."

We followed his lead and sat opposite them. Hy asked, "Who else will be there?"

"Depends on who's got the fortitude to show. My brother Matthew and his wife, Jillian, will attend. They live with Mother. He's a real-estate developer and more or less watches over the family's financial affairs. My sister, Stephanie, and her husband, Ben Mori, will come if they've got nothing better going. She's a painter, sells through a gallery down at Poipu Beach. He operates the Hawaii branch of a software firm owned by his relatives in Japan. He also dabbles in development and has done a few projects with Matthew, although they're currently at a professional impasse. And of course there'll be the other members of the film crew, the neighbors, and some of Mother's fellow clubwomen with their long-suffering husbands in tow."

"Sounds like an interesting group."

Peter waggled one hand from side to side. "I only hope it doesn't degenerate into a drunken family squabble, as so many of our gatherings do." He smiled at Glenna. "I've asked Glen why she doesn't hate me for dragging her over here and involving her with my crazy people."

She said, "When a family isn't yours, their antics are amusing. When they are yours, however . . ."

Not for the first time in the nine months I'd known her I was reminded that she'd given me few clues to her family background. I knew she'd grown up outside of Melbourne and come to the States to attend UCLA. She married while in college, but divorced shortly afterward, taking nothing away from the brief union except her former husband's surname, which she claimed sounded better for a filmmaker than her own.

I met her the day she moved into her office at the pier: a tiny woman struggling valiantly with a heavy desk that threatened to fall from the back of her Bronco and crush her. After rushing to her aid, I summoned my staff and some of the other tenants for an impromptu moving-in party that ended with us drinking beer and eating take-out Chinese food amid the clutter.

Six months later the clutter was still there—would be as long as she was—and she and I had become friends of sorts. I helped her find a tiny furnished studio in the

Outer Mission district, the best she could afford on her earnings from her films and part-time teaching jobs. She introduced me to a friend who cheaply repaired my aging Nikkormat camera when it sprang a light leak. She displayed a lively interest in my business, to the extent of borrowing manuals on skip tracing and other investigative techniques. From her I learned a lot about the way those in the visual arts looked at the world, a way that was not mine but that could be adapted to investigation in order to see details more clearly. We shared herbal tea and brandy, engaged in spirited debates about everything from sports to politics, but still I never felt I really knew the woman behind the smiles and bright chatter. Her history and inner concerns were tacitly off limits, and now I wondered why.

Hy was saying to Peter, "I understand the film's based on writings of your father's. Is he still living?"

An odd expression passed over Glenna's face. Peter got up to freshen drinks. "No one knows. He disappeared the year Hurricane Iniki blew through here, 1992. But he'd been estranged from the family for several years before that. The film's to be a memorial to him."

I asked, "The unpublished manuscript of his that the script's based on—how come it was never published?"

"I don't know. He had a literary agent who was going to market it, and he mentioned her name in the letter that accompanied the copy of the manuscript he sent to me on the mainland. A couple of years ago I tried to contact her, but she'd either died or gone out of business. I'm hoping this film will generate interest from another agent or publisher."

"Maybe it will. Glenna tells me it's terrific material."

"It is, because of my father's understanding and enthusiasm for the native culture. Our family comes from missionary stock, and while it's true that many of the missionaries and their descendants took more from the Islands than they gave, others, like my father, had a deep interest in preserving the legends and culture. He had an advanced degree in anthropology and wrote on the Pacific for publications like the *National Geographic*. The book on the Hawaiian legends was a lifelong labor of love, since he started meeting with a group of native storytellers in his thirties."

I said, "And he disappeared?"

"Ran off, and I can't say as I blame him. The family situation had become intolerable, he was drinking heavily, and I suppose he just plain burned out and decided the hell with it. My older brother hired private detectives to look for him, since there was a good deal of cash missing from the joint accounts, but they never found him. I like to think he's on some distant island, listening to yet another group of storytellers and living out his days in peace."

Glenna bit her lip. It was clear she didn't buy into such a happy scenario. Then she stood, smoothing her bright orange dress. "Peter, we'd better go up to Pali House before the party gets *too* colorful."

## 10:55 P.M.

I was standing alone at the rail of a terrace that overlooked a distant sliver of palm-fringed beach; beyond it moonlit breakers crested on a dark sea. Pali House lay behind me: a low tan structure with an aquamarine tiled roof and many wings, set among well-tended gardens. A babble of talk and laughter came from within. I tuned it out, concentrated on the rush of a stream that meandered through the property and cascaded down the slope in a waterfall.

The night was sweetly fragrant, the breeze warm on my bare arms. It took me back to my teenage years in San Diego, when velvety spring evenings had been new and full of promise. To my high school prom, the heady smell of a gardenia corsage, the touch of a special boy's hand on mine. The memory was far more pleasurable than the immediate present.

When we arrived, Celia Wellbright was playing the regal lady—a lady with a snootful of rum. Had she been even half sober she might've carried the part off: she was tall, thin, erect of carriage, her silver-gray hair pulled into a chignon, her handsome face nearly unlined, her almond-shaped eyes hinting at Polynesian ancestry. But liquor made her exaggerate her gestures and speech till she seemed a caricature of herself.

She immediately took Peter to task for being late, then swept us into a courtyard where a buffet was set up and began introducing Hy and me to an assortment of people whose identities quickly blurred, as if someone had fast-forwarded the scene before my eyes. A banker and his wife. A politician. A member of the horticultural society. A retired couple from Oregon. Glenna's scriptwriter, Jan Lyndon, whom I'd met in San Francisco and whose assurances that we knew each other fell on deaf ears.

Celia's older son, Matthew, a big pinched-faced man whose eyes peered disapprovingly through thick glasses, and his fragile-looking wife, Jillian, who seemed nearly frightened by the crowd. Stephanie and Benjamin Mori: she sun-browned and -blonded, he dark and athletic-looking, both dressed in shorts in spite of the other guests' more formal attire. Glenna's sound man, bearded Bryan O'Callaghan, leaning on a cane, his ankle in a cast. Her film editor, Emily Quentin, a heavy woman with a hearty and likable laugh. And many others . . .

Hy and I were ravenous after not eating since the meal on the plane, and we managed to down a respectable amount of sushi and hot canapés before Celia again attempted to appropriate us. Peter and Glenna had disappeared; the crew members had escaped, making their excuses. We were the only exotics Celia had not yet shown off to her guests, and show us off she would. There was a simply lovely man we must meet: Alex the mad Russian. He was also a pilot.

I pleaded a need for the rest room and, as Celia led away a martyred-looking Hy, fled to the deserted terrace.

Now, in spite of the night's warmth, I shivered. Something felt wrong here. Something elemental. Something I couldn't put a name to. It emanated from the towering scarps behind the house, from the ancient volcanic boulders that spilled down the slope. It whistled in a stand of bamboo, echoed when a breaker smacked onto the reef. Spoke to me in a voice I'd never before heard, urged me to come closer, make its acquaintance—

Shadow and motion behind me. I whirled.

"Ripinsky!"

"There you are."

"Sorry to've run off like that, but . . ."

"I know."

"How are things in there?"

"Barely tolerable. Most of the guests've left, and Celia's into what Peter calls her severe and domineering mode. I think we should all leave too."

"Then let's liberate Peter and Glenna and go."

The scene inside had turned ugly.

The family stood in a phalanx, allied against Peter and Glenna. Celia was at center: head held haughtily, hair disheveled, one strap of her long black gown hanging off her shoulder. To her right, Stephanie and Benjamin Mori assumed aggressive stances. Matthew was on her other side, features pinched unpleasantly. His delicate-looking wife peered around him with frightened eyes.

The closing of the familial ranks didn't seem to intimidate Peter; he perched casually on the back of a sofa, one foot dangling. Glenna seemed similarly unaffected; she surveyed the family with a narrow-eyed expression that I recalled from a shoot I'd attended in San Francisco, as if she were evaluating the scene's potential for filming. No one noticed Hy and me enter.

Celia was speaking. Although her words were slurred, they had considerable bite. "Of course that's what you'd say, Peter. You're exactly like your father. You've done nothing but run off on this family."

"I take the comparison to Father as a compliment," he replied calmly. "And I did not run off."

"What do you call it, then?"

"I call it attending school on the mainland and then establishing myself in my profession."

Matthew snorted. "*I* call it going to school as far away from us as you could. MIT's halfway around the world. And then, instead of bringing your expertise—which this family paid for—home where you could do some good, you chose to squander it in California."

"I thought the word 'squander' went out with the missionaries. Anyway, I don't believe it applied to founding a software firm that was bought out for a hundred million last year."

Stephanie said, "And how much of that hundred mill will these islands see? How much of it are you determined to waste on this movie?"

Glenna transferred her narrowed gaze to Peter's sister. Stephanie returned the look with one of her own. "Well, Peter?"

"Backing a documentary isn't like bankrolling a Hollywood blockbuster. I should think you'd be glad to see a memorial created to Father's work."

"That's not the point, and you know it."

"What *is* the point?"

Benjamin said, "What Stephanie's trying to get at is your reason for coming home after . . . what? Twenty years? It can't just be to make this film."

"No, that's only one among many."

"And the others?"

"You'll hear about them when I'm ready to tell you."

"This discussion is getting us nowhere," Matthew said.

Celia wasn't about to give it up, however. "No matter

what your reasons," she said, "what remains is that you've never been here for us. Like your father."

Matthew glanced nervously at Jillian, who had moved out from behind him and was looking distraught. "That's enough, Mother," he said.

"Where were you when your father ran off, Peter? When your younger brother turned to drugs? When Iniki hit?"

"Mother!"

Jillian staggered forward now, pointing a shaky finger at Peter, and I realized she was very drunk. "Yes, where *were* you during Iniki, when we needed your help? Where were you when this family was almost destroyed?"

Stephanie shook her head, rolled her eyes at Benjamin.

"Jill . . ." Matthew reached for his wife.

She slapped his hand away. "You don't know how it was, Peter. What we had to contend with. You can't imagine—"

"No, Jill, I can't imagine," Peter said evenly. "But what was I supposed to do? I was on the mainland, had no idea there would be a hurricane."

"There were warnings. You could've come back."

"By the time I heard the warnings, I couldn't've gotten a flight."

"You could've! You should've! Maybe if you'd been here, our lives wouldn't've been torn apart. You've always been the one who could control—"

Jillian's drunken tirade seemed to sober Celia up. She turned to Matthew and commanded him, "Do something about her! Now!"

He reached for Jillian, but she stumbled away, bumping into a credenza by the door. There she leaned her elbows on the polished surface, stared at her own face in the mirror behind it, and began to cry.

"Oh, shit," Stephanie said. "Not this again!"

"When it was over, the moon was full." Jillian spoke in a child's high-pitched voice. "And the forest was quiet all around us. And then everything was black and the wind peeled the bark off the trees and the forest turned to Pickup Sticks and the boulders flew through the air—"

"Stop it!" Celia shouted. She gave Matthew a shove. "See to your wife!"

He went to Jillian, tried to pull her upright. She resisted, sobbing. "Oh, Matt, why? Why us? Everything ended! And I'm so sorry . . ."

"Sssh." He put his arms around her, got her more or less erect, and led her from the room. She stumbled along, still sobbing.

Stephanie and Benjamin looked helplessly at each other. Celia brought her hands to her face and rubbed it, as if trying to erase the unpleasant scene.

I glanced at Peter and Glenna. Each seemed deep in thought, as if Jillian's outburst had told them something they were trying to fit into its proper place. When I looked at Hy, he shrugged, troubled.

Peter stood and took Glenna's hand. Said to Hy and me, "Time we leave."

Slowly Celia raised her head, her mouth going slack when she noticed us. The Moris looked embarrassed and began mumbling apologies.

The four of us left without a word. Nothing we could say would improve the situation.

"What d'you mean—the house is under surveillance?" Even in the waning moonlight Glenna's face looked panicked. I put my hand on her arm. She'd seemed fine on the way home from the party, but as soon as Peter told us good night and took the footpath through the shrubbery to his own cottage, she began to unravel from pent-up tension.

We were sitting on a long beach on the bluff overlooking the sea, a good distance from the house and its clicking sensors. Hy explained about them and their probable function, while Glenna pushed agitated fingers through her long curls. When he finished, she said, "My God, you mean somebody could've been watching everything I've done in that house? Or listening to my every word?"

"It's possible."

"No, that can't be!"

My fingers tightened involuntarily on her arm. Her voice held the same combination of outrage and helplessness that I'd felt the previous month when an unknown woman had attempted to take over my life. I took a deep breath before I let go of her.

"What's important now," I said, "is to figure out who could rig such a system. No matter how much it upsets you, I have to say this: Peter's credentials indicate considerable technical expertise—"

"He has no reason to do a thing like that. We're very . . . close."

I studied her for a moment. In San Francisco I'd attended a few parties where she'd been present, and I'd run across her in restaurants a couple of times. She'd always been with a different man, and she hadn't gone in for public displays of affection with any of them. "You're in love, aren't you?" I said.

She nodded.

"And Peter?"

"He hasn't said so in so many words. But it's going to work. It's got to. I've never felt this way before."

"Then I hope it does. And I think we can eliminate him as the person who tampered with those sensors. Who else has access to Malihini House?"

"Most anybody. The caretaker, the housecleaner, the gardeners. All the members of the family. Anybody who strays onto the property. I seldom put the alarm on. Crime isn't much of a problem on Kauai."

Some kinds of crime, anyway. "Okay, the family members: anyone suspect there?"

She considered. "Well, Ben Mori has the know-how."

"He runs a branch of a software firm owned by relatives in Japan?"

"Yes. The Moris have lived on Kauai for generations, but they've kept close ties to the Osaka branch of the family."

"Peter mentioned a professional impasse between Ben and Matthew. D'you know what that was about?"

"Cane fields that the family owns on the southeastern coast of the island. They've been lying fallow since the sugar market collapsed. Ben wanted to develop them one way, Matthew another. So they agreed to disagree, but they're still cordial. To get back to those sensors—what can we do about them?"

Hy said, "I'm going to call our Honolulu office in the morning and find out how to disable them, or have one of our technicians come over and do it. The latter's probably the better idea. Somebody who knows that particular system may be able to locate where they're hooked into."

Glenna nodded, relieved. "We'll have to be careful what we say and do till then. I don't know about you two, but I'm not planning anything more interesting for tonight than sacking out. We've got a nine o'clock shoot tomorrow."

I said, "Before you go inside, I have a few more questions. That argument at Pali House—what started it?"

"I don't know. I was in the loo, and when I came back, the battle lines were drawn. Celia called Peter ungrateful. He said he was sick of her playing the queen bee. She told him she deserved some respect. He said it was easier for him to respect her when he was living on the mainland. And that's when she lit into him with the comment about his father."

"Peter mentioned other reasons for coming home besides your film. Has he told you what they are?"

Her expression clouded. "Not yet. He can be so reserved. . . ."

"What's this about a brother who turned to drugs? Was that Matthew?"

"Mr. Stiff-and-Starchy? Lord, no! That was a younger brother, Andrew. I don't know what happened to him. There're only a few mentions of him in his father's journal."

"What journal?"

"Oh, I didn't tell you. It was the most surprising thing. Peter had a copy of the book manuscript that his father had sent him, but he had no idea there was a journal in which Elson described his life and the writing of the book. One night right after we arrived, I was helping Peter go through some boxes of Elson's personal effects that had been stored, and I found it. Fascinating stuff, and it gave me a lot of insight that my scriptwriter was able to incorporate into the narrative for the film."

"I'd like to take a look at both the journal and the manuscript, if I may."

"Certainly."

"Now one more question: what's the matter with Jillian?"

"Jill's been . . . not quite right in the head since Hurricane Iniki in 1992. When she drinks—and even sometimes when she doesn't—she flips back and relives it. Seems she was wandering around that day, didn't heed the warnings, and got caught out in it."

"Was she hurt?"

"Well, she took shelter someplace, came out pretty much okay, but she was pregnant and the next day she miscarried. Now she's unable to have children."

"That's a shame. I seem to remember hearing about that storm, but my recollection's hazy."

"There's a pictorial book about it in the house, if you're interested. It lasted six hours, and the winds hit 227 miles an hour before they blew the measuring device to pieces. The book says the hurricane released as much energy *per second* as an atomic-bomb blast, and the photos do look like ground zero. That deadfall up the beach is one example of the devastation—it used to be a forest. Peter says Kauai's kind of a magnet for nature's wrath. It's been hit by disastrous storms and tidal waves four times in as many decades."

"Well, it certainly sounded as if Jillian was reliving Iniki tonight. Wonder what she meant by 'Everything ended'?"

Glenna yawned, shook her head. "Jill says a lot of things that just plain don't make sense. Maybe that's the reason Matthew always looks like his shorts're too tight." She stood, yawning some more. "Got to get some sleep. Sorry."

Hy and I said good night and watched her go. Then I stretched my arms along the top of the bench, one hand resting against his shoulder, so I could incline my head and look up at the sky. The Milky Way spread across it, a brilliant swath of starshine.

When I was a kid my father used to round up as many of the five of us as he could find on warm summer nights and take us to the backyard. There we'd lie on the grass and he, a sailor and spinner of yarns, would tell us about the heavens. Periodically he'd gift us with ownership of certain constellations, and while my brothers' and sisters' celestial real estate often changed, mine always remained the same: Orion, the hunter.

Pa had seen through to my soul even then.

One piece of Pa's lore still had the capacity to give me gooseflesh. He told us that many of the stars we were looking at had died long before the dinosaurs walked the earth. That the light shining above could be the last gasp of a fiery mass. That it had left a dead place to travel for millions of years till it reached our eyes. Even now it chilled me to look up and think that those beams of light might be coming from a place that no longer existed, just as it chilled me to think that someday the light from the sun I took for granted would be making its way from a burned-out husk to a distant galaxy.

Now I wondered if the light from the fiery volcanic explosions that had formed this island thousands of years ago was still traveling across the universe. If so, it had left no burned-out husk behind.

Kauai was rife with the potential for further fiery explosions—of the human kind.

# APRIL 3

·

Kauai

## 9:20 A.M.

The cave cut hundreds of yards into the base of a sheer cliff, its wide mouth opening into darkness. I faced it, reminded of an even darker tunnel in an old mine and what had happened to me there years before. Quickly I tucked the memory away in the mental compartment that I reserve for real-life nightmares.

Behind me, Glenna, Peter, and two officers of the Kauai County Police Department were roping off the area between the cave and the road. People were already wandering across from the state beach to see what the commotion was about. A pair of set electricians were running cable from a portable generator mounted in the bed of a truck, and the camerawoman, Kim Shields, was setting up. Jan Lyndon, shooting script in hand, was waiting to talk with Glenna. Other people, whose functions I could only guess at, milled around drinking coffee from Styrofoam cups.

On the shoot I'd attended with Glenna in San Francisco, the crew had been much smaller. But in the car on the way here she'd explained that Peter had enlisted the aid of some locals and had arranged for her to have three interns from the University of Hawaii. Even so, by Kauai standards—parts of such films as *Jurassic Park* had been shot here—this was a minor event.

I wandered around for a bit, watching the crew set up lights inside the cave and checking for suspicious behavior on the part of any individual. None of the bystanders displayed unusual interest in either the equipment or the crew. Finally, satisfied that all was well, I sat down on a nearby trash-bin enclosure and scribbled a list of things to ask Mick to do when I called the office.

Hy hadn't come to the shoot. He wasn't really a security specialist—his work for RKI was along the lines of hostage negotiation and recovery—and besides, he had one of their technicians coming from Oahu to inspect the system at Malihini House. At Glenna's suggestion he asked Russ Tanner to fly him to Lihue Airport to meet the man, and Tanner readily agreed. He made a flashy landing in his red chopper—Hughes 500 series, Hy said—on the big lawn in front of the house and, before Hy ran toward it, I caught a gleam in his eyes that told me he'd soon hold a current rating in helicopters. Much as I hated such aircraft, I knew I'd unbend and fly with Tanner and him, and next thing you knew they'd have me at the controls.

Oh, well, life would be unsatisfying if one couldn't conquer old biases.

Glenna was conferring with Jan Lyndon now, so Peter

came over and perched next to me. "What's happening in this scene?" I asked him.

"It's part of the opening segment where, in voice-over, the actor who's playing my father talks about how the gods were said to frequently walk the earth in mortal form. In this case, the fire goddess, Pele, who was often associated with caves." He motioned at a tall young woman whose body was draped in a filmy red, gold, and orange material that created the impression of flames when the breeze moved it. "That's Sue Kamuela. Pure Hawaiian, has a dress-designing studio in Waipuna. Glen spotted her on the street the day she arrived, and persuaded her to act in the film."

With her waist-length black hair and graceful movements, Kamuela seemed a natural for the role of a goddess. "And your father—who plays him?"

"The man standing next to Sue—Eli Hathaway. He's a distant relative, bears an uncanny resemblance to my father."

"You seem to have a number of distant relatives," I said, thinking of Russ Tanner.

"These islands are practically one big family. Haoles, Chinese, Japanese, Hawaiians—you name it, many of us are related."

"Haole—that means white person?"

"In common usage. Technically it refers to any foreigner."

Peter turned his attention to where Glenna was standing, her back to us. She held both hands before her eyes, thumbs and forefingers forming a frame through which she viewed the cave. After a moment she motioned to the camerawoman, had her do the same. They conferred some more, and then Glenna called to a young man, "Are those marks in place?"

He looked blank for a moment, then hurried toward the cave and began affixing red paper tape to a rock.

"One of the interns," Peter said. "They're journalism students, know nothing about filmmaking, but Glen never gets impatient with them."

"So how will this scene play out?"

"First they'll film Eli wandering into the cave, looking contemplative. Then Sue will follow the same path, more or less mimicking his movements."

"And that's it?"

"Well, there'll be more than one take, but not that many. Glen seems to get good performances out of those two right off the bat. What I've seen of the edited footage is quite impressive. Emily Quentin's using the third bedroom at Malihini House as an editing room, and Glen rented her an Avid digital setup, so— Look at that, will you!"

The cave was suddenly illuminated in garish light that revealed cracks, fissures, and shadowy recesses. I said, "Isn't that going to look unnaturally bright?"

Peter shook his head. "The film's not as sensitive as your eye."

Glenna called, "Time to get on your mark, Eli."

Eli Hathaway moved forward to the red tape on the rock. A woman hurried after him, straightening his collar.

"Okay, Eli," Glenna said, "you can start any time after we've slated and I say 'action.'" She consulted with the camerawoman, waited, then repeated the word.

Hathaway went through his paces, telegraphing a solemn and contemplative mood with his body language.

I asked Peter, "Is he a professional actor?"

"No. He runs boat tours out of Hanalei. Glen and I ran into him at the fish market there. I hadn't seen him since he was a kid, and the resemblance to my father blew me away. When I mentioned it, Glen decided she had to use him in the film."

"So she came over here not knowing who her actors would be."

"And without knowing exactly what she'd film. The way she works on location is a fluid process, depending on what and who she finds there."

Hathaway had gone through his segment twice and came out of the cave, lighting a cigarette. "Very good, Eli," Glenna called. "Take a break now."

He waved at her and walked off toward the rope that surrounded the area.

Now Glenna, Jan Lyndon, and Sue Kamuela huddled over the script. The crew stood around, idle.

"Another thing I've learned about filmmaking," Peter said, "is that it's largely a matter of hurry-up-and-wait. There's a lot of setup, a lot of last-minute changes. This crew's drunk more coffee in the time they've been here than the entire island did last month."

The minutes dragged by. Sue, Glenna, and Jan continued to talk. Then Glenna went over to the marks on the rock, gesturing for Sue to follow. With exaggerated motions, she began walking toward the mouth of the cave. Sue mimicked her. Once there they stopped, as if reluctant to venture inside—

A whining sound.

Kamuela whirled around. As shards from the rocks at the cave's mouth peppered her, I heard the gunshot.

I grabbed Peter, pulled him off the enclosure so it shielded our bodies, all the while shouting for people to get down. Instead they stood frozen or ran in panic. Kamuela now crouched, hand to her face, blood streaming through her fingers. Beside her, Glenna stood still as a statue.

"Glenna, *get down!*" I yelled.

She started, dropped to her knees beside Sue. One of the police officers joined them, calling for backup on his walkie-talkie. The other, gun drawn, was scanning the milling crowd for the shooter. I inched around the enclosure to where I could look too. No one that I could see, except the officer, had a weapon of any kind.

Peter crouched beside me, his face ashen, glasses askew. "You see anybody?" I asked.

He didn't reply. His breathing was ragged, and his eyes were focused on the distance. I followed his line of sight to a stand of ironwoods at the southern end of the state beach across the road.

"You *did* see somebody."

He shook his head as if to clear it. Stood and extended a hand to me. "How could I?" he said. "I didn't have a chance."

I let him pull me to my feet and turned to study the trees. They were dense enough to hide a shooter, but well within the range of a high-powered rifle.

*The hell you didn't*, I thought.

                    *    *    *

Reinforcements arrived shortly from the substation at Hanalei, and the police secured and began searching the immediate area. I went over to Sue and Glenna. Kamuela was bleeding profusely from a gash on her cheek that would require stitches and possibly plastic surgery. An ambulance had just arrived, and Glenna said she would ride with Sue to Wilcox Memorial Hospital in Lihue. I agreed to follow in the Datsun as soon as possible.

When I located Peter, he was in conversation with a short balding man with an extravagant handlebar mustache whom he introduced as Detective Wendell Yamashita. The officer questioned me about what I'd seen, then turned back to Peter and asked, "So, brah, you say a stray bullet, eh?"

Peter shrugged. "Lotsa hunting on this island, lotsa guns." He had subtly altered his customarily cultured speech to reflect the rhythms of pidgin, that special language with which Hawaiian islanders of all classes and backgrounds frequently communicate. "Lotsa mokes, too," he added, motioning at the state beach.

I frowned.

"Tough guys," he explained. "Accident is all, Wen, but mo' bettah we knock off for today. Okay to get our crew outta here?"

"Okay, but keep 'em available, eh?" Yamashita turned away and motioned to one of his uniformed men.

I said in a low voice, "Who advanced the stray-bullet theory? You or him?"

Peter looked down at me, eyes deceptively innocent. "It's as good as any other."

"I don't suppose you mentioned the other problems the crew's been having?"

He grabbed my arm and steered me over by the pickup truck where the portable generator was mounted. "Look, Sharon, Wen's a good cop. If this was anything other than an accident, he'll get to the bottom of it."

"Unless he swallows your theory whole and back-burners any investigation. That's what you're hoping, isn't it?"

He hesitated, compressing his lips.

"Is there something you're not telling me?" I asked.

"All right, let me explain. If Wen suspects this shooting was anything *but* an accident, he'll shut this production down. Part—a big part—of a cop's job in these islands is to make sure they're safe for visitors, and any situation that looks as if it might result in harm to non-locals is corrected swiftly."

"What about harm to locals—like Sue Kamuela?"

"You better believe Wen cares about her, too. But his primary responsibility lies elsewhere. Tourism is the lifeblood of Kauai, and these days the island is seriously anemic. Our economy's rotten, and we still haven't fully recovered from Iniki. We can't afford negative publicity that'll drive away visitors and other film companies. So if Glen and I want to go on with this project, we'd better keep quiet about the problems we've had."

"Then your main concern is continuing with this film."

"Yes."

"But not with Glenna."

"What's that supposed to mean?"

"I didn't think I'd have to spell it out for you. Glenna was standing next to Sue, closer to the place where the bullet smacked into the rocks. Given the other attempt on her life—"

"Oh, Christ!" A sick look came over his face. "I didn't—"

"No, you didn't." And that bothered me a great deal. Glenna was in love with this man; she thought he was in love with her. But when a bullet passed within inches of her, he'd thought only of how the shooting might interfere with completing the film.

He said, "We need security on these shoots. Can Hy arrange for his firm to provide it?"

A good idea, but it still didn't make up for the fact that since the sniping he hadn't gone to Glenna, had instead spent all his time smoothing things over with the police. "I'm sure he can," I told him, "but you've got to realize that security measures aren't always a hundred percent effective."

"It's the best I can do."

The best he could do would be to propose a hiatus until I found out who was trying to stop the project. I would've suggested that to Glenna, but I doubted she'd buy the plan. Whether she was filming or not, she'd still have to pay and house the crew, as well as pay the rental on the equipment, and that could put her seriously over budget.

"Talk to Ripinsky about security," I told him. "And when you do, tell him I've gone to Lihue."

## 12:47 P.M.

Sue Kamuela's husband had already arrived at the hospital by the time I got there, and as soon as the doctor had assured us that she was being treated and would be released promptly, we were on our way back to the north shore. I took the wheel while Glenna slumped in the passenger seat, looking totally demoralized.

"I should've seen it coming," she said as I pulled into traffic.

"The sniping? How could you?"

"Not the sniping specifically, but I should've known disaster was right around the corner. This has been a bad-luck project from day one."

"If you feel that way, this might be the time to put the film on hold."

"I can't do that! The expense . . . If I do, I might as well give up entirely."

"And you feel the film's worth risking people's safety—including your own? That shot was probably intended for you."

She shook her head in confusion, as if the possibility was occurring to her for the first time.

"Peter's hiring RKI to provide security," I added, "but we all know that's not a magical solution. Not if someone's determined to do you harm. And whoever it is seems damned determined."

"As determined as Peter and I are to get this film made."

"I understand why *you* are, but why is he? Not just because it's to be his memorial to his father?"

"Well, it's all tied up with his feelings for Kauai, I think. It's almost as if he wants to make amends for staying away so long."

"He's that deeply attached to the island?"

"I guess so. When you're born in a place like this, when your family's been part of the fabric of its society for generations, you can't help but feel a fundamental attachment."

"I suppose," I said, but doubt was apparent in my voice. I'd never felt that way about San Diego, even though my family had lived there for generations. "D'you feel attached to Australia?"

"No, but that's different." Her tone was clipped.

"How so?"

Silence. I waited.

"Look, Sharon, I don't like to talk about Australia. I never felt I belonged there." She sighed deeply. "My home life was . . . I don't know if you could call it difficult, or merely nonexistent."

"Tell me about it."

"My family were all takers. They didn't give anything to society the way the Wellbrights have. My father made his money in construction, mostly by bribing government officials. My brothers would've followed in his footsteps, but they were both killed in an accident on one of the job sites. I loved my mother, but she was never home. She was a photojournalist and traveled a lot, so I was raised by nannies and then shipped off to boarding school in England. When I was at UCLA, Mom ran off with another man, and Dad bought himself a trophy wife. I never met her. By the time he died last year, she'd already left him. I had to go back there to settle the estate, and I felt like a foreigner. And the ironic thing is that after all my father's taking and taking, what was left was the house and a stack of unpaid bills. I sold the house to settle them, packed up a few mementos, and left. I'll never go back again."

There was unresolved anger behind her words—conflict, too. She'd turned her back on her family home and her native country, but she'd still carried away those mementos.

I said, "It sounds like a lonely childhood."

"It was, but it made me creative, because I was forced to fall back on my own resources. And it made me want to promote a sense of community in my work, to make the world a place where people understand and respect each other. If I own any artistic vision and purpose, that's it. So you can see why I'd hate to give up on this film when it's so near completion."

"How many more shoots do you have scheduled?"

"Two major ones tomorrow—during the day and at night—and then a lot of retakes and some little stuff. Plus I'll have to find another Pele and reshoot Sue's scenes. And of course I may see something else I need as it's edited."

"And the whole process will take . . . ?"

"A couple of weeks."

Going forward seemed too big a risk to me, but I'd already counseled her, so I said, "Well, talk it over with Peter."

We reached the congested area near the Coconut Marketplace at Kapaa, and I took advantage of the creeping pace of traffic to call Hy.

"Peter told me what happened this morning," he said when he heard my voice. "We've worked up a plan, and three of our best people're on their way from Honolulu.

The crew is moving out of the B-and-B's where they've been staying and into the compound here."

"What did the technician say about the house's security system?"

He laughed wryly. "He's already gone back to Oahu. Nothing for him to do here. Seems somebody restored the sensors to their normal function while we were away this morning. The tech did confirm that they can easily be modified for audio and video monitoring."

"So whoever it was suspected you'd spotted them."

"Right. When d'you plan to be back here? I want to go over the security plan with you."

I considered. "That depends. D'you know where Tanner is?"

"He had a charter at noon, should be back by one-thirty."

"Then I think I'll stop in to see him. Glenna'll drop me there. I'm going to have a busy day, so I'll see you whenever. Glenna can give you her impressions of what happened at the shoot when she gets to the house."

*The shoot.*

*The shooting.*

I glanced at Glenna. The irony of it hadn't been lost on either of us.

After Glenna dropped me at the shopping center, I went to the shed that served as the office for Ace Tanner's Tours and got directions to the helipad from a young Filipina who was minding the store in the boss's absence. Then I bought a sandwich and a Coke and took them to a bench in the parklike grounds of the shabby church across the street. After I ate, I called my office. All was running smoothly, Rae told me. I asked to speak with Mick, found he'd taken time off for a dental appointment, and dictated to Ted a long list of details that would get my nephew started on some background checks I wanted. Then I set off on foot down a sandy side road to the helipad.

It turned out to be in the backyard of Tanner's small brown bungalow. The house, an A-frame with a lanai extending across its front, stood in a clearing surrounded by tall palms. The red chopper was on the pad, and Tanner was on the lanai, his bare feet propped up on the railing.

"Hey, pretty lady!" he called. "If you're here for that lesson, can't do. My noon charter got put off till two."

I mounted the steps and took the lawn chair he motioned at. He was dressed in the same type of camouflage-cloth jumpsuit as the day before—his professional trademark, I supposed—and sipping at a can of Diet Pepsi. Through the screen door behind us I could hear the familiar mutter of a scanner.

Tanner saw me glance that way. "I'm one of those nosy folks who need to know what's going on all the time, so I monitor the air traffic. You want a soda, help yourself." He jerked a thumb at the door.

"No, thanks. You hear about the sniping at the shoot this morning?"

"Yeah, from the police chopper pilot. Tough for Sue. Will she be okay?"

"The doctor says so. Peter's hiring guards from Ripinsky's firm for the remaining shoots."

"Should've done something like that when the whole business started. So you want to schedule that lesson?"

"Not now."

"Yeah, Ripinsky told me you don't like choppers. You'll get over it."

". . . Maybe."

"No maybe. Ripinsky took the controls on the way back from Lihue this morning, handled her like a pro. And he claims you're the better pilot." He glanced at his watch. "They're late. Korean developers checkin' out a piece of property they're interested in. I can't afford to lose this charter. Business has been the pits lately."

"How come?"

"Not much film work this year, except for this gig with Glenna and Pete. A lot of my other business was with Asians, both corporate and tourist, but with the collapse of the financial markets there, that's slacked off. Happening all over the Islands. Waikiki, they overbuilt hotels and shopping centers for the Asian tourists and now they're not comin'. Or they're comin' but not buyin'. I tell you, you go into one of those malls and there's nobody in the stores. It's kinda creepy."

A car appeared at the edge of the clearing, moving slowly as if the driver was unsure he was in the right place. Tanner stood up and waved. "Better late than never. Hey, you want to come along? There're only three of them, and I seat five. We can talk while we fly."

"Won't they want commentary from you?"

"Not that kind of charter. These guys want to go to the site, set down for a look-see. You and me, we'll have us a good time."

* * *

Good time my ass, I thought as I belted myself into the chopper. The three Koreans were already in back, brief-cases open, comparing site drawings and other papers. Tanner handed me a headset and I adjusted it so it fit comfortably.

"Don't go gettin' nervous," he told me. "I'm not gonna do anything tricky with paying customers on board."

"Good."

"Christ, what a wuss!" He winked, then turned to the passengers and asked them a question in what I assumed was their native language. They nodded and returned to their discussion.

"You speak much Korean?" I asked.

"Speak a little a this, a little a that. You got to, in this business." He started the engine, checked his gauges, tuned the radio to 122.7. "We'll take the long way, give you an overview of the island."

As he engaged the rotors, I leaned forward, ready for liftoff. The land began to fall away through the transpar-ent wall at my feet. This was my favorite moment of any flight, breaking free of the earth. As Tanner hovered, then swept the chopper forward, I smiled.

"You could get to like it, huh?" he said.

"Okay . . . I could get to like it."

He turned the big bird and headed out toward the sea.

For a few minutes we rode in silence. Because of the lower speed and altitude, I could make out more detail than on takeoff in an airplane. I looked down at the sea, studying the configuration of the coral reef, then stared at the cloud-draped peaks that crowned the island. Glenna had said that the summit of Mount Waialeale was the source of Kauai's seven rivers and the wettest place on the face of the earth.

Tanner said, "So tell me about yourself. You live in San Francisco, right?"

"Right."

"And Ripinsky lives on a ranch in the high desert, but the two of you are building a house on the Mendocino coast."

"He told you that?" Normally Hy wasn't so forthcoming with relative strangers.

"Male bonding. Or maybe it was pilot bonding. You guys've got an interesting arrangement."

"Well, we both value our independence."

"Last woman I had who valued her independence tried to make off with all my money. You like being a private detective?"

"Yes, I like it."

"Why?"

He seemed genuinely interested, so I replied, "It makes me feel valuable, that I'm helping people. I suppose if I were of a scientific bent, I'd've gone into medicine. Or if I dealt well with authority figures, I'd've gone into law enforcement. As it is, I've found the perfect niche."

"Kind of a maverick, huh?"

"I suppose. Often I don't do the acceptable thing. I don't like routine, find things funny that most people don't, like skewed situations, oddball people."

"*Mahalo*. Thanks."

"You're welcome."

He changed course, heading out to sea. "This is your

typical route for tour operators, in order to avoid wind shear along Kilauea Point. You should take a look at a sectional for the island; you'll see the word 'warning' more times than on practically any other chart."

"What else besides wind shear?"

"High-volume traffic, military operations, national defense operations, even electromagnetic radiation."

"Sounds like an interesting place to fly."

"It is. You know, I never did get at your reason for stopping by my place."

"I hoped you might be able to answer some questions. It's difficult trying to investigate when you don't know the territory or the people."

"Fire away."

"First of all, d'you know anyone who might want to stop this film from being made?"

He frowned, considering. "Well, you can bet old lady Wellbright ain't too happy about a film that's supposed to be a memorial to her long-lost, but I can't see Celia taking up a sniper's trade, or even hiring it done. Nobody in that family's pleased to see Pete spending money on the project, but with them money's not really an issue."

"There was an argument at the party last night, and money sure sounded like an issue."

"Ah, hell, whatever they argue about is just camouflage for the fact that they don't like each other very much." He slid the chopper closer to shore, slowed it. "There—take a look. All of that belongs to the Wellbrights. Pali House, Malihini House, La'i Cottage—that's Pete's—and Lani House—Stephanie and Ben's."

I looked down, recognized the aquamarine tiles of Pali

House and the lawn in front of Malihini. A smaller building was nestled in the trees to the west, and beyond that was a structure with many wings and a blue-tiled roof.

"Does everybody here name their houses?" I asked.

Russ laughed. "Only the rich folks. La'i means peace, and Lani means heavenly."

I was studying an area on the other side of Lani House—a wild tumble of trees and other vegetation that looked to be a deadfall. "What's that?" I asked, pointing.

"What's left of Elson's forest after Iniki got through with it. He was quite a horticulturist, took virgin forest and introduced other native plants. He'd sure as hell hate to see it now."

The deadfall looked hazardous as well as incongruous next to the well-maintained estate.

"The point I'm tryin' to make," Russ added, "is that the Wellbrights're too rich to worry about gettin' their hands on Pete's money. The only comparable properties on the north shore are those parcels right below us, between their land and the state park. Plus they own ranch land at Haena and cane lands on the southeast side."

I nodded, watching as we passed over the large parcels, then studying a crowded beach fringed with trees and protected by a rocky point and a reef. The road appeared to end in its parking lot.

"Tell me about Elson Wellbright," I said.

Tanner's face became thoughtful. "He was an odd duck, even for that family, but I liked and respected him. My people're poor relations, we've got mixed blood—mostly Hawaiian, some Portuguese, some haole. For all they claim these islands're a melting pot, it's still a class society, and the Hawaiians're considered the lowest of the low, so that made us undesirables to people like the Wellbrights. But for some reason Elson liked me. Loaned me books and taught me things about my culture that made me proud as any man. And twelve years ago when I wanted to start my own charter company, he gave me the money to buy this bird. I owe him big-time." He paused. "Listen, I want you to do something for me."

"What?"

"Close your eyes and don't open them till I tell you."

I looked ahead at the miles of treacherous folded cliffs that dropped hundreds of feet to rough waters. "Tanner, what're you going to do?"

"Stop being a wuss and trust me."

"All right." I closed my eyes, vowing serious revenge if he did anything scary.

Flying with your eyes closed causes a curious lack of orientation. You may think you know whether the aircraft is straight or turning, ascending or descending, but more often than not when you open your eyes you'll find it's at an attitude and altitude you didn't anticipate. Now, since I wasn't all that familiar with helicopters, I lost my bearings completely.

"Tanner?" I said after a minute or so.

No reply.

"Tanner!"

"Okay, open 'em."

We were hovering off the cliffs, so low and close that I felt I could reach out and touch them. Red and brown and deeply furrowed, they rose from crescent-shaped beaches and crashing surf to an impossibly blue sky. The westerly sun cast golden light over their deep green crevasses and obsidian scarps, but it did nothing to mellow their severe countenance. Nothing could mellow that—not even the passage of thousands of years.

My breath caught and I looked at Russ. He nodded, emotion tugging at the corners of his mouth. "The Na Pali Coast," he said.

"What a wonderful way to see it for the first time! Thank you. I mean, *mahalo*."

He nodded brusquely.

I glanced into the backseat. Two of the businessmen had their heads together over a diagram, and the other was punching a calculator. My eyes met Tanner's, and we howled with laughter.

"Skewed situations," I said.

"Right." He manipulated the controls, and the chopper darted around a series of outcroppings, suddenly enough to make me grip the seat's edge. "Now look down there."

We were hovering above a flat reddish brown area atop one of the cliffs. It was bottle-shaped, the bottom to the sea, the neck opening into a deeply forested valley. The tangle of vegetation went on for miles, flanked by craggy palis; a waterfall cascaded down one of the peaks and disappeared into the underbrush.

Tanner said, "This is where Sweet Pea's filming tomorrow. Took us a whole day to find the right location."

"Why here, in particular?"

"Well, you see those stones?"

I looked down where he pointed. "Uh-huh." They were in the center of the bottle—large slabs of volcanic rock piled one upon the other.

"What we call a *heiau*. Ancient altar. There're a lot of them scattered along the coast."

"People worshiped here? How'd they get to it?"

"The ancients were a hardy people. These valleys're crisscrossed by their trails. Now look at that grove of trees by the cliff's edge. Breadfruit. The combination of them and the *heiau* fits the legend Sweet Pea's documenting—the leaping-off place."

"Tell me about it."

He pulled on the stick, and the chopper began a sweeping ascent over the sea. "The legend concerns the desolate ghosts. Real losers, people who didn't have zip in their lifetime. After they die they become the invisible homeless, wandering around the island and tryin' to scam their way down into the underworld. The paths to the underworld—*leina-a-ka-uhane*—are always on cliffs, facing west and marked by breadfruit. The desolate ghosts take to hanging out under the trees, looking to hitch a ride below with a friendly spirit."

"Sort of a supernatural freeway on-ramp."

"You got it. Rides don't come along very often, though, and after a while the ghosts crack up. They climb the trees and hurl themselves off the cliffs, hoping to find a way below through a sea cave. I don't think too many of them make it."

Even though he was smiling, there was an intensity to his words that told me the legends and spirits lived for him as they had for his ancestors. There was a lot I could learn from a man like Russ—and a great deal I'd never understand.

"About tomorrow," I said. "Hy and his people will

want to be first cn location, and I'd like to come along, too."

"How many guards did he ask for?"

"Three."

"Then I better pick them up at Malihini House at first light, come back right away for you and some of the equipment. It'll take a few trips to get everybody and everything up there, and I've got a midmorning charter."

"Appreciate it."

"It's just the aloha spirit, pretty lady." He put his hand on my knee and briefly squeezed it. "Besides, I like you."

The gesture, coming from someone I barely knew, surprised me, but I didn't feel uncomfortable with it. Maybe I was getting into the aloha spirit myself. I said, "What about Elson and Celia? Was it always an unhappy marriage?"

"As long as I knew them, but they must've really loved each other in the beginning. She was a beauty—still is. Daughter of a rich cattle rancher on the Big Island and his Balinese wife. Elson was a handsome intellectual, had a doctorate from some Ivy League college. But they both turned into heavy drinkers, and you'd hear about wild parties and affairs. Around 1990 when Drew got radically out of control, the marriage went to hell. Celia threw Elson out of Pali House, and he went to live at La'i Cottage. You seen it?"

"Not yet."

"It's a great place. Primo examples of every Hawaiian art and craft. Tons of books on the culture. This was a man who cared about how the past had molded the present. And he believed in the sacred trust to care for and protect the *'aina*—the earth. He was part of this island, and it was part of him."

He paused to listen to the radio. Another pilot's voice said, "Hey, brah. Who's your charter?"

"Koreans lookin' at real estate."

"Catch ya latah at the Shack?"

"Be there by'm'by." Tanner grinned at me. "We'll stop by the local watering hole when we get back, have a couple a beers with that guy. He was a buddy of Drew Well-bright's, might be able to tell you something about the family."

"Drew is the youngest son?"

"Right."

"How'd he get out of control?"

Tanner's expression grew grim. "Drugs. Both usin' and dealin'."

"What happened to him?"

"Don't know. Maybe my friend can tell you."

"One more thing about Elson: if he cared so much for Kauai, why d'you think he ran off?"

He shrugged. "Maybe there was a woman he cared about more than the *'aina*. We'll scoot over to that property now, set the customers down so they can check it out. And while they're busy, you and I, we'll have some *fun*!"

The chiseled and striated walls of Waimea Canyon closed in on us as the chopper sped toward an immense rust-stained peak. Without the weight of the three Korean businessmen it seemed as light as a dragonfly. I clutched the edge of my seat as Tanner slid it sideways only yards from the cliff and we soared upward toward the sky.

He looked at my face and laughed, a bark of sheer pleasure, throwing back his head so his straight black hair tossed exuberantly. "You know," he said, "helicopters are basically unstable in any mode of flight."

"Thank you for sharing that."

"The true definition of one of these birds is 'ten thousand movable parts, each trying to do you serious bodily harm.'"

"Russ!"

He laughed again. My anxiety evaporated and I joined him. We crested a peak, flying backwards, dropped down into another gorge, and ascended in a series of quick spirals.

It was *great*!

"Tanner," I said, "you're nuts."

"You wanna try your hand at it?"

"No!"

"You don't watch, I'll start calling you Wussy."

"I'm not yelling for you to stop, am I?"

"Nope."

"I haven't thrown up, have I?"

"Thank God."

"Well?"

"Well?" He put the chopper into a steep glide toward the canyon floor, then climbed and hovered next to a wide rocky ledge. "Tell you what: why don't I leave you here for a while?"

"*Leave me?*"

"Yeah. I'll put down on the ledge, let you get out and sit there while I pick up my customers. You want to experience this place, really feel it. This might be the only chance you'll ever get."

The idea was appealing, but suddenly I was seized by an irrational fear that he would abandon me. Night would fall, the temperature would drop radically at this high altitude, and by morning I'd be fodder for vultures. Hy would scour the island for me, eventually come to suspect what had happened. If he could coerce Tanner into talking, all he'd find would be a few bare bones, not even enough to hold a funeral over. Of course, my family set no store by funerals anyway . . .

I chuckled, remembering my grandfather's ashes, which still resided in my father's coat closet. None of us had ever gotten organized enough to scatter or bury them.

Tanner frowned. "You're not crackin' up, are you?"

"Just thinking of one of those things that nobody but me considers funny. Actually, I'd like to stay here awhile."

As he set the chopper down on the ledge, I remembered what he'd said in conversation with Hy the day before and repeated, "Without disturbing any of the dancing angels."

He flashed me a grin and said, "Get outta here. I'll be back by'm'by."

I stepped down, ducked, and ran away from the wash of the rotors, then watched as he tipped the chopper forward and rolled smoothly into the air. He climbed and then was gone over the peaks. When the engine and rotor noise had faded, the canyon was as still as if this was the beginning of time.

I went to the edge and looked down. Steep red-brown

walls fell away to a deep green crevasse. Nothing moved down there but cloud shadow. I looked up, saw dark-bellied cumuli blowing in.

The ground at my feet was pebbled. I picked up a medium-sized stone and threw it into the canyon. It disappeared without a sound. I thought of the leaping-off place where the desolate ghosts disappeared silently into the sea. I gathered more stones and hurled them at the opposite ledge, but they fell far short. Finally I sat down, my legs dangling into nothingness, and listened to the silence.

There was a time when, as a lifetime city dweller, I found silence intimidating, too much a reminder of my own unimportance. Hy, who loved the silence of the mountains and the desert, had shown me its beauty. Now Tanner, by his absence, had allowed me to discover the silence of thousands upon thousands of years. And rather than reminding me of my own mortality, it was telling me I was a part of something that possibly had no end.

*Enjoy the moment, McCone. It may be the last peaceful one you'll experience for quite some time.*

## 6:45 P.M.

The Shack was strictly a gathering place for locals, a small frame bar and grill on one of Waipuna's meandering side streets, with tables on wooden decks that were staggered down a rise above the beach. No tourist decor here—no decor to speak of, except for candles in hurricane lamps and latticework overhung with flowering vines. Tanner's regular seat was the third stool from the end at the outdoor bar, and when he and I came in, a dark, wiry man on the fourth stool raised his hand in greeting.

"This is the fella you heard on the radio," Russ said. "Joey Chang, meet Sharon McCone. I been givin' her the island tour, and she's one hell of a passenger. I hear she's one hell of a pilot, too."

Chang grinned and shook my hand. "Choppers?"

"No."

Tanner said, "She will be. Took her on the canyon run, and she really got into it."

"Good for you," Chang told me as we settled onto stools and two mugs of beer materialized immediately. "He gives you his old free-lesson come-on, you should take him up on it. Man's the best, no kiddin'."

"Come-on, huh?" I narrowed my eyes at Tanner, who feigned innocence.

"Uses it all the time to drum up business. 'Course, lady like you, he'll give a cut rate."

Tanner said, "Hey, don't be givin' away my secrets, eh?" After a pause to drink he added, "You useta hang with Drew Wellbright, didn't you?"

"Drew? Sure. We was tight till seven, eight years ago, when he got so fucked up."

"Drugs, right?"

"Oh, he did a little a this, a little a that. But he sold more than he used. No, what it was, the guy was crazy. All that money his family's got, and he wouldn't sleep in the house. Started campin' all over the island. Last I saw him, he was stayin' down on those cane lands, Barking

Sands side. Was squattin' in his family's old sugar mill. Then he left Kauai."

"For where?"

"Who knows? Why you askin'?"

"Somebody mentioned him today, is all."

"You know, somebody mentioned him to me not so far back." Chang thought for a moment. "Who was that? Damn!"

"Somebody here on the island?"

"Nah. It was . . . yeah! Guy I know works at Honolulu Shipyards said he saw Drew down on Sand Island Access Road."

"Doin' what?"

"Don't know. Guy just said he saw him." Joey looked at his watch. "Hey, gotta *hele* on. Promised the wife I'd pick up a video for tonight. Stop by some night. You too, Sharon. We'll knock back a few, hangar-fly."

When Chang was out of earshot, Tanner said, "Sounds like things've gone downhill for Drew. Sand Island Access Road's near the docks in Honolulu—area's mostly industrial, though some people live there. Tough neighborhood. He's gone a long way from Pali House."

He signaled for another round, and we sat in silence while the barman brought it. The day was edging into dusk, the sun sinking behind the peaks. In spite of the fading light, it was still warm and a breeze moved the flowers on the overhead latticework, sending forth their perfume. Tonight the scent brought to mind parties in dimly lighted apartments near U.C. Berkeley, where the night promised any adventure you were bold enough to try.

"You know," Tanner said, "what Joey told us about Drew made me think about what you asked before—who would want to stop this film from being made. There's a small supermilitant native Hawaiian faction here on Kauai that might see disrupting the movie as a good way to promote their cause."

"And that is?"

"Hell, I don't know where this particular bunch is comin' from. I can't disagree with a pro-native stance; I'm mostly Hawaiian myself. My ancestors were flat-out robbed by the haoles and taken advantage of by damn near every other ethnic group. Like I said before, the natives're still last in line. It's a situation that's gotta change."

"How?"

"If I could tell you that, I'd be on my way to Sweden to pick up my Nobel Prize. There're no easy answers, because discrimination's been built into our society since the day the missionaries landed. Some people think they can cure it by legislation, others think they can cure it with guns. There's the Hawaiian sovereignty movement—Kanaka Maoli. Some activists want to enter into a process of decolonialization under supervision of the United Nations. Others want to secede from the Union immediately, return Hawaii to the twelve percent that's Hawaiian. I heard one leader of that faction say that if the others don't want to live our way, they can leave."

"Kind of tough talk."

"Especially for people like Elson Wellbright who were born here and treasure the Islands. Or people like me, who're Hawaiian, but basically American. And then there're the nuts, like this faction I'm thinkin' of, who use the movement as an excuse to cause trouble."

"You know any of them?"

He shook his head. "Only by reputation."

"So why did what Joey said about Drew make you think of them?"

"Because I've heard they're squattin' in the old sugar mill on the Wellbright cane lands east of Waimea, where Drew stayed."

It was a lead worth checking out. "Tell me how to get there."

"Uh-uh. No way. You're not goin' there, not alone. Wait till tomorrow. I'll fly you."

"No, I need to be at the shoot tomorrow. Besides, if it was one of them who shot at Glenna, it means they're stepping up their activities. I need to check them out tonight."

"Take you a couple a hours to get there. Be dark by then."

"Mo' bettah."

He grinned at my use of pidgin. "You're the pro; guess you know what you're doin'." He reached over the bar for a napkin, and I provided a pen so he could sketch a map.

"You follow Route Fifty outta Lihue. At Eleele you go west on the Kaumualii Highway. Take it all the way past Waimea and Kekaha and the Pacific Missile Range installation. There're a lot of cane roads out there, but the one you want's marked by a grove of papaya trees, only one of any size along there. Follow it for maybe half a mile, you'll see another road on the left. Take it, half a mile more, you'll see the old mill."

"You know the way well."

"Ought to. Those cane fields were in production till the eighties, but the mill was shut down years before. When we were sowin' our wild oats, Pete and I used to take girls there." Suddenly his face went somber and he put his hand on mine. "You go there, you watch yourself, pretty lady. Those people're tough and stupid. It's a bad combination." Then his eyes moved past my shoulder and he added, "Well, well. Here's Pete, Sweet Pea, and Ripinsky, come lookin' for us."

I swiveled, slipping my hand out from under his. Glenna and Peter waved, and Hy nodded. His eyes were neutral, calmly assessing Tanner and me. The three came over to us and, after some initial confusion about seating places, we decided to move to one of the tables on the sea side. As the others headed for it, I drew Hy aside.

"Did you all come in one car?"

"No. I drove the Datsun; Glenna and Peter came in his car. Why?"

"I've got a lead I want to follow up, and I need transportation." Briefly I outlined what Tanner had told me.

Hy said, "It's worth checking. You sure you want to go down there tonight?"

"I don't think I should wait."

"Want me to come along?"

I hesitated. "Yes, but one of us should stay with Glenna and Peter, just in case. Better you, since you're carrying." I'd seen the outline of the gun concealed under his loose shirt when he came in.

"Is it that obvious?"

"Only to somebody who's looking for it. After what happened this morning, I expected you'd get hold of a weapon."

"Peter loaned it to me, from his father's collection at the cottage. Nice Colt Government Model forty-five."

"You could get in a lot of trouble, carrying in this state."

"Let me worry about that." He took a set of car keys from his pocket and pressed them into my hand, then closed my fingers over them. "I'll mind things here; you go on. But, McCone, from here on out, I want you to be very careful."

His words held a level of meaning that I immediately identified. Dammit, why could he so easily read me?

## 9:53 P.M.

It was full dark by the time I reached the Pacific Missile Range facility. Clusters of low buildings lay to my left; the airfield's rotating beacon flashed green-white-white, green-white-white against the sky. The naval weapons testing installation occupied many acres along the shore, but soon it was behind me and walls of cane screened the highway. I met with no other cars, saw nothing but a road-killed chicken. Finally the grove of papaya trees loomed up on the right.

The old cane road was just beyond the trees—narrow, rutted, and overgrown. I checked the odometer, then turned and followed the road up a gradual rise. The Datsun's headlights showed red dirt dotted with hummocks and scrub vegetation; the near full moon shone down, silvering cracks and furrows.

After close to a mile, I spotted the secondary road that led to the mill, a flat, straight track that disappeared into the undergrowth. I stopped the car and grabbed a pair of binoculars I'd found on the littered backseat, trained them along the road till I caught a glimpse of faint flickering light. I'd driven almost as far as I dared, would have to continue on foot.

Several yards farther along the main road I came to a dumping ground: doorless refrigerators, dead washers and dryers, a burned-out truck, tattered mattresses. I pulled the Datsun behind it, shut off the engine and lights, and got out. The night was so still that I could hear the wash of distant surf; the moon laid a path to the foot of the secondary road, but its light couldn't penetrate the thick underbrush.

I took my small flashlight from my purse, fumbled around till I found my Swiss Army knife, grabbed Glenna's binoculars. Then I locked the purse in the Datsun's trunk, stuck the knife in the pocket of my shorts, and moved quickly toward the road. The flashlight beam revealed recent tire tracks in the red dirt.

A stand of stunted trees with three tall palms sticking up from it lay to one side. I burrowed into it, and something with thorns raked at my arm. A buzzing noise, then a sting. The mosquitoes were out in force. There had been relatively few at the Wellbright property since, Glenna said, it was frequently sprayed. But here in this wasteland the little pests were hungry for a feast of wild McCone.

I tried to ignore them and kept burrowing on a course parallel to the road. The lights were close now—

Somewhere ahead of me an engine started. Tires crunched on the ground, and headlights washed over the brush. I crouched as a dark vehicle rushed past. It drove quickly along the road, bumping in and out of potholes, stopped, and idled at the intersection.

The Datsun! What if whoever was leaving the mill spotted it?

I started back the way I'd come, angling toward the dumping ground where the car was hidden.

Too late. The dark vehicle turned that way. I drew deeper into the thicket; there was too much barren land between there and the car to chance running for it. Besides, even if I reached it, where would I go?

I heard the other vehicle idling again. Then its door opened. Footsteps slapped on the hard-packed ground. The Datsun's door squeaked.

He or she must be looking to see who it belonged to. Was there anything inside that would identify Glenna or Peter? I couldn't recall.

After a bit the door slammed and something else creaked open. The trunk, where I'd put my purse? No, I'd locked it. About thirty seconds passed, and then there was a clang.

The hood. Damn! Whoever it was had done something to disable the car.

After a moment the other vehicle moved, its transmission whining in reverse. Then it turned and headed back toward the highway. I tried to catch sight of it, but I was too deep into the thicket, and by the time I emerged, its sound had faded. I ran to the Datsun, slipped inside, tried to start it. Nothing, not even a click.

Great! I was stuck in the middle of a cane field in the dark of night with a dead car!

I pulled the hood release, got out, and raised it. Turned my flash on the car's innards. I know a fair amount about the internal combustion engine—you have to, when you're sister to two automobile nuts and you're also a pilot—and what I saw told me the person had pulled enough wires to seriously damage the electrical system. The Datsun wouldn't run again without the aid of a mechanic. And where would I find one at this hour, when the nearest town of any size had been closed up and asleep at nine o'clock?

Well, at least I had my cell phone. I could call Hy, ask him to borrow Peter's car and come get me.

I liberated my purse from the trunk, dug for the phone, pressed the power button.

Nothing. Dead battery.

I resisted the urge to hurl the phone to the ground. It wasn't the fault of the manufacturer or the cellular provider that the instrument's owner repeatedly failed to check its charge.

Okay, McCone, what now?

Might as well press on toward the mill.

The underbrush ended at a cleared area where an old sedan nosed in to a corrugated iron wall that leaned at an angle. Other walls slanted toward it, and the roof was tipped back so the structure was partially open to the sky.

The flickering light I'd glimpsed earlier came from inside.

To the right of the cleared area was a second mound of trash. I sprinted toward it and squatted down in its shelter. Smells assaulted me: rotten fish and what was probably human waste. I pulled a tissue from my shirt pocket and pressed it over my nose so I wouldn't gag.

Voices came from inside the partially collapsed mill—the low rumble of at least two men and the high-pitched stridency of a woman. Due to some acoustical quirk caused by the angles of the walls, I could make out tone, but not words.

The charged emotional climate inside the mill quickly communicated itself: the men were hostile and agitated, the woman derisive and insistent. As she spoke, they grew silent. She went on for some minutes, ending in a crescendo of scorn. For a moment no one spoke, but then a man said something in conciliatory tones. The others muttered, obviously defeated.

A spate of activity now: footsteps, bumping, scraping. The motion was reflected in the firelight that bounced off the rippled surface of the canted roof. I remained where I was, very still, gritting my teeth when a mosquito planted its proboscis deep in my shoulder. Twitched my arm futilely against another.

After several minutes a figure came through a gap between the front and side walls. Man? Woman? I couldn't tell. Glenna's binoculars hung around my neck, so I raised them for a closer look, but there were too many shadows here and everything came out a blur. Rather than try to fool with the focus, I let the glasses drop and stared intently as four more figures emerged. One was supported between two others—drunk, probably.

I expected the people to go to the sedan and drive away, but instead they skirted the mill and disappeared into darkness, the drunken person and his supporters bringing up the rear. After a moment I followed, moving slowly and cautiously, feeling my way on the uneven ground. The little procession was perhaps twenty yards ahead of me, and now I could make out what they were saying.

A man's voice: "Damn, Amy! Why we gotta do this?"

"We've been over that before."

Another man: "What it mattah now?"

"One's beliefs should always matter. That's what we're all about."

After that they were silent, climbing a rise that was covered in scrub vegetation. At its top they stopped, silhouetted by the moonlight: four men in jeans and T-shirts and the woman they called Amy, featureless and clad in a voluminous garment that moved with the breeze. The sound of the sea was louder now.

I moved as close as I could, crouched behind a fragrant shrub.

One of the men said, "We wastin' time, Amy. We got big trouble."

"The gods will protect us."

"Bullshit!"

"Quiet! This is sacred ground. We'll begin now."

Silence. The drunken man swayed between his supporters. I could make out little about him except for a silver earring shaped like a scimitar that dangled nearly to his shoulder and glinted in the moonlight.

Amy said, "Buzzy?"

One of the men cleared his throat and began a melodious chant in what I assumed was Hawaiian. His words drew the others forward, into a close circle. As the cadence rose and fell, the branches of trees that ringed the clearing cast eerie moving shadows. A strong breeze caught Amy's clothing, making it billow like the wings of a giant dark bird.

Suddenly for me they were no longer a group of argumentative, ragged squatters but a gathering of ancients performing their magical rituals. In spite of the night's balminess, my flesh rippled as the chant rose to a climax, then fell off into silence.

The squatters remained in their circle, heads bowed. Finally Amy said, "*Ahi wela maka'u*. We are all suspended somewhere between fire love and fire terror. When one strays too close to either extreme, he is burned."

Then, as if by prearrangement, they all turned and moved slowly toward the far side of the rise. Disappeared over it. I waited a moment, then scrambled up there, lay flat, and peered after them. The land sloped steeply and ended in a cliff above the sea. The people were turning away from its edge, coming back.

I slid down the rise and took shelter behind the shrub again. Soon they passed by in single file, close enough that I could make out the rustle of Amy's clothing. I noted four shadows, four pairs of feet.

A cold suspicion settled on me, and I parted the leaves

and stared at their departing backs. Three men, one woman. No drunken man.

As soon as the darkness had swallowed them, I scrambled up the rise and slid down its other side to where they'd stood at the cliff's edge. The ground dropped away sharply, and I felt a flash of vertigo as I looked at the boiling surf hundreds of yards below. It smacked hard on the jagged rocks, sprayed high.

No one could survive in such surf. Especially one who was drunk on his feet.

Or dying.

Or perhaps he was already dead.

I crouched down, scanning the water. No body. A skittering noise nearby made me pivot in alarm. Some night bird, settling in the branches of—

A breadfruit tree. The moonlight showed the peculiar scalelike pattern of the fruit's skin.

A breadfruit tree. A leaping-off place.

A desolate ghost, taking a forced plunge into the sea.

As I crept back toward the mill I heard doors slamming and an engine starting. The squatters were leaving, their dreadful ritual over. I waited till the night was still again, then moved to where the group had stood earlier. Stones lay there: great slabs of lava rock, arranged in a platform of sorts.

A *heiau*, similar to the one Tanner had shown me from the air on the Na Pali Coast. But for what sort of ritual?

Given what I'd seen here tonight, human sacrifice was a good guess.

I stepped up to the altar and touched one of the stones.

It was smooth from the passage of time. I imagined the intense heat that had formed it, drew my hand away.

*Fire love, fire terror.*

I knew both extremes well. Had strayed toward terror and nearly been paralyzed. Had strayed toward love and nearly been burned.

For a long time I remained there beside the ancient altar, listening to the crash of surf below the leaping-off place. Feeling the magic in this sacred spot. Imagining myself pushed and pulled between the extremes that fire creates in the human heart.

The mill smelled smoky and musty. I peered cautiously through the gap between the front and side walls, ready to retreat if someone had remained behind. Embers glowed in an old galvanized tub that served as a makeshift fireplace, and some crates that looked as if they might have been used to sit on were arranged around it, but otherwise the place had been cleared out.

Hastily cleared out. Trash that hadn't made it to the heap outside drifted in the corners, and some foodstuffs—dried fruit and ramen noodles—sat in a carton by the gap in the walls. A pot hung over the steel tub on a device improvised from a coat hanger.

The squatters weren't coming back here.

I stepped inside, took out my flashlight. Then I began my search.

Wine bottles—a cheap, sweet brand. Several unlabeled jars that smelled of okolehao, the potent home brew that I'd sampled on a previous visit. Take-out cartons from McDonald's and KFC. Newspapers: the Honolulu *Adver-*

*tiser* and Kauai's *Garden Island*. A used syringe, lying in
the middle of the floor. A ruled pad covered with childish
writing that was mostly scratched out in a different color
ink. That I'd take with me.

I continued prowling, locating a flimsy blouse whose
flame-like hues resembled the dress Sue Kamuela had
been wearing at the shoot that morning. I put it with the
ruled pad. A used condom was stuffed into a crack between the wall and the rotting floor. That gave me an
idea, and I examined every crack in the place—a time-
consuming task that paid off: I found a postcard mailed to
Ms. Amy Laurentz at a post office box in Waimea, a scrap
of paper with a phone number scribbled on it, another
giving an address in Honolulu, and something resembling
a campaign button that said, "Out of Union Now!"

When I was sure there was nothing left to find, I gathered my treasures and went to pass the night in the Datsun. There I settled into the passenger seat, my legs
propped up on the driver's side, and examined my dis-
coveries.

The blouse I'd show to Sue Kamuela; perhaps she'd
made it and could tell me something about Amy Laurentz. The phone number and address I'd ask RKI's people to check out for me on Monday. The "Out of Union
Now!" button probably had to do with the secession
movement. I'd show it to Tanner.

The handwriting on the ruled pad was difficult to decipher. I held the flashlight over it, made out a few words
through the strikeouts and scribbles: "the *'aina*," "listen
to the Hawaiians," "self-rule," "decolonization." The

phrases hinted at a political tract that the writer was having difficulty drafting.

Next I held the card in the flashlight beam. It was plain, postmarked Lihue, dated last Tuesday. The address and message were typed: "Friday, 9:00 A.M. Dry cave."

I'd heard someone refer to the place where the sniping had taken place as a dry cave. And the shoot had started at 9:00 A.M. Someone who had access to the shooting schedule had notified Amy and her ragtag band of the time and place.

Someone who had hired them to disrupt the filming?

Someone close to Glenna?

The discovery unsettled me, took away the possibility of sleep. I told myself I had to rest, shut my eyes. They felt gritty, and there was a throb above my right eyebrow. My stomach growled; I hadn't eaten since my sandwich and Coke. I wriggled around, searching for a comfortable position. Grabbed a sweater from the backseat and bunched it up under my head. Warded off the advances of mosquitoes.

When I finally dozed off, I dreamed of a sea cave where violent waves dashed a man's limp body against the rocks, their phosphorescent foam turning blood red in the darkness.

# APRIL 4

•

Kauai

**10:29 A.M.**

Malihini House slumbered peacefully in the sun against a backdrop of sparkling sea. Hens pecked on the lawn while a rooster strutted nearby, crowing proprietarily. It wasn't till I got out of the Datsun that I noticed an odd stillness.

I ran up the steps to the lanai, calling out to Hy and Glenna. No one answered. The screen door was pulled shut, the inner door locked. I took out my key, let myself in, called again. No response.

For an instant I felt a flash of panic—perhaps something had happened in my absence? Then I remembered the shoot on the Na Pali cliffs. I'd been so preoccupied with what I'd witnessed at the cane lands last night and my problem with the disabled Datsun that I'd totally forgotten Tanner was to begin picking up and transporting people at first light. By now everybody was on location, Russ was out on his charter, and I was stuck here.

It had taken me forever to hitch a ride on the highway, even longer to get a mechanic out from Waimea to tend to the car. Once the Datsun was running, I thought of going straight to the police with the story of what I'd seen, but decided it would be an exercise in futility. The man who had been thrown into the sea was probably food for sharks by now, and even if the police could find the squatters, it would come down to the word of a visitor from the mainland against that of four locals. In the light of day, the scene on the bluff seemed surreal even to me; to the police, it would sound like an okolehao-induced delusion.

I went to the small desk in a corner of the kitchen to check the answering machine and spotted a note in Hy's handwriting: "McCone—Hope you're okay. Call me as soon as you read this." Quickly I dialed his cellular number, was told by an electronic voice that the unit was outside the service area. Of course, on those remote cliffs; Hy hadn't counted on that. I hung up and stood there, feeling deflated and at loose ends. What now?

A walk on the beach to clear my head and think things over.

The path to the beach wound through ironwood, papaya, and banana trees, flowering shrubs crowding in beneath them. A pile of branches and a cut-up trunk lay beside the trail, indicating the place where the tree had nearly fallen on Glenna. I went around and looked at the indentation where it had once stood, but could see no evidence of digging. Of course the gardeners who'd been working here had obliterated any signs.

Around a curve, a series of steep steps formed by gnarled roots led down to white sand that was littered with driftwood. Shiny-leafed morning glories trailed toward the water. I left my rubber flip-flops there and continued on bare feet, turning west at the tide line and splashing through the cool surf. To my left the land rose sharply, thick vegetation screening the Wellbright property. The ironwood roots clung precariously to the eroding soil—near casualties of Iniki—and only the peaked roofs of the houses were visible.

As I walked, the beach became rocky and the coral reef curved in to meet it. A stream cut through the sand beyond Lani House, clear and fast, spilling into the sea. On its other side black boulders cascaded down the slope from the tangled deadfall—the ancient lava field, and what remained of Elson Wellbright's forest.

I stepped into the stream, was startled by its iciness. Bent and cupped up some water in my hands and tasted it. Pure and fresh, straight from the wettest peaks on the face of the earth. I waded across, and a rustling in the deadfall brought me up short.

A dog bounded out, a husky, its beautiful fur wet and muddied, wearing that smug expression they get when they know they've just cost their owners a trip to the groomer's. It was followed by a brown Lab, no more than a puppy and equally damp and dirty. They wagged their tails as they cavorted toward me.

I squatted down, bestowing pats and checking the tags on their collars. The husky was called Sitka, the Lab Belle Isle—tropical-dwelling dogs named for their cold-weather origins. The address on the tags simply said "Wellbright Estate."

"Hey!" a man's voice shouted.

I straightened, saw Matthew Wellbright coming along the beach in a tight, fast stride. His face was red and scrunched up in anger, but when he recognized me he relaxed and slowed down.

"Sharon! I didn't realize it was you. I thought some stranger might be harming the dogs."

If the dogs sensed his concern, they didn't show it. Sitka gave him a bored look and ran off in the opposite direction; Belle Isle yawned and sat down at my feet, her tail thumping on the sand.

I said, "Why would anybody harm them?"

"Well, given what's been going on lately . . . I don't suppose you've seen my mother or Jillian?"

"No, neither."

"Damn! Mother's been missing since early this morning, and it isn't like Jill to take off without telling me. Stephanie and Ben're gone, too."

Did he usually keep such close tabs on his family members? Or was he prompted by the same kind of concern he'd shown for the dogs?

"Well, I'm sure everybody'll turn up eventually. If I see them I'll send them your way."

Matthew nodded his thanks but made no move to leave. "How come you're not at the shoot?" he asked.

"Business to attend to elsewhere," I replied vaguely.

"You found out anything?"

"I've got a few leads."

"Oh?"

"Nothing I care to discuss yet."

He frowned but didn't press me. "I stopped by Malihini House last night to apologize, but nobody was there."

"Apologize? For what?"

"Our behavior at the party Friday. We weren't ourselves. Haven't been, since Peter returned."

"You mean, because of the problems with the film crew?"

"Let's just say that his being back has raised a lot of old issues." He glanced down the beach, where Sitka was heading into the deadfall, and bellowed for him to come back. The dog ignored him.

"I wouldn't worry about anything happening to him in there."

"Maybe you wouldn't, but I do. There're drifters camping out all over this island. I caught a pair of them building a fire in there just last month."

"That area does look like an attractive nuisance. Why not clear and landscape it?"

"No." He shook his head emphatically. "That was my father's forest; it contained over fifty different native plants and trees. I want it left that way, as a memorial to him."

What was it with the Wellbright sons and their memorials to Elson?

As if he knew what I was thinking, Matthew added, "Peter's trying to immortalize him on film. I have my own way of preserving his memory." He paused. "So where were all of you last night?"

I opted for a half-truth. "At the Shack with Russ Tanner."

He pursed his lips, eyes narrowing behind the thick glasses. "Ah, good old Ace."

"You don't care for him."

He shrugged. "It's more that I don't care for the way he's insinuated himself into my family."

"Isn't he a relative?"

"Distant. His great-grandmother was a Wellbright missionary daughter who scandalized the congregation by running off with a full-blooded Hawaiian. That's not enough of a connection to require us to invite him to Sunday dinner. The Tanner surname comes from another missionary family on Maui, but you don't see him flying over there to suck up to them. Anyway, I don't want to talk about Russ. He's been a serious source of aggravation his whole life."

Again Matthew called for Sitka. This time the dog wandered our way, looking as if it was his own idea. Matthew's expression grew defeated and somewhat wistful. If he couldn't convince his dog of his authority, how was he to police his family? Then his eyes brightened with relief. I followed his line of sight along the beach to where a slender figure in a loose white dress was walking. Jillian, her long light hair trailing out from under a straw sun hat.

"Well," I said, "there's one of your missing persons."

"About time, too. Maybe she knows where Mother's gone." He waved to his wife and she waved back. "Oh, while I think of it," he added, "why don't you and Hy stop by Pali House this evening? We'd like a report on the security arrangements, as well as one on your investigation."

The request surprised me and put me off. "It's not my practice to make reports to anyone but my client."

His lips twitched in annoyance. "It's Wellbright money you're being paid with. That makes us all your clients."

Jillian had stopped a few feet away from us, was bending over, writing something in the sand. "Jill?" Matthew said.

She ignored him, erased the writing with her foot, started over.

"Jillian!" He went to her and took her hand. She straightened. To me Matthew said, "Eight o'clock, and casual." Then he began leading her away.

No, I thought, I wasn't going to spend another evening watching the Wellbrights drink and bicker. And I wouldn't share my findings with anyone but Glenna. It was her signature on the bottom of my contract.

Out of curiosity I went over and looked at what Jillian had been writing. Only one word was legible: "Please," in a childish backhand. Well, I could imagine the damaged woman had any number of things to ask for.

After a moment I started off in the opposite direction, the dogs following. The lava fall extended into the water, and I waded out onto the flat, smooth rocks. Waves sloshed around my ankles, and in the tide pools I saw small crabs and shells. I reached down for a spiral of purple and white, examined it, and then began to hunt for others.

Not that I was a serious beachcomber or even had much interest in shells, but it struck me as a good way to focus my thoughts on my investigation. Both activities required you to examine small segments and look for details you wouldn't notice at first glance; both forced you to go slowly, not get ahead of yourself. Unfortunately, I soon realized I was doing far better with the shells than with the thoughts.

## 12:38 P.M.

The four-engine plane banked low off the coral reef, its landing lights turning the water to quicksilver. I straightened, adjusting my balance on the lava rock. The day had become overcast, hot and muggy; before I shaded my eyes against the glare I wiped moisture from my forehead.

Although it was a big plane, I hadn't heard it approach, as sometimes happens, depending on flight path and wind direction. I watched as it headed out to sea, blending into the murky gray of the sky. For the past five minutes or so I'd been aware of an increase in offshore helicopter traffic but thought little of it. Tanner had told me that the tour aircraft followed the same route we'd taken past here yesterday, and I assumed business was brisk because it was Saturday. But now I saw a veritable swarm of choppers homing in on the cliffs to the west.

Something unusual going on there.

The plane was coming back at around 500 feet above the surface, in slow flight, looking for something. A C-130, I guessed, military transport. I squinted at its fuselage, trying to read the insignia.

U.S. Coast Guard.

Search-and-rescue mission.

My stomach prickled with anxiety. A drowning off one of those isolated beaches I'd seen from the air? A hiker falling from a high trail? Or . . . ?

"Okay," I said, "don't go jumping to conclusions."

The C-130 neared the reef, its engines droning and chattering. Again it headed out to sea and looped back, farther to the west now. It was searching the water in segments, much as I'd searched the tide pools for shells. More choppers had joined in the effort, which centered near the cliffs. The cliffs where Glenna and her trouble-plagued crew were filming. The cliffs where Hy was . . .

I scrambled off the rocks and ran along the sand to the path to Malihini House, the Wellbright dogs yelping at my heels.

Tanner and his chopper weren't at the helipad, but the scanner muttered inside his house and the door was unlocked. I stepped into a simple white room furnished in rattan, spotted the unit on top of a low bookcase, and went over there. It was tuned to 118.9. I turned the volume up and heard the unmistakable calm, clipped tones of an air traffic controller's voice, probably at Lihue.

". . . taxi into position and hold, expect one-minute delay for wake turbulence."

"Five-eight-tango will waive the delay."

"Five-eight-tango, cleared for takeoff."

I didn't want to monitor the airport. I wanted to hear the traffic near the Na Pali Coast.

Dammit, why didn't Tanner have a sectional lying around here so I could check the frequency? Well, why would he need one? He was as familiar with Kauai airspace as I was with that between Oakland and Mendocino County.

*122.7*

That was it. I'd noticed yesterday that the frequency was the same as at Mendocino County Airport, near Hy's and my property on the California coast.

I tuned the scanner, at first heard only static. Then a man's voice said, "Three-two-five, say again, please."

"Four-niner-niner, I have the floater. I'm, ah, half a mile southwest of Makaha Point."

"Three-two-five, do you need assistance?"

"Negative. I have it covered, will hold for the cutter."

"Roger, Three-two-five."

"*Mahalo*."

As he spoke his thanks, the pilot's voice was flat, lacking in urgency. Someone had drowned, the body had been located, and now the Coast Guard would recover it.

Outside I heard the flap and drone of a chopper. Tanner, returning. I ran onto the lanai, watched as he set it on the pad with a feather-light touch. He saw me and waved as he shut it down.

As I started over there the door opened and two middle-aged couples spilled forth.

". . . awful, just awful!" one woman was exclaiming.

"Damn fool, if you ask me," the man behind her said. "Should've stayed off those cliffs."

"Well, we're not going up on them," the other woman announced. "No way, not us!"

The second man nodded. "Why should we, when we've got a world-class golf course at our doorstep?"

The kind of customers Tanner called shirts.

Russ got out and came toward me, arms outstretched, concern etching his forehead and muddying his blue eyes. He took both of my hands in his. "You hear?"

A chill washed over me, set my limbs to tingling. "Only that somebody drowned and a body's been recovered. Was it—"

"Hey, Ace!" one of the men called.

Tanner looked at him, mouth pulling tight in annoyance. "What d'you want?" he snapped.

The man took a step backward. "Uh, just to thank you for the tour, even if it was cut short."

"Sorry, man, the lady and I are upset about the accident, is all. Come on back tomorrow, we'll finish the trip."

The four exchanged looks that said it was the last thing they wanted to do, and beat a hasty retreat to a convertible that was parked nearby.

I clung to Tanner's hands, asked, "What happened up there?"

"I don't know much more than you do, just what I could get over the radio. Guy I know, flies outta Lihue, spotted somebody go over the cliff at the location where Sweet Pea's filming. Current took the body right away. Pilot got on to the Coast Guard—"

"Jesus!"

"Okay, cool head, main thing. We'll fly up there, find out."

The bottle-shaped area on top of the cliff lay flattened and foreshortened as Tanner guided the helicopter in on a shallow approach for a quick-stop landing. Setting it down was complicated by the presence on the ground of another chopper.

I said, "Police?"

He nodded, the set of his mouth grim as he manipulated all four controls with quick, consistent movements. I remembered what he'd said about helicopters being basically unstable in any mode of flight, and swallowed hard, fighting the tension that infected me.

As we neared the ground, the space assumed its natural configuration and I could see people. They were unrecognizable at this angle, but I stared hard anyway, trying to pick out faces. Tanner hovered briefly, set it down, and then I spotted Hy standing a few yards away and peering anxiously into the bubble.

Tanner reached across me and opened the door. "You go on ahead. I'll catch up with you."

I undid my seat belt, slid out, ran to Hy with ducked head.

"McCone! I was worried!" He pulled me close.

I hugged him, felt his warmth and the steady thump of his heart. Realized how truly scared I'd been that he might've been the one who went off the cliff. After a moment I stepped back and scanned the crowd. Glenna and Peter were over by the police chopper, talking with a uniformed officer. She looked drained; Peter was pale and stone-faced. Jan Lyndon and Bryan O'Callaghan stood by the *heiau* with Kim Shields, the camerawoman. They were whispering and glancing at Hy and me. All the other members of the crew seemed to be here, and two men and a woman in tropic-weight RKI blazers patrolled near the cliff's edge.

"Who . . . ?"

Tanner came up to us. "Ripinsky," he said, "what the hell happened here?"

Hy motioned us toward the neck of the bottle-shaped area, where the valley seemed to spill forth between the palis. In a low voice he said, "Celia Wellbright fell off the cliff."

Tanner's face went slack with shock, then flushed, as if he'd had some complicity in her fall.

I exclaimed, "*Celia*? What was she doing here?"

Russ said, "She called me this morning after I'd brought everybody up here, demanded I bring her too. I couldn't check with Pete to see if it was all right, and Celia . . . well, she can be imperious as hell. So I brought her." He glanced at the sea. "Wish I hadn't."

"No way you could've known, man," Hy said. "She tell you her reason for coming?"

Tanner shook his head. "She hardly spoke the whole way. Nipped a couple of times at her little silver flask, but I didn't think much of it. Celia never goes anyplace without that flask."

"Well, she didn't nip here, that I know of," Hy said. "Maybe because Peter gave her a damned cold reception."

"Did they argue?" I asked, remembering the scene at Pali House.

"No. She got out of the chopper, said hello to him. He told her she wasn't welcome here and turned his back on her. She seemed shaken at first, but made a fast recovery. Went over by those rocks"—he motioned to our right—"and made one of my men set up that chair."

The chair still stood there, a green-and-white canvas sling that when folded would look like an umbrella. Celia Wellbright's body had left its impression on the seat, and a woven tote bag leaned against one leg. I was struck, not for the first time, by the irony of how well our possessions survive us.

"What happened then?" I asked Hy.

"The filming started, and everybody more or less ignored her. To tell the truth, I almost forgot about her myself because I was concentrating on the crew members. They were rolling on a scene where Eli Hathaway, playing a middle-aged Elson Wellbright, steps out of the shadow of those breadfruit trees and walks slowly toward the stones. And that's when it happened." He shook his head at the memory.

I glanced at the breadfruit trees, then at the *heiau*. Caught Tanner doing the same.

Hy went on, "Eli was about halfway there, had just come out into full sunlight, when Celia let out this sound . . ." He paused again, plainly distressed. "If I had to describe it, I'd say it was like the scream of a coyote being mangled in a trap. Of course, everybody froze. And then she was up and running, straight for the cliff edge."

"Didn't anybody try to stop her?"

"We all tried. But she was running fast and blind. Almost took Eli and one of my men over with her."

Tanner let his breath out in a long sigh.

I asked, "Where'd she go off?"

"There, straight out."

"She didn't yell anything? Give any indication of what made her do it?"

"She didn't even scream on the way down."

I looked at the cliff's edge and shuddered.

Tanner asked Hy, "How's Pete holding up?"

"Seems okay, given the circumstances. He and Glenna told the police the whole story of this production company's troubles. I'd say it's a matter of hours before they shut it down."

I said, "If Peter and Glenna haven't already decided to."

"They'd be fools not to." Hy glanced around at the milling crowd. "Russ, will you do something for me?"

Tanner was staring at the *heiau* again. "What you need?"

"Start getting the people out of here. Take anybody the police say is free to go."

"Roger." He touched his hand to his forehead in a mock salute. There was a sarcastic quality to the gesture that seemed out of character.

When he'd left us, Kim Shields came over. "We need to talk," she said.

"About?" Hy asked.

"What I should do with the film." She patted her tote bag.

I said, "Don't tell me the camera was rolling the whole time."

"Uh-huh. I've got everything on film. Should I turn it over to the cops?"

Normally that would have been the correct course of action, but once the police got hold of it, I'd never be able to view the footage. I hadn't witnessed the actual event, but I might be able to pick up something from the film that would explain what had pushed Celia Wellbright over both the psychological and physical edge. "Where have you been getting it developed?"

"It goes overnight to a lab in Honolulu. They develop it, transfer the negative onto tape that can be digitalized into the Avid computer, make a simultaneous copy that can be screened on any VCR. We have it back by the following afternoon."

"Then why don't you follow that procedure, only ask them to put a rush on it and deliver it to Malihini House tomorrow morning?"

"I'll do that." She looked around bleakly. "What d'you suppose is going to happen with the project now?"

"Offhand, I'd say we're all out of a job."

## 6:57 P.M.

The police chopper had left, and Tanner had evacuated everybody but Hy and me. The afternoon's overcast had cleared, and the sun was making its leisurely descent toward the horizon. I scuffed my feet on the pebbled ground by the ancient *heiau*, touched my hand to one of its smooth slabs.

Hy said, "Jesus, McCone, I can't begin to make any sense of this!"

I'd just finished telling him what had kept me away all night. "Neither can I."

"Somebody disabling the car at the cane fields, Hawaiian militants, a body being thrown into the sea. And now the grande dame of the Wellbright clan has hurled herself over a cliff."

"Sounds like an episode of *The X-Files,* doesn't it?"

"Worse." He didn't look amused. "I'm beginning to wish we'd stayed in San Francisco."

"Are you?" I was, and yet I wasn't. These islands held an allure that I hadn't responded to on previous visits, something seductive that hinted of dangerous elements lurking just below their tranquil surface. I'd always responded to the pull of danger, and now I was feeling it in an almost sexual way.

He said, "The other day when Glenna told us about feeling a presence just before the papaya tree almost brained her, I chalked it up to artistic temperament. But from what you tell me about Tanner, we're dealing with a gonzo chopper pilot who talks about ghosts and goblins as if they're his best friends."

"They're not ghosts and goblins, Ripinsky. The man's mostly Hawaiian; he's talking about the legends of his ancestors, tales that go back to before *our* ancestors crawled out of their caves." I didn't bother to disguise my annoyance.

He gave me one of his cool analytical looks. "Don't tell me you're starting to believe in that stuff?"

"I think there has to be some validity to stories that have survived so long. There are layers and layers of meaning in this culture that're difficult to tap into."

"You sound as if you want to tap into them."

I was silent, watching the leaves of the breadfruit trees catch the wind and play against the red-and-gold-stained sky.

"Well?"

"Maybe I do, on some level."

"McCone, I don't understand. You've always been the most rational person I know."

"Maybe that's the problem. Maybe I'm too rational for my own good."

He shook his head, still watching me. I felt a distance opening between us. I didn't like or understand it, but somehow the effort to bridge it was more than I could summon. I just didn't care. Not now, not in this place.

I pictured a volcanic crater, glowing red. Saw Hy standing on its other side, much as he was now standing on the other side of the *heiau.* Flame licked at the crater's edge, then shot up toward the sky till I could no longer see him.

"McCone, what's wrong?"

I shook my head, turned at the distant sound of the chopper. Watched the red bird approach and slide into position for its descent.

Hy watched it too, his gaze still and thoughtful. When it touched down, he walked toward it without waiting for me.

## 8:39 P.M.

A high-pitched cry tore the velvety fabric of the night and sounded a tremulous counterpoint to the wash of the surf. Hy and I stopped walking along the beach and looked toward Lani House. Down the path came a figure in white—a woman in a loose dress, running swiftly and sobbing. She turned north, moving in an unsteady gait, and stumbled into the stream, her dress trailing in the water.

Another figure in light clothing emerged from the path and went after her. A big man, jogging clumsily on bare feet. By the time he caught up with the woman, she had crossed the stream and was scrambling over the boulders toward the deadfall. He grabbed her around the waist, began dragging her back the way they'd come.

"Jillian and Matthew," I whispered to Hy. "Peter said they're staying at the Moris' tonight."

The moon silvered the couple now. She was offering no resistance, leaning heavily on him. He put both arms around her, but her feet kept getting tangled, and finally he picked her up. I could hear her ragged sobbing.

Hy touched my arm, and we turned discreetly toward the water. Jillian said, "Oh, Matt, now everything's *really* over."

"Hush."

"I'm so sorry. So sorry."

"It's going to be all right."

She kept on sobbing, and after a moment the sound faded in the distance.

When I was sure they were out of earshot I said, "What d'you suppose that was all about?"

"She's not terribly stable, and she's taking Celia's death hard."

"Did you hear what she said? The same as the other night, at the party."

"Broken-record syndrome. Drunks're that way."

"And where did she think she was going?"

He shrugged. "Away from the others, I guess. None of them seemed particularly upset when we got back here."

"Except Peter."

"Well, he saw it happen."

I turned, peered through the trees toward the lights of Lani House, then at La'i Cottage, where Peter and Glenna were spending the evening in seclusion. At Pali House the members of the crew were making arrangements to go back to the mainland. Glenna had been adamant about giving up on the film, and Peter had agreed with her. They'd told the crew they wanted them back home where they'd be safe, and Tanner had already picked up the three interns from the university and flown them to Oahu.

I looked back at the water, watched the phosphorescent waves breaking on the reef. Hy stood silently beside me, arms folded across his chest. This walk hadn't been a good idea; the soft night and sound of the surf should have fostered closeness between us, but they'd only emphasized the distance that had opened on the cliff top.

I asked, "So what should we do now?"

"Go back to the house, I guess."

"No, I mean about the investigation."

"That's for you and Glenna to decide. I don't see any reason she'd want you to go on with it."

"Unless she wants closure. I know I'd hate to leave with so many questions unanswered."

He didn't reply.

"Ripinsky . . ."

Someone else was coming across the sand from the Mori property. Stephanie, jogging toward us. "Hey, you guys," she called. "I guess you witnessed that little scene between Jill and Matt."

"Is she okay?" I asked.

"She will be, once she sleeps it off." Stephanie came up beside me. Her close-cropped blond hair was wet and smelled faintly of chlorine. Her face showed no signs of grief.

"Jillian's upset about Celia, I suppose," I said.

"Celia's just an excuse. She's upset about life."

Hy made a sound halfway between a grunt and a groan, and walked away from us. Not like him to be so rude, but Stephanie didn't seem to notice.

I asked, "Why? Because she lost her baby after Iniki and can't have others?"

"That's what Matt says, but I doubt it. Jill never was a cheerleader for the blessed event."

"Is she in therapy?"

"She doesn't want it, and Matt doesn't believe in it."

"Maybe the problem's medical. She looks physically frail."

"She's got a strong constitution, but she doesn't eat properly. I've tried to get her on a decent diet and exercise program, but she doesn't care."

Stephanie's face was earnest and concerned. In her way, she probably cared for her sister-in-law, but they might as well have been from different planets. Stephanie could no more comprehend the depths of clinical depression than Jillian could understand a physically centered approach to life's problems.

I asked, "How're the rest of you holding up?"

"Oh, we're okay. The Wellbrights have always prided

themselves on their stiff upper lip. We've been sitting around the pool all evening trying to figure out what to do next."

"You mean about funeral arrangements?"

"That, and settling Mother's affairs. She left a lot of loose ends. Matt and Ben were always after her to establish a trust, get a proper will drawn up. But could she be bothered? No, she could not."

"Well, I'm sure you'll get it sorted out."

"We'd better—and quickly. There's a lot at stake here. Frankly, we could do with a little help from Peter. But is he with his family at a time like this? No, he's closeted in the cottage with his sweetheart."

"He was pretty shaken up, Stephanie. And I know Glenna feels responsible in a way."

"Well, she shouldn't. Mother always did as she pleased, and nobody could control her. And I'm sorry if I sounded snotty about Glenna; I know she's your friend, and probably the best thing that ever happened to Peter. But he has this tendency to run away at the first sign of trouble, and we really could've used his input tonight. In fact . . ."

"Yes?"

"Well, now that Glenna and Peter have decided not to go on with this film, your work for them is finished, right?"

"I assume so. Why?"

"We—Ben and I—were wondering if you could do some work for us. The estate's going to have to be probated, which means eventually Father will have to be declared legally dead. In order for that to happen, we'll need to conduct a search for him."

"I thought you had that done when he disappeared."

"Yes, but Ben thinks we'll need a more current report. Don't you?"

"I'm not sure. Why don't you consult your family attorney?"

"If he says yes, would you be interested in working for us?"

"Certainly." It would give me the opportunity to stay on Kauai longer and try to get to the bottom of recent events.

"Then we'll talk with him and get back to you. Matt will have to agree, of course, but I doubt he'll raise any objections. And Peter . . . well, he'll just be glad somebody's taking charge for him."

She sighed, shaking her head and staring out to sea. "It hasn't been easy, you know. All that time Peter was on the mainland having a good time and making tons of money, Matt and Ben and I were stuck here. Mother wasn't easy to deal with—her drinking, her notion that she was the queen and we were her obedient subjects. And then Jill went Looney Tunes. We can't keep her off the booze any more than we could Mother. No matter how well we lock it up, no matter where we hide it, she manages to get at it. Matt spends most of his time tending to her, which means he can't keep his mind on our finances, so it all falls on Ben's shoulders. And then Matt has the nerve to disagree with Ben's decisions, and the friction's driving me so crazy that I can't paint any more. . . . Forgive me for dumping all this on you."

"That's okay. I know it's a difficult time."

She nodded, turning and looking over my shoulder. I followed her line of sight, saw she was focused on the lights of Malihini House. "That house was built for Matt and Jill. When Mother threw Father out, they went to be with her, and Ben and I moved in. I loved it, thought we'd stay there forever. But Ben had bigger ideas." Her gaze moved to the roof peaks of Lani House. "Ben always has bigger ideas."

What had Tanner said the name of the house meant? Heavenly. Apparently, the name didn't reflect reality.

Suddenly Stephanie looked embarrassed, as if she felt she'd revealed too much about herself. She said, "I'll let you know what our attorney says." Then she turned and jogged back the way she'd come.

I caught up with Hy, and we walked back to the house. As we crossed the lawn, I smelled tobacco and saw something glowing red in the corner of the lanai. A figure sat up in the hammock that hung there and called, "It's only me—Peter."

Hy went to rinse the sand from his feet at the spigot next to the steps. I asked, "Is Glenna with you?"

"No, she's totally exhausted, going to try to get some sleep. I need to talk with you, Sharon."

"Let me rinse off first." I took Hy's place at the spigot, momentarily recoiling from the rush of cold water. On the porch I heard him excuse himself to Peter, saying he had to make a call. When I mounted the steps Peter was standing, pipe in hand.

"How're you holding up?" I asked.

"At the moment I'm numb. Can we talk?"

"Sure." I sat down on a lounge chair, but he remained on his feet.

"Ben called earlier," he said. "He told me Stephanie was going to talk with you about undertaking a final search for our father. Did she?"

"Yes. I'm willing, if all of you want me to."

"Then we have an agreement. How d'you plan to proceed?"

"I'll start here, by talking with people who knew your father."

"I can put you in touch with someone who was very close to both of my parents. And, Sharon, while you're still on the island, I want you to keep looking into the other matter. Even though we've scrapped the film, Glen and I need to know who wanted to stop it."

"Good. I hate to leave an investigation unfinished."

Peter went to the rail, began lighting the citronella candles that stood in clay holders. There was a restless quality to his movements, and a tension, as if he was holding back something he badly needed to talk about. I decided to probe.

"Thursday night at Pali House," I said, "you alluded to reasons for coming back to Kauai, other than to make the film."

He nodded and sat down next to me. "The family doesn't know what those reasons are yet, so I'd like you to keep this confidential."

"Of course."

He was silent for a moment, contemplating the embers in his pipe. "The reason I'm here is twofold: now that

I've sold my company, I need a new challenge; and I want to do something to improve Kauai's economy. It's service-based, highly dependent on tourism, and very sensitive to events like the crises in the Asian markets. We need to diversify, to be brought into the information age, and I plan to join the handful of high-tech entrepreneurs who're trying to bring that about all over the state."

"By starting another software company."

"Right. My strategy is to bring in some of the best minds from the mainland and to train locals as well. There's been a brain drain to places like Silicon Valley in the past couple of decades, but a lot of those people will jump at the chance to come home, and others will be eager to live in paradise."

"Sounds like a good plan. But why keep it from your family?"

"Two problems." He got up, moved to the rail again, knocked the embers from his pipe into one of the candles. Leaned there facing me and used the pipe stem to tick off points.

"First, Matthew. He lacks expertise, ambition, and vision, and his personal problems consume most of his energy. He'll expect to be included in the enterprise, but that's just not the way it's going to be. Next, Ben. I don't like or trust him, and I wish to hell Stephanie hadn't married him. She'd've been better off with Russ."

"Was that an option?" I asked, surprised.

"Once, but then Russ all of a sudden married somebody else, and Stephanie grabbed Ben on the rebound. Anyway, the problem with him has to do with the cane lands we own down near Waimea."

The cane lands where I'd witnessed a probable murder last night. Should I tell Peter about that?

Before I could decide, he went on, "The kind of operation I'm talking about will require a substantial physical plant and employee housing of a better quality than what's currently available. That tract is perfectly suited to both purposes, but I'm going to meet with opposition from Ben. He's got his heart set on building an exclusive resort area like Poipu Beach there, has already had surveys done and plans drawn up. That project is stalled right now because Matt's against it, but if he hears I want the land, he'll quickly come around to Ben's way of thinking. Until I've figured out how to deal with the two of them, I'm putting off telling them anything."

"That's reasonable."

A wave smacked hard onto the reef, and Peter flinched. Probably thinking of the waves that had claimed his mother—just as I was thinking of those that had claimed the man at the cane lands. Tragedy permeated the darkness tonight. Tragedy and strangeness. . . .

"Peter," I said, "there's something I have to ask you. After the sniping yesterday morning, you saw something or someone in the grove of trees across the road from the cave."

He looked surprised, shifted uncomfortably from foot to foot. "I told you—"

"I know what you told me, but if I'm to work for you, I need the truth."

"I . . ." He sighed. "All right, but this is going to sound crazy. I saw . . . I *thought* I saw my father standing under

the ironwoods, smoking a cigarette. Now do you understand why I didn't want to tell you?"

After Peter and I had signed a contract and he had left,
I went to the bedroom door and looked inside. Hy was
asleep, breathing deeply. Just as well, I thought as I
turned away. I wasn't at all optimistic about how he'd
react to my continuing the investigation.

I went to the kitchen, poured a glass of wine, and took
it to the lanai on the inland side, away from the crash of
surf. Lighted some candles and sat on a lounge chair and
sipped. And thought about what Peter had told me.

I didn't believe he'd actually seen his father under the
ironwoods. He'd only glimpsed the figure briefly as I was
pulling him to the ground, and impressions received
under sudden stress are notoriously unreliable. His
thoughts had been focused on Elson Wellbright lately;
that alone was enough to trigger a visual memory. In contrast, his plans to redirect Kauai's flagging economy and
his anticipated problems with Matthew and Ben sounded
well thought out and authentic. But because he'd told no
one about them, they could have no bearing on the film
company's troubles.

The candles guttered and flickered. I watched them
die, then raised my eyes to the towering palis—craggy
humps against the starshot sky. Thought about flying
over them with Tanner.

And that was a subject I was avoiding: Tanner. Fascinating man, suspended as he was between the past and
the present. The blood of the ancients flowed through his
veins. The legends and stories of thousands of years lived

on in his consciousness. How did a person connect like that? I had one-eighth Shoshone blood, from my great-grandmother. I even looked like Mary McCone, but I felt no pull from her culture, only a mild curiosity as to why she had left her own people to become the deeply religious Catholic wife of a much older white man. How did one tap into one's genetic roots to the degree that Tanner had?

More to the point, why had Russ and I connected to such a dangerously high degree?

I'd been fighting the feelings for hours, ever since I'd felt the distance grow between Hy and me as we stood on the cliff top, but now I let them steal over me. I pictured Russ at the controls of the chopper, working them with such precision. Throwing his head back and laughing exultantly as we soared over the peaks. Putting his strong hand on my knee and saying, "It's just the aloha spirit, pretty lady."

It was more than that, and we both knew it.

God, I couldn't give in to this! Hy was all the things Tanner was, and more—a man whose life had molded him into something fine and valuable. He'd spent his childhood shuttling between his crop duster father, who taught him to fly as soon as he could reach the controls, and his mother and her second husband, who had taught him to mediate fights. An ugly nine-year period flying charters in strife-torn Southeast Asia, the untimely death of his wife, his often heartbreaking work on behalf of the environment and human rights—all of that had served to make him strong and compassionate. True, he hadn't tapped into his Russian heritage the way Tanner had into his roots, although he did speak the language. Instead, he'd tapped into my mind and heart.

I finished my wine and suddenly felt sleepy. Something rustled in the shrubbery at the far side of the lawn. Moved slowly and stealthily in the darkness. Had I heard such a sound at home in San Francisco or on the property Hy and I called Touchstone, I'd have immediately gone on the alert. But here it had no power to alarm me.

Not here, in this land where the past lived on in the present. Where spirits walked at will through the warm, scented night.

# APRIL 5

.

Kauai

**10:28 A.M.**

*Elson Wellbright steps out of the breadfruit grove and
moves into sunlight. He walks toward the heiau. . . .*

And a figure that was not in the shooting script came
running into the frame from the left. A tall, slender
woman in a loose sky-blue dress, her long silver hair
falling from its pins and streaming out behind her. Her
face was contorted by shock, fear, rage. Hands outstretched, she careened off Eli Hathaway, who tried to
grab her, but she was already gone—crashing off the RKI
guard, pitching toward the cliff's edge.

As Celia Wellbright went over, the blue of her dress
bled away into the sky.

"Are we not seeing something?" I asked Hy after we'd
viewed the videotape and gone over the script for the
third time.

"I don't think there's anything *to* see. Celia snapped,
went berserk, and fell to her death."

"But why?"

"Who knows?"

"Wish I'd been there. I'd've kept an eye on her. Maybe somebody said or did something to set her off."

"McCone, you wouldn't've kept an eye on her because you wouldn't've known what was about to happen." Hy's voice crackled with impatience. "And I don't think anybody said or did anything. They were all concentrating on filming the scene."

I didn't reply, just got up and shut off the TV and VCR. Hy was badly out of sorts this morning, had been since I told him I'd signed a contract to work for Peter.

He seemed to have heard the echo of his tone because he said in a conciliatory manner, "So what's on your plate for today?"

"Any number of things, starting with dropping this tape off at the police substation and scheduling an appointment with Sue Kamuela. And you?"

"My job here's finished. I'm off to the skies."

"With Tanner?"

"Uh-huh. He says he can sign off on my currency in choppers in a couple more hours."

A rating that he probably wouldn't use again for years, but why shouldn't he go ahead if he wanted it? I felt a stirring of envy, wished I were flying too.

He was watching me with that still, thoughtful expression again. "What?" I asked crossly.

"Nothing. At least nothing that won't keep till later."

On my way to Sue Kamuela's shop I took a closer look at the town of Waipuna. Most of the buildings, including the church, were shabby, but that was part of their charm. The establishments that lined the highway were eclectic, with a distinct countercultural cast—New Age throwbacks, with a bit of the sixties for flavoring.

In addition to stores selling life's necessities there were vendors of crystals and scented oils, beads and hand-dipped candles, self-help literature and tapes, baskets and wind chimes, natural foods and vitamins. A large organic nursery occupied an entire corner. The roster of a weathered green shopping arcade, with a playground and picnic area in its center, listed enough therapists—aroma, hydro, holistic, massage—to cater to every malady. Something called Ergomania caught my eye, but I decided life was too short to delve into it.

Sue Kamuela's shop, KauaiStyle, was on the second floor of the arcade, off a gallery that overlooked the central area. Three skylights allowed natural light to enhance the brilliant colors of sample garments on headless mannequins that stood among padded wicker furniture in the showroom. No one was there when I entered. I called out to Sue, and she answered me from behind a curtained doorway at the rear.

"I'll be right out, Sharon. Have a seat."

I chose a chair next to a mannequin dressed in layers of teal, purple, and gold. Half a minute later Sue joined me. Her cheek was bandaged and there were minor abrasions on her forehead and chin.

"How're you feeling?" I asked.

"Not too bad. I look terrible, but these little cuts"—she motioned at her forehead—"won't even leave scars. The deep cut'll require plastic surgery, but that gives me an excuse to get my eyes done, since our insurance will pay for the hospital stay. I was lucky it wasn't worse."

"And it could've been, which is why I'm here. I have something I'd like to show you." From a tote bag I took the blouse that I'd found at the mill and handed it to her. "Did you make this?"

She turned it over in her hands, feeling the cloth and examining the stitching. "It resembles one of mine, but it's not. Probably whoever it belongs to bought it at the open-air market in Kapaa; they sell a lot of cheap knock-offs. Does it have something to do with the shooting?"

"Possibly." I replaced the blouse in the bag. "I think it may have belonged to a woman named Amy Laurentz. Have you heard of her?"

"Amy, the crazy haole? Sure. She's a modern-day nomad. Moves to a place that interests her, stays till she's sucked everything she can from it, then moves on. You know the type: one year it's Montana, the next Taos, then Big Sur, the north shore of Oahu, and finally here. At least, that was Amy's progression."

"You sound as though you know her well."

"As well as I want to. Back when she was still reasonably sane, she was living here in Waipuna with my husband's cousin, selling drugs for a local distributor. She got interested in Hawaiian culture, read a few books, and all of a sudden she was an expert on our people. Then she started writing letters to the editors of the *Garden Island* and the free shopper."

"Letters about what?"

"Protecting the environment. Self-rule for the Hawaiians. At first the letters made sense in a way, but then they got less coherent. Probably she was using a lot of what she was selling. The *Garden Island* quit publishing her ramblings, and even the shopper ignored most of them. Amy got frustrated and started running around to meetings and rallies."

"What kind of meetings and rallies?"

"Of the people who want to see Hawaii leave the Union. That's where she met Buzzy Malakaua. He's a low-life half-wit. Claims to be a lobbyist for Hawaiian rights, but that's just his excuse to make trouble. God help us all if we do secede and the Buzzys of the world get control—or lack thereof."

I took the "Out of Union Now!" button from the bag and showed it to her. "Would this be something they'd pass out at the rallies?"

She nodded. "I've seen a few people wearing them."

"So Amy met this Buzzy . . . ?"

"And took off with him. My husband's cousin was relieved to see her go. Letters have started coming to the shopper again, supposedly from Buzzy, but I suspect Amy's writing them and having him sign his name."

"Does Buzzy have family on the island?"

"A sister, Donna. She owns the bead shop across the street. Buzzy came here from Maui a couple of years ago, after his parents kicked him out, and started living off Donna. Every now and then she'd force him to take a job as a dishwasher or a busboy, but mostly he surfed, did drugs, and sat around the house watching TV."

"Okay to use your name if I go see Donna?"

"Sure. If he and Amy had anything to do with this"—

she touched her bandaged cheek—"I want them stopped before anybody else gets hurt."

I would have liked to visit Donna Malakaua immediately, but I had scheduled another appointment for one o'clock, and it would take some time to get there. Regretfully I set off on the road to Princeville, where I'd arranged to meet with Celia and Elson Wellbright's close friend, Mona Davenport.

The planned community was light-years removed from the towns I'd passed through on my drive there. Spacious homes and condominium complexes sat on well-barbered lawns where a corps of gardeners ministered to exotic plantings. A sense of everything's-in-its-place-and-don't-you-dare-touch-it pervaded the place. I followed the signs to Hanalei Bay Resort, past a golf club whose parking lot was full of cars. Even though the development was too tidy for my taste, I could appreciate the planning and attention that had gone into creating it.

When I stepped into the resort I realized that it was one of two I'd seen from the road far across the bay, spilling down the cliffs toward the water. The Bali H'ai was an open-air restaurant with a splendid view of the island's mist-shrouded peaks; a muumuu clad hostess showed me to Mrs. Davenport's table by the railing.

I recognized her from the party at Pali House: a reed-thin woman with crisply styled white hair, whose fingers now toyed with the stem of an empty martini glass. When I came up to the table her blue eyes were focused blankly on the distant palis, and it took her a moment to reorient herself. Then she let go of the glass and clasped my hand with icy fingers; I treated them gently, afraid the slightest touch would hurt them.

After I was seated and had ordered wine and she'd asked for another martini, I said, "Thank you for agreeing to see me today. Peter told me how close you were to his parents, and I'm sure his mother's death must've upset you greatly."

She nodded distractedly, watching a small redheaded bird that hopped onto the table and cocked its head at us. When no crumbs were in the offing, it flew to the railing and stared at another pair of diners. "It was so sudden," she said. "I could scarcely believe it when Peter called me. Celia and I . . . I guess you'd call us best friends. We go back a lot of years."

"When did you meet?"

"As teenagers, at boarding school outside of Boston. I was from Connecticut, the lonely and depressed product of a newly broken home. She was away from Hawaii and her family for the first time, and delighting in independence. She brought me out of my depression, showed me that life could be an adventure. We shared many of those, and then, on a visit to her home on the Big Island, she introduced me to my future husband, a college friend of her fiancé. The four of us—Celia, Elson, Harold, and I—remained close friends all our lives."

"Did you move to the north shore to be near the Wellbrights?"

"Not at first. Harold was in resort development, and we lived all over the Pacific, but we visited and kept in touch. On one of those visits we bought our property, and when Harold took an early retirement we built our house.

He's been gone four years, and now so is Celia." She blinked back tears, ran the tip of her tongue over dry lips.

"And Elson, of course, has been gone longer than either of them."

"From the island, yes."

"Do you have any idea why he disappeared?"

"I do not. When Peter called and asked if I'd speak with you, he said you're attempting to trace Elson. May I ask why?"

"It's a formality, prior to probating the estate."

Mrs. Davenport flushed angrily. "They're already putting it into probate? Celia's not in the ground yet!"

"It struck Peter as premature too, but Ben Mori wants to get moving on it."

"Yes, of course he would. The man's a dreadful opportunist. Stephanie only married him on the rebound, you know."

"Peter told me that. She doesn't seem very happy."

The waitress brought us our drinks and we paused to study the menu and order. After she'd gone I said, "I gather that Elson and Celia's marriage wasn't a happy one, either."

Mona Davenport looked down into her glass. For a moment I thought she'd refuse to answer. Then she raised curiously conflicted eyes to mine and said, "I suppose you expect that as Celia's best friend I'll take her side and say all manner of dreadful things about Elson. But the fact remains that it takes two to make a miserable marriage, and they both contributed their full fifty percent."

"In what way was it miserable?"

"Oh . . . the usual. What started out as a passionate

love affair between two good-looking and well-off people degenerated into incompatibility. Elson was far more intellectual and better educated than Celia. She was intuitive and artistic—Stephanie gets her talent from her mother—but she had no real means of expressing it. Celia resented Elson's work and the traveling it involved, wanted him home with her and the children. He didn't need the money and could have turned down the magazine assignments, but then he would have been as rudderless as Celia. Eventually they both drifted into infidelities and alcoholism, and weren't particularly attentive to their children."

"Peter seems to have fond memories of his father, though. Matthew, too. That's not usually the case with neglected children."

"Peter and Matthew worshiped Elson. So did Stephanie. But it was more the way a fan adores a celebrity than a child does a father."

"And Andrew?"

"Andrew was a difficult, disturbed child."

"A drug addict?"

" . . . Eventually."

"What became of him?"

She shook her head, lips pressed tightly together.

"To get back to Elson's relationship with his other children . . ."

Mrs. Davenport seemed relieved at the change of conversational tack. "It wasn't that he didn't love them; he simply wasn't good with children. In fact, the only young person I ever saw him relate to was a distant relative, a hapa haole named Russell Tanner."

"Hapa haole?"

"The term means half white, although I believe Russell's mainly Hawaiian. Celia resented their closeness, felt that Elson was robbing her and their children of his affection. She even went so far as to suggest that Russell was Elson's illegitimate son. Of course, there was no evidence to support that. I think there was just something about the boy that touched Elson in a way his own children did not. They didn't need him, you see. Russell did."

The way Mona Davenport spoke told me more about her than about Elson or Russ. There had been some unusual attachment between this woman and her best friend's husband—a friendship, certainly, perhaps an affair. Its exact nature wasn't important, but she might know more about the circumstances of his disappearance than even she realized. I decided to probe that again, and her mention of Tanner had given me a good starting point.

I said, "I understand that a dozen years ago Elson Wellbright gave Russ Tanner a substantial amount of money to start his charter service."

Mona Davenport looked surprised. "How did you learn about that?"

"Russ told me."

"Oh, you know him. Well, yes, the gift was quite large, and Elson could make no secret of it. It dealt the final blow to the marriage. When Celia found out about it, she made Elson move out of Pali House. Russell had always been grudgingly welcomed there, but he, like Elson, became persona non grata. It must have hurt him badly; he'd always valued his Wellbright connection."

"And did being made to leave hurt Elson badly as well?"

"He was relieved to be out of that chaotic household. He settled down to his work in the little caretaker's cottage on the estate and, when he wasn't traveling, seemed quite content."

"Then why did he vanish?"

She shrugged. "I'm sure he had his reasons."

"Are you sure you have no idea what they were?"

" . . . I have no idea."

"You were close to Elson Wellbright, weren't you? He told you things he didn't tell others."

She sighed. "He told me things."

"Things you didn't tell his wife? Your best friend?"

Mona Davenport's eyes grew stern and her lips pulled into a taut line. "Young woman, there are some things one doesn't tell one's best friend. Things that would hurt her. Things that would hurt others. There was a great deal I didn't tell Celia."

"Such as?"

"If I didn't discuss them with her, I'd hardly discuss them with you, now, would I?" She shook her head emphatically, staring into the sunlight at the far shore of the bay.

"Celia Wellbright is dead, and Elson—"

"Would have been seventy-two years old this year and had not taken good care of himself. It's not likely he's still living. Let him be."

"The family needs to establish—"

"The family! You mean Ben Mori. Peter doesn't need that estate probated quickly; it's common knowledge that he made millions from the sale of his company. Matthew's so weak and ineffectual that he wouldn't know what to do with his share. And neither Stephanie nor Jillian cares about money. But Ben needs funds badly. I've heard he's overextended because he counted on developing those cane lands west of Waimea. He even wanted to develop the land Elson's forest used to stand on. Thank God Matthew showed some backbone for once and stood up to him. I say, let Ben Mori wait for his share of the spoils!"

"Mrs. Davenport, with or without my conducting a search, the Wellbright estate will be put into probate. Elson will be declared legally dead."

"I know that. I'm only asking that it be done in a fashion that won't destroy his or Celia's memory. I'm sure that's what Peter wants, too." She paused, eyes focused on the distance once more. "Look over there, Ms. McCone. That's Lumahai Beach, where scenes of *South Pacific* were filmed. That was the romantic drama of my youth. Have you seen it?"

"Yes." Now where on earth was this going?

"You remember Bali H'ai? The special island? You're there—what they filmed was actually the palis of Kauai." Her lips twisted wryly. "In reality, Kauai doesn't measure up to Bali H'ai, even though our tourist board claims it does. This island has always been and always will be full of real people, with real problems. Some of them quite insurmountable."

"People like Celia and Elson Wellbright."

"And Matthew and Jillian. Stephanie and Ben. Russell Tanner. Peter. Let it be, Ms. McCone. Do enough of an investigation to satisfy the attorneys and the courts. Please let it be."

And that was all I could get out of her. Our meals arrived then, and she proceeded to relate a series of chatty reminiscences about the Wellbrights, anecdotes that were curiously at odds with our earlier conversation. Perhaps she regretted talking so frankly and hoped to distract me with her stories.

It didn't work. She only whetted my appetite for more information.

When I got back to Waipuna, I parked in front of Donna Malakaua's bead shop and remained in the car while I called Mick's condo in San Francisco. He was home, sounded grumpy, and when I asked why he and Keim hadn't gone away for the weekend, he replied, "Girlfriend of hers came into town unexpectedly. They're off someplace. It's raining so hard I'm thinking of drawing up plans for an ark. And there's nothing good on TV."

"Feel like working?"

"Might as well. What d'you need?"

"A background check on a person who's been missing for almost six years." I gave him the particulars Peter had supplied about his father.

"We're supposed to find this guy?"

"Find him, or find proof that he's deceased."

"All right! I'll get cracking on it." Now he sounded cheerful. Nothing like a difficult case to inspire Mick. I told him I'd check back later, and headed for the bead shop.

It was called Crystal Blue Inspiration, and the curtain

that hung in the doorway was of iridescent beads in various shades of blue. They clicked and swayed as I pushed my way through. Inside was a small space—more of a stall than a room—with counters on three sides covered with wooden trays much like the ones that printers once stored type in. Each space was filled with a different kind of bead, some plain, some fancy and hand-painted. Two teenagers with long silky hair stood over one of the trays, pawing through the wares and discussing them with utmost solemnity.

Instantly I was transported back to the days when my high school friends and I would drive all the way from San Diego to Laguna Beach to visit a special bead shop. We too had discussed our potential purchases as if the decision were life-altering. It was nice to see that things, in places like Waipuna at least, hadn't changed all that much.

A large woman who might have been in her late twenties was sorting through plastic bags of beads at the rear counter. She had curly black hair, a wide pleasant face, and troubled eyes. When I came in, her gaze jerked nervously to me. Quickly it returned to the merchandise.

"Ms. Malakaua?" I said. "My name's Sharon McCone. Sue Kamuela—"

"She told me you'd come by."

"Can we talk?"

"About what?"

"Your brother, Buzzy."

She glanced at the teenagers. "Adrian? Debi? You guys cool with me going outside awhile?"

They kept on sorting through the tray. "Sure, Donna," one said.

Donna Malakaua came around the counter and motioned for me to follow her. Without speaking she led me across the street to the shopping arcade, where we settled on a bench near the play area. The day had grown hot, and there were only a few children on the swing set. Malakaua sighed heavily, took a pack of cigarettes from the pocket of her pink shift, and lighted one.

"So what you want with Buzzy?" she asked.

"I was hoping he might be able to put me in touch with Amy Laurentz."

Her lips pursed as if she'd tasted something sour. "That bitch. Junk, you know? Was a bad day for Buzzy, he found her."

"I'd say so. He's been with her for how long?"

"Two, three months? Long enough."

"And you last saw him when?"

She dragged on her cigarette, watching the kids on the swing set. "Sue said you workin' for the Wellbrights. What's a rich haole family want with Amy?"

"She may have some information I need."

"Yeah?"

"Something to do with the old cane lands where she and Buzzy've been living."

She shook her head. "Don' know how Amy can help you. Wellbrights oughta know about that land. Belongs to them."

I tried another tack. "The three other men who are living down there—do you know them?"

"Three?" She frowned. "Only one I know is Tommy Kaohi."

"Who's he?"

"Kid from out Hanalei Valley. He's junk, too."

"How so?"

"Just junk. You know."

I watched Donna Malakaua as she tossed her cigarette on the ground and crushed it out with her flip-flop. Dark circles under her eyes, stress lines around her mouth. Worried about her little brother.

I said, "This Tommy Kaohi, does he wear an earring—a long, curved silver one?"

"Dangly, down to here?" She measured with her forefinger.

"Yes."

"That's Tommy."

And it meant Tommy Kaohi was the man whom the others had tossed into the sea.

"Where does Tommy hang out?"

She looked at me for a minute, then sighed. "You got a piece of paper?"

I took a small notebook from my purse, handed it to her along with a pen. She wrote Tommy's last name, drew a small map. "Don' tell him I told you," she said, passing it back to me. "Tommy's bad. Real bad. He the reason Buzzy's in trouble."

"What kind of trouble?"

No response.

"Maybe I can help."

The look she flashed me was disbelieving. Why would

a stranger from the mainland who was working for a rich haole family want to help her brother?

"Look," I said, "I've got a brother too." I conjured up an image of Joey who, last any of the family had heard, was working as a waiter in McMinnville, Oregon, but might be anyplace by now. "He's really dumb and screwed up, but I love him. And he's always getting into trouble. One time? He was drunk and rear-ended a cop car. And when the cop came back to look at the damage, Joey jumped out of his car and punched him. Now, *that's* trouble."

Donna Malakaua smiled faintly. "That's trouble, but Buzzy, he got worse."

"He tell you about it?"

She took some time lighting another cigarette, smoked for a while. "Okay, you got a brother, you know how it goes. But it's that bitch Amy's fault, I swear."

"I hear you."

"That Amy . . . *Damn*, why does he go with her? He got a job, was workin' steady. And then there *she* is, talkin' about the Hawaiians, but all the time she's peddlin' dope to them for that Tommy Kaohi. I tell you . . . okay, Buzzy, he come to see me yesterday morning while it's still dark. Asked for money. Said stuff'd gone crazy. What stuff, I ask him? He won't say, 'cept he and his friends got hired for a job, and Tommy decided to score big, and it all went wrong. Buzzy say him and Amy, they gotta leave the island. So I give him what cash I got."

"Did he say where they were going?"

She was silent again, staring at the swing set. The kids had run off, but the swings still swayed back and forth. I watched her worried eyes move with them. When she raised her cigarette to her lips, her hand trembled.

"He didn't say, but probably Oahu. Amy got business associates there."

"Who?"

"Oh, hell!" She put her hand to her eyes. When she took it away, it was wet with tears. "Amy never had no business associate wasn't a drug pusher. Buzzy, he got big plans, but you know what? He talks and talks and talks, but he's a loser. Just a loser!"

After I said good-bye to Donna Malakaua, I headed for the car, but halfway there I spotted Tanner walking along the sidewalk with a slender, ponytailed girl of about thirteen. They were both eating ice-cream cones.

His daughter? It had never occurred to me that he might have a child.

I waved; he waved back and waited for me to catch up. "Sharon," he said, "this is my daughter, Sarah. Sarah, this is the lady detective I was telling you about."

She regarded me solemnly, her lips smeared with pink ice cream. Her hair was a lustrous dark brown, her eyes gray, her oval face delicate. "Casey," she said.

Her father grinned. "Sorry, I forgot." To me he added, "She changed her first name for Christmas. Said it sounded too missionary. I haven't gotten used to the new one yet."

"I like the name Casey," I said.

"*Mahalo.*" She kept eyeing me as if I were some unfamiliar species that she wasn't sure she could relate to.

I asked Tanner, "Is business slow today?"

"Had some shirts this morning, and signed off on your boyfriend's currency, but nothin' going for this afternoon. Casey and me, we're just hangin' while her grandma does her shopping."

"Well, then, how'd you like to fly me someplace? I'm working for Peter now, so he'll pick up the tab."

"Sure, where?"

I showed him the map Donna Malakaua had drawn.

"Hanalei Valley, eh? What's this about the Kaohis?"

"You know them?"

"Yeah, they're relatives. Which Kaohi you lookin' for?"

"Tommy."

"Rob and Sunny's kid. What's he done now?"

"He may be mixed up with those militants you steered me to."

"Wouldn't surprise me. Kid's in his early twenties, has been a pain in the butt since the day he was born. High school dropout, doesn't work, into drugs. Got caught smoking *pakalolo*—local word for grass, means 'crazy weed'—when he was only eight. I heard he took over Andrew Wellbright's customers after Drew left, and I suspect he puts his profits up his nose."

"Does he live with his family?"

"When he can't find some other place to crash." Tanner glanced at Casey. She was sucking melted ice cream through the bottom of her cone and listening intently. "Your grandma gonna be shopping for a while, honey?"

She nodded.

"Want to go fly with us?"

A more emphatic nod.

"Okay, why don't you run over to the grocery store, tell her what we're gonna do and that I'll bring you home later?"

She nodded and skipped off toward the road.

"Cute kid," I said.

"Good kid, too. Smart, but not smart-ass. Gets good grades, stays out of trouble. Lives with my mother, since I'm gone so much, but we spend a lot of time together."

"And Casey's mother . . . ?"

"Died when she was five. Drug overdose. We were already divorced." Something flickered in Tanner's eyes. Anger? Sorrow? Whatever, he was aware I'd noticed it, because he fished his aviator's sunglasses from his pocket and put them on.

Casey came running back. "Let's *hele* on!" she called.

Tanner said, "Kid loves to fly, but she'll never make a pilot."

"Why not?"

"You'll see."

"She doesn't throw up, I hope?" An unpleasant image of the one and only time I'd taken my brother John's boys flying flashed before me.

"Nothing like that. You'll see."

"Take a look back there," Tanner said. We'd lifted off a few minutes ago and were headed for the island's interior.

I glanced into the backseat, where Casey had hopped in, refusing a headset and popping plugs into her ears. She was slumped to one side, fast asleep.

"Does she do that every time she flies?"

"Like clockwork. Loves the takeoff, but after that it's dreamland for her."

"Well, at least she's getting her rest."

"And giving us a chance to talk. What'd you find out about those militants?"

"Enough to make me suspect they had something to do with the disruption of the filming. I found a postcard in the mill dated last Tuesday and mailed from Lihue. It said 'Friday, nine A.M. Dry cave.'"

"The shoot that was hit by the sniper."

"Right. I think somebody who had access to the shooting schedule hired them."

"Somebody close to Pete and Sweet Pea, then. Christ!"

"At least that narrows it down. By the way, I had lunch with Mona Davenport today."

"Mona . . . ? Oh, right, Celia's friend. Why'd you see her?"

"Peter suggested she might be able to shed some light on where Elson went after he left the island." I explained about the need for a search before the estate could be probated. "Mrs. Davenport told me I should turn in a report that would satisfy the attorneys and the court, and let the rest be."

"Really." Tanner fell silent, concentrating on the controls as we encountered slight turbulence. Or maybe he was really concentrating on something else; behind his sunglasses his eyes had narrowed, and now he compressed his lips thoughtfully.

I said, "Russ, I've been thinking about Mona Davenport. She admits she and Elson were close. He told her things that she kept from Celia. Would you know what they might've been?"

"No."

Too quick on the denial. Tanner wasn't a very good liar.

"You sure? He might have told you the same things."

"Why would he have told me anything? I was just a kid—"

"You were no kid when he gave you the money to start your business—a very substantial sum that caused his wife to throw him out of the house. The other day you made it sound as if the marriage had just run its course, but Mona Davenport was very specific about what ended it."

"Okay, so there was a blowup over the money—but Mona's wrong. That was a good four years before Celia made Elson leave Pali House."

"Why would Mona lie?"

"She's probably just not remembering clearly."

"What *did* cause the split?"

"I don't know." Again, too quick on the denial.

"Could Mona be confused because that also had something to do with you?"

"Where're you getting these ideas?"

"It's a logical assumption."

"I don't—" He broke off, touched my arm, motioned ahead of us. "Look—Hanalei Valley."

Convenient, I thought, but I let the subject drop for now.

The terrain here in the interior was a brilliant green, crosshatched by red-dirt roads, the river snaking among them. Standing water glinted throughout acres of what must have been taro patches, and here and there stood clusters of iron-roofed sheds and houses.

"A lot of this land belongs to the Fish and Wildlife Service," Tanner said as he put the chopper into a glide. "Farmers grow crops in a way that benefits endangered waterfowl. Kaohis've got themselves a nice little business: Along with taro, they grow organic produce, sell it to the fancier restaurants down at Poipu. Whole family's in on it; they all live together in those buildings you see over there. Four generations and some *hanai*—adopted folks. It's the Hawaiian way."

Soon we were skimming along over the top of a windbreak near the buildings. We cleared the iron roofs so low that chickens scattered across the packed dirt. A big black-haired man who was spraying water onto seedlings set out on a table looked up and waved.

Tanner said, "My cousin Rob. You'll like him. Anything you want to know about plants, Rob can tell you." As he brought the chopper into a hover he added, "Reach back there and wake up the kid, will you?"

I took hold of Casey's foot and shook it gently till she opened her eyes. For a moment she looked puzzled— Where am I? Then she gave me a quick grin and sat up straight.

People were converging on the helicopter now: Rob Kaohi, several children, and a tall woman with long tawny hair. "The kids I can't keep straight," Tanner said. "The blond lady's Rob's wife, Sunny. She's from Kansas City, came here on vacation, met him, and never went back. Missouri's loss."

He shut the chopper down, and as we climbed out, more people emerged from the cluster of weathered buildings. Tanner made introductions while Casey ran off with a pack of kids, and after the seventh or eighth person, I gave up trying to keep names and relationships straight. Sunny and Rob ushered us toward a long house with a fiberglass awning over a patio, shooed a mongrel and two cats of equally dubious origin off the plastic furniture, resisted the clamoring of a child for a Popsicle, provided sodas for the rest of us, and all the time chatted about friends and relatives and crops and Russ's charter service.

I relaxed and sipped my soda, putting aside for a while the grim reason I was here and enjoying the cheerful chaos that went on around us. The Kaohis seemed to take it for granted that Tanner and I were an item, and he said nothing to disabuse them of the notion. I supposed they'd made the assumption because of the easy way Russ and I related; Hy was the only other man I'd ever felt so comfortable with on such a short acquaintance.

Comfort with an edge, though, I reminded myself. The kind that's always present when a man and woman are starting to feel an attraction. It was present now, and I warned myself against letting my guard down any more than I already had.

During a lull in the conversation, Russ asked his cousins, "Say, how's your firstborn?"

Sunny's tanned face grew solemn. "Well, now, Tommy's a subject we'd just as soon stay clear of."

"More trouble, eh?"

"Bad trouble, if you believe Grandma."

"Your *tutu*? What's she sayin' this time?"

To me Sunny said, "Rob's grandmother thinks she's got psychic powers, at least where our kids're concerned. She's always making dire predictions, but fortunately most of them don't come true. This time she claims something awful's happened to Tommy and that we'll never see him again."

The hair at the nape of my neck tickled.

Rob muttered, "Might be the best thing ever happened to us."

Sunny gave him a reproachful look, but didn't seem shocked. Apparently it was a remark he'd made before.

I glanced at Tanner. He nodded in a way that told me it was okay to be frank with the Kaohis.

I said, "The reason Russ asked about Tommy is that I'm trying to locate him. I'm a private investigator, working for the Wellbrights. Some of Tommy's friends may have been behind a number of accidents that happened to a film crew Peter Wellbright was backing."

Rob said, "Pete's worried about that film crew? What about his mother? Now, *that* was an accident."

I nodded agreement, didn't offer an explanation.

Rob turned troubled eyes on Tanner. "Thought this was a social call, cousin."

"Partly it is. Sharon's a friend, and good people." He rested his hand on my shoulder.

His cousin looked closely at me, then at Sunny. "Well, no sense protectin' the little shit. If he done something wrong, he got to answer for it."

I leaned forward, mostly to escape Russ's disturbing

touch. "I don't know as he's done anything. I take it he's not home?"

"Hasn't been home in weeks. Only comes here when he wants something."

Sunny shook her head. "That's not true. He was here last Wednesday when we were at the show. George said so."

"Lucky I wasn't home when he showed up."

Sunny sighed but didn't respond. "George is Tommy's younger brother. He's here, if you want to talk to him."

"I do."

"Then come with me." She stood and motioned for me to follow.

As we set off across the yard I heard Rob say to Tanner, "Nothing but trouble. Little shit's been nothing but trouble."

George lived in his own trailer behind the sheds and greenhouse: an ancient silver humpbacked vehicle that looked impossibly cramped. Probably that was why we found him seated at a picnic table under a nearby tree, tapping away at a laptop with an intensity that reminded me of Mick. When he noticed us, he held up one finger, finished what he was doing, and turned around, pushing back a shag of dark hair from his forehead. His eyes were lively, his round face open and cheerful, but when his mother told him who I was and why I wanted to talk with him, he became somber and somewhat remote.

I asked, "Okay if I sit down?"

He nodded stiffly and motioned at the opposite end of the bench.

Sunny said, "I'll leave you to talk," and walked back toward the house.

George's eyes followed her. "She doesn't want to hear any of this," he said. "Pop gave up on Tommy a long time ago, but she's still hoping."

"And you?"

He shrugged. Which meant he hadn't given up on his brother, either.

Perhaps, I thought, I was doing the Kaohi family a disservice by not confiding my suspicions about what had happened to Tommy. But they were only suspicions. A glimpse of a long silver earring shimmering in the moonlight really wasn't enough to base them on. Besides, Tommy Kaohi's people were already suffering enough; better to spare them the real pain till his death could be confirmed.

I said to George, "I understand why you're hesitant to talk with me, but I don't intend to report anything you might tell me to the police."

"I don't know you. How can I be sure?"

"Russ Tanner'll vouch for me. D'you want to talk with him?"

He shrugged again, fingers playing on the edge of the table. "I guess if he brought you here you're okay. What d'you want to know?"

"Actually, I'm interested in Tommy's friends."

"Friends!" He snorted. "He doesn't have any."

"What about Buzzy Malakaua and Amy Laurentz?"

"Those people're shit. At least Amy is. She used to run drugs over on Oahu, now she's doing it for Tommy.

Buzzy, he's just plain stupid. Tommy and Amy lead him around by the nose, can get him to do anything."

"Is he dangerous?"

"Buzzy? Hell, no. He runs from a fight."

"What about Amy?"

"She likes to push people around—especially guys—but I don't think she gets physical."

"Who else is working for Tommy?"

"Those two are the only ones I know."

"Okay, your mother said Tommy was here last Wednesday night."

"Yeah. Most everybody else went to the show, but I'd pulled an all-nighter the day before, cramming for an exam—I'm studying computers at the community college—and I went to bed early. Tommy woke me up, tappin' on the window. He was high. Nothin' new. Tommy's always high."

"He was alone?"

"Stoned and alone. Except for the movie camera. Big one, professional-quality. Had to be expensive. He gave it to me for safekeeping."

"He say where he got it?"

"Oh, sure. He said some guy he knows got in a jam, sold it to him for airfare to the mainland. But Tommy's never had that kinda money laying around. Most of what he makes he spends. You ask me, he cockaroach that camera."

"Cockroach?"

"Steal."

"You still have the camera?"

"Yeah."

"May I take it to show to the person I think it was stolen from? I'll give you a receipt."

"Don't need a receipt for something that's not mine—or Tommy's." George got up and went to the trailer, returned with a camera similar to the one Kim Shields had been using.

"Tommy say anything else to you?" I asked.

"Sure. When he's high he can't stop talkin'. He say he's stayin' down at the sugar mill on the old Wellbright plantation with Buzzy and Amy and a couple a guys from Maui. Somebody told them it was okay to use the place, but I don't believe that. He told me he had some radical plan, was gonna get rich. What plan? I ask him. He can't say. Why not? Because it involves people in high places. What people? I'd know if he named them. And so on. Yada, yada, yada. None of it means shit, comin' from Tommy."

George's eyes were bleak and angry. A love-hate relationship with his brother, if I ever saw one. I suspected the whole family—even Rob—felt the same. It would make losing Tommy even more painful.

## 6:10 P.M.

The chopper settled gently onto the lawn in front of Malihini House, its rotors setting the branches of the trees to blowing as if in a gale. I took off my headset and seat belt, got out, and extended my hand to Casey.

Tanner had offered to fly me there, and back to Waipuna later to fetch the Datsun. He wanted, he said, to deliver his formal condolences on Celia's death and to introduce Casey to her relatives. I agreed to the plan because I sensed he had an ulterior motive. Besides, his presence would probably forestall the family summoning me to Pali House to report on my investigation. I had no intention of doing so—the only Wellbright entitled to one was Peter—but would just as soon avoid an unpleasant confrontation.

Casey hopped to the ground and looked around, her eyes widening. "Cool," she said. Then, "Awesome." It was clear she'd had no inkling of how wealthy these distant relatives were.

Tanner joined us, carrying the camera. "Big bucks here, honey, and this ain't the half of it."

She gave him a disbelieving look as we started toward the house, Tanner putting his hand on my shoulder and jokingly grumbling about me making an old man lug a heavy camera uphill.

Hy had come out on the lanai, was leaning on the railing, watching us. His stance was loose, his expression welcoming, but as we came closer I caught a hint of underlying tension. And in his eyes . . .

I'd seen that look before, often enough to know it spelled trouble. A carefully controlled anger, reminding me that despite his domesticity and good humor, this was a man who could be very dangerous.

His gaze moved from my face to where Tanner's hand rested on my shoulder and back again. Then he nodded slightly, as if confirming something. Russ's fingers tightened, but I pulled away, the spot where he'd been touching me feeling unaccountably hot.

Hy smiled ironically. "I see you found the missing camera. And a young woman." He nodded to Casey.

I introduced them, went up on the lanai, and stood beside him while Tanner and Casey flopped down on the steps.

"I'm pretty sure this is the camera Glenna had on rental," I said. "Where is she?"

"Peter's. He called her around an hour ago, all agitated over something concerning his father's will."

"They're reading wills already? Celia hasn't even been buried, and Elson's not legally dead."

He shrugged. "All I know is what Glenna told me. She was out of here like a shot. Guess she wanted to check out the situation, safeguard her financial future."

Tanner was sitting up straighter now, thoughtful and alert.

I said, "*Her* financial future? I don't understand."

"There seem to be a number of things you don't understand lately, McCone. I'll spell this one out for you: My take on Glenna is that she came over here, saw all this, and decided she wanted a piece of it. The best way of accomplishing that was to sink her hooks into Peter. For a while it looked good. She had something to barter—the ability to get the film made—in exchange for his affections. But now everything's fallen apart, and she's getting desperate."

"I can't believe she's that mercenary."

"Something about her behavior's been off since we've been here."

"But she's never been interested in money. She lives from hand to mouth."

"That was before. A place like this changes things, now, doesn't it?" He was looking at Tanner.

"What does that mean?" I demanded.

"I said I'd spell out one thing for you. Now you're on your own." He turned and went into the house.

I watched him go, my cheeks flushing as his meaning came clear. Then I looked at Russ; he'd grasped it, too.

Why had Hy felt compelled to bring it out into the open?

Russ sent Casey to explore the beach, and then he and I took the path to the cottage, under papaya trees hung heavy with unripe fruit. Silence lay between us. The unspoken was now out in the open, and neither of us seemed able to deal with it. I didn't know what he was thinking, but I was hoping that if we didn't speak of it the problem would simply go away. Unfortunately it had been my experience that problems usually hung around till confronted.

When no one answered our knock, we went inside the cottage. Tanner called out to Peter, but received no reply. "Guess they've gone someplace."

"Where, d'you suppose?"

"Well, his Volvo's here, so he's probably at Pali House or Stephanie and Ben's." He noticed how I was looking around the room and added, "Some place, eh?"

La'i Cottage was a smaller version of Malihini House: one bedroom and another room combining living space and kitchen. As Tanner had told me, it was crammed with bookcases and cultural artifacts. An elaborate feather cloak decorated one wall; musical instruments hung between two bookcases; shell leis, a quilt, several paintings, and a collection of wood, gourd, and coconut calabashes were only a few of the objects tucked here and there, wherever space would permit. The furnishings were old but well tended, of a heavy dark construction, and had probably come around Cape Horn with the Wellbright missionaries. A freestanding cabinet held a gun collection extending from the Revolutionary War to modern times. To me, the total effect was extremely claustrophobic.

Or maybe it was because Tanner and I were alone there.

"Is this exactly as Elson left it?" I asked him.

"No. Hurricane Iniki hit right after he went away, and the roof was blown off this cottage. Did a lot of damage, but La'i Cottage—like Pali House—was strongly built and survived. Matt had it repaired and had what was salvageable of his father's stuff put back as he'd left it. Pete hasn't changed it much."

"The hurricane—it was a real watershed for the island."

Russ nodded.

"You say Pali House survived. What about Malihini House?"

"It was flattened. Stephanie and Ben lived there at the time, but they'd taken shelter with Celia. Otherwise they would've been killed. Afterward Ben wanted to build their own house, and Celia had Malihini rebuilt as guest quarters." He paused, shaking his head. "Iniki was like nothing any of us had ever experienced, and we're used to punishing storms. I could tell you stories, and maybe someday I will, but right now I prefer not to relive it."

"Then let's find out where Peter and Glenna are instead."

I went to a phone on an end table; it had an automatic-dial feature and the card on the handset listed several numbers. There was no answer at the Moris', but Peter picked up at Pali House.

"Tanner and I are at your cottage," I told him. "We located what I think is the missing camera and brought it to show to Glenna."

"Russ is with you?" He lowered his voice.

"That's right."

A pause. It sounded as if he'd covered the mouthpiece. "You two might as well come up here. Bring the camera."

I replaced the receiver. "He wants us there."

"Both of us? That's a surprise. I haven't been allowed to set foot in Pali House for years."

"Maybe now that Celia's gone the ban's been lifted. Anyway, he sounds stressed."

"That whole goddamn family's permanently stressed." He hesitated. "Sharon, before we go, we ought to talk."

"About what?"

"You and me."

"This isn't the time for that."

"When is?"

"I don't know. Maybe never."

He moved closer, put his hand to my cheek, brushed back a strand of hair with his fingertip. I felt the heat of his body, the heat rising in mine.

He said, "We can't ignore what's happening here."

Oh, Christ, he wasn't going to let it go! And Hy wouldn't, either. Why was I the only one of the three of us with any sense?

"Look, Sharon, maybe we could've willed it away if Hy hadn't forced the issue. But he did, and now—" His hands grasped my shoulders, pulled me toward him.

"No!" I jerked free, stepped back. "We won't do this, we won't go there. If we talk about it, we may say things we can't take back." I spun around, heading for the door. "Come on. We're expected at Pali House."

"Stop—"

"No, you stop! I didn't ask for this to happen. I have a life, I have a future planned. Don't you interfere with that."

For a few seconds he didn't move or speak. Then he picked up the camera and followed me. As he shut the door behind us, he said softly, "I'm not the only one who's interfering."

Peter met us at the door of Pali House, looking haggard. When he saw Casey—Tanner had insisted on bringing her along—he seemed surprised but greeted her warmly.

Tanner said, "I'm sorry about your mother, Pete."

"Thanks," he replied, slapping him on the shoulder.

It occurred to me that the two of them seemed more like real brothers than Peter and Matthew did. Some kinship of spirit there, a curiosity about the world and what it had to offer, as well as a willingness to take risks. Compassion, too: Peter noticed that Casey looked uncomfortable and took her hand as he led us into the central patio.

Good that he did, because the tension there was so thick
it would have taken more than the proverbial knife to
hack through it.

Stephanie and Ben sat side by side on a wicker sofa,
stern and watchful. Looking out for business, I supposed.
Glenna perched on a nearby hassock, surveying the scene
as if she were about to start filming. I half expected her to
raise her hands to her eyes and frame it. Matthew was
pacing in jerky strides along a row of decorative aquamarine tiles set amid the terra-cotta. His brow was knitted in
concentration, and he appeared to be having an intense
conversation with himself. When we came out of the
house he stopped and turned, hands balled into fists at his
sides.

"Who the hell's that?" He pointed to Casey.

Tanner touched her head in reassurance. "Relative of
yours, Matt—my daughter, Sarah."

This time Casey didn't object to his use of her "too
missionary" name. She did stand her ground, however, as
Matthew scrutinized her rudely, looking him in the eye
with a directness unusual in one of her age.

Russ added, "Guess you know her momma was Liza
Santos." There was a needling quality to his tone.

Matthew's cheeks colored, and his eyes jerked to Russ.
For a moment he glared at him, compressing his lips as if
guarding against saying something he might later regret.
Bad history there, I thought, watching Tanner return
Matthew's look with a level stare.

Matthew broke eye contact first. "Well, Russ," he said,
"this is an adult conference."

Peter asked Casey, "How'd you like some ice cream or a soda?"

She looked to Tanner for direction and, when he nodded, said, "I would. *Mahalo*." Peter told her the cook's name and gave her directions to the kitchen. As she left the patio, she threw Matthew a parting glance that said she found this relative seriously weird.

Glenna cleared her throat. "Sharon? Is that the camera you recovered?"

I nodded, and Tanner took it to her. She examined it, checked the serial number. "Yes, it's the one that was stolen. Where'd you find it?"

"I'd rather go into that later, if you don't mind."

"Whenever."

At Peter and Stephanie's urging we sat down—all except Matthew, who had resumed his pacing. Ben said, "We asked you here, Russ, because a situation's come up, and you seem to be part of it."

Tanner waited, looking only mildly interested.

"The situation concerns . . . Let me start at the beginning: Elson's and Celia's wills were in the safe here, and I delivered them to our attorney, Michael Blankenship, this morning. They were drawn up in the early eighties. Very similar to each other, except for specific bequests to charities, with the bulk of the estate going to the surviving spouse and to be divided among Stephanie, Peter, Matthew, and Drew at the time of that party's death. A codicil to Celia's, dated 1990, removed Drew as an heir."

Tanner shifted in his chair. "Must've been hard for you to deal with such matters, in your grief."

Ben flushed. "Look, Russ, if you're going to start on me, you can wait to hear this from Michael!"

"Sorry. Go on." Tanner glanced at me, his eyes glinting mischievously. I couldn't blame him for baiting Ben.

"All right. Michael called me this afternoon. The situation is irregular: Celia's property goes to Elson. But as we all know, Elson's missing and by now could very conceivably be dead. Sharon's probably told you that we've already set the machinery in motion for getting him declared legally dead." He nodded at me. "But since the estate will be in limbo until we can do that, Michael wants to petition the court to have one of us declared conservator."

"Ben, will you get to the point?"

"Dammit, Russ, stop interrupting! This is a complicated situation." Ben looked around for help from the others, but none was forthcoming. Stephanie and Peter sat very still, their eyes on Tanner, and even Matthew had stopped pacing. Glenna perched expectantly on the edge of the hassock. Now I could feel their collective tension infecting me. Only Tanner seemed at ease.

Ben grimaced, began speaking again. "In the course of our conversation, Michael pointed out that the copy of Elson's will that I delivered this morning is no longer in force. He has in his safe the original of a *later* will, drawn up in 1990. It differs from Celia's in only one significant point: the estate is to be divided among Stephanie, Peter, Matthew"—he paused dramatically, pointed at Tanner—"and *you*. Certain provisions would make it extremely difficult for Celia—or for us, now—to challenge the bequest."

Tanner nodded. "That's correct."

Ben's eyes widened. Stephanie, Peter, and Glenna made astonished sounds. And Matthew, who had been standing several feet away, strode over to Russ. "You *knew* about this?" he demanded, his voice shaking with anger.

"Your father gave me a copy of the will after he made it."

"For God's sake, why?"

"I assume so I could protect my interests."

"No, I mean why were you included at all?"

"He had his reasons. And they're private."

"Goddamn it, all your life you've been sucking up to us—"

Peter said, "Matt, there's no point in rehashing old resentments." To Russ he added, "I can't believe you've known about this since 1990 and never told any of us. Did my mother know?"

"She found out a couple of years later."

"When she threw Father out of the house."

Tanner nodded.

Ben said, "What I want to know, Russ, is what these so-called private reasons of Elson's were. He's dead, so you can tell us."

"You know," Russ said, "for somebody who's only a relative by marriage, you seem awfully eager to get your hands on the Wellbright fortune."

"Russ!" Stephanie exclaimed. "That's not fair!"

I glanced at Peter; he was nodding slightly in agreement with Tanner.

"Sorry," Tanner said easily. "I guess we're all on edge. But in answer to Ben's question, no, I can't talk about Elson's reasons. I will tell you one thing: I am *not* his illegitimate son."

The silence that followed held both relief and surprise. Apparently they'd bought into the rumor.

Ben exclaimed, "This is outrageous! You owe us an explanation!"

"I owe you nothing."

Matthew said, "Russ is right."

Even Tanner stared at him. Then comprehension flooded his face and he smiled. "Good call, Matt."

Matthew nodded weakly, said with an effort, "We'll proceed as Father wished."

Ben's face twisted in rage, and he gripped the arm of the sofa till his knuckles went white. Stephanie closed her eyes and put her hand to her mouth, shaking her head. Peter and Glenna fixed analytical eyes on Matthew.

Tanner stood and extended his hand to me. "Sharon and I need to be going. Sarah's *tutu* will be wondering where she's gone to."

I hesitated. Part of me wanted to question him about this turn of events, part of me wanted to get as far away from him as possible. Finally, without taking his hand, I stood. Said to Peter and Glenna, "I'll see you later at Malihini House."

*  *  *  *

I waited till we were walking along the gravel track to the house and Casey had run off toward the chopper. Then I said, "All right . . . what about this bequest from Elson?"

"You heard what I told them."

"That's it?"

"So far as it goes, that's the truth."

"And the rest of it?"

"Nobody's business but Elson's and mine."

We turned off the driveway, onto the grass by the springs where the ginger plants emitted their fragrance. Tonight it seemed to hint at corruption and decay. I looked up at the lighted house, thought of Hy and the confrontation we'd have there.

It was as if I were being pulled at from all directions: by Glenna, by Peter, by the rest of the Wellbrights. By Hy. By Tanner. I didn't want to continue with this investigation. I didn't want to go up to that house and face my lover. I didn't want to get on board that chopper again—not with this man, whose pull was strongest of all. I didn't—

God, everything was in negatives!

I stopped walking. Just stood there, tired and confused.

Tanner kept going, noticed I wasn't with him, came back, and put his arm around my shoulders. His touch only deepened my sense of being cut off from everything that was sane and familiar. I let him lead me away from the lawn, into a stand of palm trees. Offered no resistance when he leaned against the thick bole of one and pulled me close. Stood passively in his arms as he kissed me, feeling wretched beyond belief.

"I'm not good with words," he said.

"You do all right."

"I mean the kind of words that'd make you feel better about all this."

"Words won't help."

"What will?"

"I don't know. Nothing, probably. I'm just all of a sudden so damned tired."

"Then let's take you back to Waipuna so you can get that car. Something like this, it's better if you sleep on it."

*Sleep on it? Next to Ripinsky? I don't think so.*

He released me and we started for the chopper, walking a couple of feet apart. A figure was coming down the hill from the house. Hy, carrying his travel bag.

*Oh, God, now what? A call from RKI? A crisis situation in some far-off place?*

He set the bag down next to the chopper and waited for us.

"What's happenin'?" Tanner asked.

"I need you to run me to Lihue to catch a flight to Honolulu."

His voice was level, even pleasant, but he wasn't looking at me.

"Sure. Some problem?"

"Yeah. Let me talk to McCone for a minute, would you?"

"I'll preflight."

Hy took my arm, steered me uphill to the lanai.

"What's the trouble?" I asked.

He looked down at me and, in the flickering light of

the citronella candles, I saw his eyes were somber and pained. "You and me."

"If that's what's making you leave, don't go. We can talk—"

"I don't think this is a good time."

A replay of my earlier conversation with Tanner, but now I'd assumed his role. "Then when will there be a good time?"

"I don't know. When you're ready."

"When *I'm* ready?"

He put his hand on my shoulder, held me at arm's length, as if he was afraid his resolve might weaken if I came any closer. "Look, McCone, all three of us know exactly what's going on here. He saw you and wanted you. The two of you connected. Rules of attraction. I could see it coming from the beginning."

"So why didn't you—"

"Stop it? I can't tell you what to do. Can't tell you what to feel."

"I don't *know* what I feel!"

"Exactly. That's why I'm giving you the space to sort it out. You need to do that. But I don't need to sit around here and watch you do it."

I grabbed his arm, feeling as if he were threatening to cut a lifeline. "Where'll you be?"

"Honolulu, for a day at least. I need to meet with our people there."

"And then?"

He shrugged.

"How will I know where to find you?"

Gently he took my hand and removed my fingers from

his arm. "I doubt we're so far gone that you won't be able to find me when you're ready. You've always known how to do that."

The night was warm and silent, except for the murmur of the surf. The scent of ginger drifted on the breeze. It made me want to throw up.

Finally I rose from the chair where I'd been sitting since Tanner's chopper lifted off, went into the house, and fixed myself a gin and tonic that was mostly gin. Wandered back to the bedroom, turning on all the lights as I went.

The unmade bed confronted me. It bore the imprints of Hy's body and mine, where we'd lain after making love that morning. It had been oddly unsatisfying; his mind seemed elsewhere, and mine had been unfocused. Well, at least I now knew what was bothering him.

I took off my T-shirt and shorts, pulled on the long black-and-gold cotton dress I'd worn to the Wellbright party a century ago. Its primary color suited my mood. Then I went back to the living room, sipping my drink and turning on more lights. They did nothing to brighten my outlook.

Hy and I had never owned an easy relationship. We weren't like Rae and Ricky, who agreed so completely on the most minute details that it seemed spooky. Or Anne-Marie Altman and Hank Zahn, the attorneys who shared my suite of offices at Pier 24½. They believed in compromise—whether by negotiation or by flipping a coin. Hy and I disagreed frequently and fought spiritedly over our differences. If we'd flipped a coin to settle an argument, the loser would have made off with it and spent it.

We probably lived apart too much: I at my house in San Francisco, he at his ranch in Mono County, both of us often away on business. But we always came together at the place we loved most, the coastal cottage we'd named Touchstone. And while separated we felt an intuitive connectedness that to others might have seemed as spooky as Rae and Ricky's complete agreement.

When I met Hy I'd felt that connection almost immediately. And from the day I was first with him, I'd never given a serious thought to any other man.

So what had changed that?

*Maybe you're having a midlife crisis, McCone.*

I don't believe in them.

*You're forty. As Ricky said in one of his songs, it's an itchy age.*

And what does Ricky know? He's only thirty-seven!

I set my glass down on the breakfast bar, reaching for the gin bottle. If I was to spend the night holding inane conversations with myself, I might as well do it drunk. My eyes rested on a newspaper—the Sunday edition of the *Garden Island*—and a headline below the fold on page one. Quickly I slipped onto one of the stools and scanned it: "Body Found at Salt Pond Beach, Police Seek Leads to Identity."

The article said that the shark-mangled body of a male had washed up at a county park beach early yesterday morning, and the remains had been flown to the forensics lab at the Honolulu Police Department so that the skull could be reconstructed and artist's sketches made. Anyone with information as to the victim's identity should contact the Kauai County Police Department.

I got up and rummaged through the drawer of the kitchen desk till I found a map. Salt Pond Beach was between Hanapepe and Waimea, on the south shore. From what I'd observed of the sea's current, it seemed possible the man who'd been tossed in at the cane lands would have ended up there.

Out of kindness to Tommy Kaohi's family, I knew I ought to go to the police in the morning and tell them what I'd witnessed. But how would I explain why I'd held off so long? As an investigator unlicensed in this state I'd be on pretty shaky ground, even with RKI's sponsorship. Perhaps it would be better to make an anonymous call—

Voices outside. I went to the lanai, saw Glenna and Peter walking along the driveway. They seemed to be arguing, and when they saw me they fell silent. I waved and went back inside to freshen my drink. Hesitated, wondering if that was wise. Said, "The hell with it," and freshened it liberally.

The two of them came into the house, and Peter joined me at the gin bottle. "Jesus, what a day!"

I nodded. "Quite a few surprises."

"You get anything out of Russ about why my father made that bequest?"

"No." I didn't want to discuss anything remotely related to Tanner.

Glenna sat down on one of the stools. "Where's Hy?"

Another subject I'd just as soon avoid. "He had to go to Honolulu on business."

My reply sounded short; Glenna raised her eyebrows.

I ignored the implied question. "Glenna, I need to talk with you in the morning, and I also need copies of Elson's journal and the manuscript you based the film on."

"There're a couple of copies in the editing room."

"Thanks."

"About where you found the camera—"

"You know, it's late, I'm tired, and I'm sure you are too."

"God, yes," Peter said. "That family of mine . . . I spent most of the last hour trying to get them off financial affairs and onto planning Mother's service."

"At least your family buries its dead." I was thinking again of Grandpa's ashes in the coat closet.

They both looked at me as if I'd said something extremely bizarre, and I supposed I had. I didn't explain, however.

It struck me now that one of the reasons the Wellbrights made me so edgy was that they were as fully dysfunctional as my own people—sort of the way the McCones would have been if we'd had money. I'd always assumed we liked each other pretty well, but as I thought back to the last time we were together as a family, I began to doubt even that most basic of my premises.

It had been Ma and Pa's last wedding anniversary—before she divorced him and took up with a man who owned the chain of coin-operated laundries she frequented, and Pa said he would never set foot in the same room with the Bastard Who Stole My Wife. Even then they didn't act like the poster couple for marital bliss. He didn't want to come out of his garage workshop for the party we threw them, and she didn't like being banished from her kitchen.

On the other hand, my sister Patsy and her husband, who had volunteered to prepare the food, didn't enjoy being confined to the kitchen. They owned a restaurant and belatedly realized they'd signed up for a busman's holiday. Patsy's three kids flat-out hated the Little Savages, Charlene and Ricky's brood. The Little Savages ganged up on John's boys, who in turn ganged up on Patsy's brood, taking them into the canyon behind the house and tying them to a tree. Charlene and Ricky, as usual, weren't getting along. John had just broken up with his girlfriend, and wasn't getting along with anybody. We were all pissed off at Joey, who failed to show up or send a card. And I, who had been known to defensively tipple at family gatherings, got rip-roaring drunk and ended up in our tree house singing dirty songs with Pa at three in the morning.

Families!

The memory of the monumental hangover I'd suffered quelled my desire for more gin, however. I set my glass on the counter, excused myself, and went outside and across the prickly grass on bare feet to the bench where Hy and I had sat with Glenna on our first night here. Perched there, my legs folded under my long dress, and watched the moon path on the shifting water. A helicopter on night flight passed; I stared at its red, green, and white winking lights and thought of Tanner and Hy. What had the two of them talked about on the way to Lihue? Had Tanner been defensive? Apologetic? Had Hy spoken angrily? Repeated his giving-you-space line? Had they come to some man-to-man understanding that excluded me? Turned me into little more than a piece of property to be assigned or discarded as they saw fit?

*Unfair, McCone. Neither of them is that kind of man.*

More likely Hy hadn't bothered with a headset, had sat silent the whole way.

And now what? Tanner had said he'd return for me in the morning so I could fetch the Datsun. But what if he took it into his head to return tonight? How would I handle that?

*More to the point, do you want that?*

Yes and no.

*And tomorrow when he comes—what do you want then?*

I'm not sure.

I continued to listen to the sea and watch the moonlight. Quite a few choppers were out tonight, and each time I saw one's lights I felt a mixture of hope and dread. The gin haze had cleared, and I became wakeful, as I usually did after I drank the hard stuff. I wanted to sleep, but it wasn't possible.

At a little before midnight I went to the house to locate the background checks on the Wellbrights Mick had sent over, as well as Elson's manuscript and journal.

# APRIL 6

•

Kauai

**12:18 A.M.**

June 19, 1955
Kauai

These storytellers I have found are amazing! They make the legends come alive in a way that the turgid written sources can't. Today when they talked of Pele, the fire goddess whose rage turned rivals to stone, I closed my eyes and pictured Celia. Beautiful, fierce Celia, her love for me as strong as Pele's for Chief Lohiau. Lohiau died of despair after Pele left him for her home in the crater of Kilauea, and she moved heaven and earth to bring him back to her. Would Celia do the same for me?

The journal and manuscript were photocopies, well thumbed, with notes in the margins in Glenna's hand. Some were detailed ideas on how to shoot a particular scene, others were points she needed to clarify. This passage was marked, "Parallels?"

July 26, 1962
Kauai


Spent a few hours with my storytellers today, exploring the migration version of the Pele legend: a tale of disjointed wandering in search of a home. Home, something that Celia holds dear above all else. This afternoon when I told her about the *National Geographic* assignment in Bali, she cried as if I were leaving forever. It's only for two weeks, and not even until next spring, for God's sake! But she says the children are so difficult, her responsibilities so great. I told her she has the housekeeper, the maids, the nanny, and if she wants companionship she can pack everyone up and take them to her parents' place on the Big Island. She brightened at the suggestion. My Pele, returning to the land of the fires that nourish her.

Glenna's marginal note said, "Bali, 1962 and 88." I thumbed forward, saw several entries written on Bali in 1988.

October 17, 1969
Djakarta


Quite unthinkable that Celia would do this to me! She sent Mona Davenport, who is vacationing here with Harold, to my hotel today, to persuade me to abandon this assignment and return home. Of course Mona had no real expectation or desire to accomplish that and said she sympathizes with my annoyance at Celia's dependence.

But equally unthinkable is what happened between Mona and me, a consequence, I think, of several factors. She is a very lovely woman whose husband leaves her alone even more than I leave Celia. She bears up very well, but her loneliness and my feeling of having been betrayed by my wife brought us together. We both agreed that it can never happen again, and I believe we'll keep that promise and each become the kind of friend the other can rely on.

In the Hi'iaka myth, Pele sent her sister to fetch Lohiau and bring him to their home on the Big Island. In many ways, Celia and Mona are as close as sisters. Hi'iaka seduced Lohiau after finding that Pele had broken their compact and burned her beloved lehua groves in her absence. When I pointed out the obvious parallel to Mona, she asked that I plant lehua in my forest on Kauai in her honor. I shall try to oblige.

Glenna had written, "Consequences consistent with myth?"

January 28, 1972
Kauai

Russell Tanner stopped by this evening to borrow yet another book and bring me a gift—a kukui wood good-luck charm that he had carved himself—to take on assignment in Samoa. He's an intelligent boy, struggling to make connection with his culture and to make sense of the position of the Hawaiians in our society. There's a great deal I can teach him.

Celia doesn't approve of my fondness for Russell, and I suppose it hurts her to see me spend so much time with him rather than with my own children. But I have little to offer a son as determinedly serious as Matthew or of such a scientific bent as Peter. Stephanie is a darling, but she's her mother's child, too wild and contrary. At ten months, it's difficult to imagine what Drew will be like.

I'm looking forward to this trip to Samoa. Sometimes it's best to back off and gain some perspective on one's life.

I found myself reading every reference to Tanner with more than casual interest.

April 4, 1978
Zamboanga, Philippines

Mona flew here from Manila this morning, and we spent the day together, mainly drinking at the seaside bar of this quaint old hotel. Bought her a turtle shell from one of the boat vendors who paddle around. She tells me Celia's at it again—juggling two men and making no secret of it, hoping someone will tell me and I'll come home and take charge of the marriage. How little she knows of me. I can barely take charge of myself.

My only concern is what effect her behavior will have on the children. Matthew's his mother's boy; he approves of her every action and would do anything for her. But Peter, Mona tells me, has turned very cold to her, and Stephanie's running wild. Drew acts out in tantrums, and Celia's harsh on him.

More and more Celia resembles the hag from the fire pit, spreading blackness and ruin all about her.

Glenna had circled "hag from the fire pit," and put a question mark next to it.

August 18, 1981
Kauai

Up too late last night, too much drinking, plus a dreadful argument with C. And now this piece for the in-flight magazine is due, and I've lost my focus. How did life get so out of hand?

November 8, 1983
San Francisco

Here for a meeting with the West Coast editor of that new travel magazine, and to escape the turmoil at home. C. depressed and drinking heavily over the breakup of yet another affair. She found out where I'm staying and constantly calls, trying to bait me, claiming Drew isn't my son. Good try, Celia, but it won't work. The poor devil looks exactly like me.

May 27, 1985
Tokyo

This JAL in-flight pub could turn into a regular assignment. And a good thing, as it takes me away from the fire pit. Sent the first half of the legends book to that agent my editor at the *Geographic* recommended, and she's agreed to represent me. Still, the major work on it is yet to come, and how can I accomplish anything, given the situation at home? I wish Celia would stop drinking, but how can I expect her to when I can't stop myself? At least Mona and Harold are now living on the island and can be there for both of us.

In my last conversation with her Mona told me that Celia is extremely upset over Stephanie dating Russ Tanner. We can't have tainted blood mixing with our pure missionary strain! (C. has conveniently forgotten that her own mother was Balinese.) I'll have to warn Russ to be discreet, but I refuse to ask him to stop seeing my wild daughter. A fine young man like him is bound to have a settling influence on her.

October 29, 1985
Kauai

Russ Tanner came by to see Stephanie this evening and brought along a friend who wanted to meet me—Liza Santos. She's a lovely girl who's studying cultural anthropology at the University of Hawaii. Russ is enjoying his work flying helicopter tours, but he's lost none of his enthusiasm for reading about the ways of his people. They were both very excited about the prospect of my work with the storytellers becoming a book.

I wonder about that, though. Do I have the stamina to go on with it? Perhaps I've lived too much in the past, or at a distance. Perhaps if I'd paid attention to the present, stayed here at home, none of this ugliness would have happened. I badly crave warmth and brightness in my life, but I fear it's too late for that. Too late for C., certainly. She's drinking even more these days, and Mona says something must be done for her.

April 11, 1986
Kauai

Mona warns me that something must be done to protect them, and I know she's right. But the only alternative that's been suggested is so extreme, and bound to hurt her. The future must be secured, however. At least I have true friends to turn to.

December 12, 1986
Kauai

This is the saddest day of my life. I've gained, but lost. Irrevocably.

February 20, 1988
Bali

I have not visited here since my first *Geographic* assignment, thirty-two years ago. Cannot help comparing the young, ambitious, and very, very hopeful man I was then to this burned-out, used-up shell. Yet there's a specialness here, and I feel myself coming alive in subtle ways. We'll see.

February 26, 1988
Bali

Yes, alive again! The passions of the Polynesian people live on in this beautiful land.

At this point the journal entries became sporadic, as if Elson Wellbright's emotional rebirth had freed him from chronicling the details of his largely unhappy life. What few passages he did commit to paper had a cryptic, guarded quality. Glenna had stopped making comments many pages before; I sensed she'd become as immersed in the man's personal story as I had.

January 5, 1990
Kauai

The draft of the book is finished, but there's much rewriting to be done. I've no fear I can manage it, however. This fireproof sanctuary (in reality, my den) that I've established in the pit (a.k.a. Pali House) has proven invaluable. And then there are my eagerly awaited excursions into the real world with my Special One.

February 1, 1990
Kauai

Could I have prevented this tragedy? I doubt it. I only did what I could, given the nature of the situation. But I realize now that I haven't provided for the future as well as I ought, and again Russ Tanner has come up with the solution. I can depend on him for my peace of mind, just as he can depend on me for what he will need.

July 10, 1990
Kauai

C. found out about the new will. I'm not sure how, although I suspect that Blankenship (with whom she once had an affair, and who is still fascinated by her) violated confidentiality and told her. He's done me a good turn, though, since C. banished me from Pali House forever. I'm now settled in the caretaker's cottage with all the things I really care about, poised to push ahead with the manuscript. A lovely sojourn in Taipei in late August (JAL magazine), with plenty of time to make plans.

September 5, 1992
Kauai

The manuscript is finished! My Special One arrives tomorrow. On the twelfth the book will be delivered to my agent, and I will be delivered to freedom in Santa Fe. It will be difficult to leave this island: the palis, the sound of the waves on the reef, my gentle storytellers, who have received the wisdom of their elders, those same elders with whom I began my exploration of the ancient Hawaiians so many years ago. I'll miss the ironwoods and the lava fall. I'll miss my forest, where Mona's lehuas bloom so brilliantly. I'll miss Mona and Russ. They have been and still are a great source of strength in difficult times.

I'll miss Matthew, Jillian, Stephanie, and even Ben. I've mellowed toward my children, and they've forgiven me my failings. I'll miss seeing my first grandchild. I worry about Peter. He seems determined to keep his distance, and I'm afraid he'll never experience the joy in these islands' heritage that I have. I've sent him a copy of the manuscript to remind him of his roots here. If I were a praying man, I'd pray for Drew, but I'm afraid he's as beyond hope as his mother. I'll always think of the little one and wonder.

I always thought I would live and die on Kauai. Be buried in the graveyard behind the little mission church beside my forebears. That my bones would become a part of this sacred soil. That my spirit would leap free from the cliffs at our cane lands and dive into the otherworld.

Not to be.

That was the last entry in the journal. Glenna's comment, in large black letters: "Yes!"

Around it she'd drawn a zigzag pattern that reminded me of flames gone out of control.

### 3:02 A.M.

"Shar, do you *know* what time it is here?" Mick's voice sounded aggravated in the extreme.

"Three hours later than where I am. Arise and face the new week."

"Jesus! Most people go to Hawaii to lie on the beach, drink too many mai tais, and fuck. You go there so you can stay up all night and call me at an ungodly hour!"

I didn't want to think about the reasons people customarily came here. With Hy gone I wouldn't be doing any of those things. Particularly not the latter, if I had any sense left at all.

"Sorry," I said, knowing he wasn't really mad. "How far did you get with the background check on Elson Wellbright?"

Mick yawned loudly. "I could download a ton of articles he wrote for journals and magazines, but I doubt you'll want to wade through scholarly treatments of the Polynesian myths and chants as they influenced Hawaiian legend. The rest is just pop anthropology and travel features—the kind of stuff you read on a plane if you forget to bring along a paperback."

"Nothing else?"

"A huge blank. That Social Security number you gave me doesn't turn up anyplace. None of the other usual checks worked, either."

"No death certificate, though?"

"Well, I'm not halfway through on that. It takes—"

"Try Santa Fe, New Mexico. He may have gone there."

"I'll get on it right away. Anything else?"

I hesitated, thinking of the scraps of paper with the Honolulu address and phone number that I'd found at the sugar mill. I'd planned to ask one of RKI's specialists to check both out, but now I didn't want to call there. If Hy heard I had, he might think it a ruse to get him to speak with me. Maybe I was being overly coy but, dammit, he'd hurt me. I didn't want him flattering himself by picturing me alone and desperate.

Even though I did feel that way every time I thought about his defection.

"Yes, there is something," I told Mick. "Hold on." I set the receiver down and went to the bedroom, rummaged in the bureau drawer where I'd stowed the squatters' leavings. Both pieces of paper were gone.

"I don't believe this," I whispered. Someone had entered the house in our absence, searched it without leaving any sign, and taken my potential leads. I closed my eyes, trying to recall either the number or the address. Gave up and went back to the phone.

"I've misplaced the information," I told Mick.

"Well, I'll get on to Santa Fe vital stats, then."

"Wait, there *is* something else, although Wellbright takes priority. Glenna Stanleigh."

"You want me to run a check on our *client*?"

"Only when you've exhausted every possible method of looking for Elson Wellbright."

"But why Glenna? I thought you guys were friends."

"So did I. All I want is a standard background workup."

"Well, you're the boss."

"And don't you forget it. Keep yourself available today in case I need anything else, okay?"

"Sure. Available as a roofless house in hurricane season."

God help me! Now he was picking up Charlotte Keim's Texasisms.

## 9:17 A.M.

Glenna and Peter weren't at La'i Cottage and his Volvo was gone, but a note to him in her handwriting was taped to the door. I hesitated before reading it, then thought, What the hell? If she hadn't folded or enveloped it, there wasn't anything in it that she didn't want others to see.

"P— I've borrowed your car to drive to the airport. Will fly to Honolulu and return the camera to the rental house. Don't know when I'll be back. —G."

Curt, and it seemed presumptuous of her to take the car without asking. Maybe after I went outside last night they'd picked up on the argument they'd been having when they got to Malihini House.

No matter what was going on with them personally, I needed to talk with Glenna. As soon as I'd hung up on my call to Mick, I'd begun to regret asking him to check her out, and now I badly wanted to give her the chance to explain herself. Last night I'd told her we had to talk. Perhaps she'd gone to Oahu to avoid a confrontation.

The sound of the chopper alerted me to Tanner's arrival. I took the path through the papaya trees and watched the big red bird settle onto the grass. Russ waved through the bubble, shut it down, and got out. As he came toward me I saw a tentativeness in his usually confident step. His dark glasses were in place, and his expression seemed purposely polite and remote—a good charter pilot picking up a client who, if well treated, might tip generously.

He's afraid, I thought. Last night he overstepped a boundary line we'd tacitly drawn between us, and now he's afraid he's ruined everything and we can't even be friends.

I thought of the things I'd read about Tanner in Elson Wellbright's journal. This was a man who'd overcome a fatherless childhood in a tin-roofed shack. Who as a boy had been foisted off at every opportunity on his wealthy relatives by an overly ambitious mother. Who had endured indignities from most of those relatives and from society at large. Who had put himself through community college, earned his pilot's license and helicopter rating, and emerged into adulthood with pride in himself and his roots. A good man.

Like Hy.

When he first spoke, Tanner's voice was as tentative as his step. "Morning. You okay?"

"Yes. You?"

"Uh-huh. Want to go get that car now?"

"Not yet. Come on up to the house, have a cup of coffee first."

"Well, I'll take a soda, if you've got one."

We walked up the slope, keeping a careful distance from each other. He sat down at the table on the lanai while I went inside and returned with two soft drinks.

"So," he said.

I sat down next to him. "You got Ripinsky to Lihue in time for his flight?"

He nodded.

"He say anything to you? About . . . the situation, I mean?"

"Only that we all need time to sort things out. That nobody's to blame for what's happened. And he asked me to go easy."

"Go easy?"

"Give you as much space as you need."

"Nice of him to watch out for me," I said sarcastically.

"Look, he wasn't being condescending. The man really loves you, and I can sure understand that."

I sighed. "I really love him, too."

"I know that. So why is this other thing happening with us? In my case, it's pretty straightforward, but in yours . . ."

"I wish I knew. Last night I considered that I might be having a midlife crisis."

"And?"

"Too simple an explanation. Besides, if you're having one of those, aren't you supposed to chuck everything, dye your hair, buy a Porsche?"

He smiled faintly. "I think that's only one variation on the theme."

"Well, I don't believe in them, anyway."

"Oh, no?"

"Nope."

"Well, if *you* don't believe in them, obviously they don't exist."

"You value my opinion that highly, do you?"

"I value everything about you."

We fell silent, suddenly embarrassed. It was a moment before Tanner asked, "So what did you do last night?"

"Tried to get drunk. I was well on my way when I remembered a horrible hangover I had one time. So I stopped."

"You've only had *one* hangover?"

"God, no. But this was the granddaddy of them all. Whenever I feel like really tying one on, the memory helps me apply the brakes. What did you do after you got back from Lihue?"

"Flew past here twice and used up all my willpower telling myself I shouldn't stop. I would've liked to get drunk, but I had an early-morning charter. Eight hours, bottle to throttle."

We were silent again. On the lawn a rooster set up a hideous screeching, and another answered him in kind from somewhere near La'i Cottage.

"Russ," I finally said, "there's something I need your input on."

"Sure, what?"

"I think Tommy Kaohi's dead." I described the scene I'd witnessed at the *heiau* near the sugar mill.

Tanner listened, eyes narrowing. When I finished he said, "You had me take you out to Rob and Sunny's, knowing their kid was dead?"

"I didn't *know* anything for sure. I was hoping he'd be there or that they'd've seen him since Friday night. But either way, I needed to know."

"Still, it was kind of a cold thing to do."

"No, it would've been cold to alarm them unnecessarily. But now this body's washed up at Salt Pond Beach. The HPD has it and they'll do a facial reconstruction, circulate artists' sketches. But if the Kaohis can provide dental or medical records, it'll speed up the identification."

"Why didn't you go to the police right after this happened?"

"Because I was afraid they wouldn't believe me. It's a bizarre story, you've got to admit."

"Yeah, it is. So are you going to talk to them now?"

"I'd rather avoid that, if possible. Technically I'm able to investigate here because I'm under Hy's firm's umbrella, but I should've cleared it with the KPD first."

"And why didn't you?"

"Peter and Glenna wanted to keep the production company's problems under wraps."

"So because of them and their stupid film, you let the scumbags who killed Tommy get away?"

"Look, they were already long gone."

"You had a name—Amy Laurentz. You got another name—Buzzy Malakaua."

Oh, God, he was right about everything! Not going to the police had been stupid, illegal, and uncaring. Not telling the Kaohis what I suspected *had* been cold. And now I was in an untenable position.

I couldn't stand to see the reproach in Tanner's eyes. I shaded mine with my hand and stared at the distant palis. "I really screwed up, didn't I?"

"Everybody does sometimes. Your business isn't an easy one, and you're operating in unfamiliar territory." He took my hand away from my eyes, held it. "Didn't mean to jump all over you."

"You only stated the truth. Russ, how am I going to make this right?"

"I'll take care of it."

"No, I should—"

"Leave it to me. I've been cleaning up other people's messes my whole life. Leave it to the expert."

"I guess you are an expert."

"What does that mean?"

"After I decided not to get drunk last night, I stayed up reading Elson Wellbright's journal."

"Didn't know he kept one."

"Well, he did, and he said quite a few things about you. Implied quite a few others. Much of it was cryptic, but I've got a pretty good sense of what it was you promised him."

His fingers tightened on my hand. "If you do, you know it's best to let it be."

I watched him for a moment. This wasn't the time to press him, especially in light of his offer to fix the Tommy Kaohi situation. Instead I kept silent and twined my fingers through his.

It was not the worst thing I could do on a sunny morning in paradise.

## 2:13 P.M.

I pulled the Datsun to the side of the road where a tangle of palms and ironwoods screened a beach, and I stepped out into their shade. A warm breeze rustled the brittle fronds and swayed the drooping branches. I moved through them to the narrow strip of sand.

A white-haired couple sat on a blanket a few yards away, sharing a bottle of wine and looking at the water. They smiled as I passed, and I smiled back, envying them. There was an ease in the way their shoulders touched, a peaceful closeness in the way his hand rested on her knee. A settledness that I'd never known with any man. Perhaps in time Hy and I might have achieved that, but now our relationship was derailed, possibly would never get back on track again. And as for Tanner . . .

No way I could envision a future for us. Too many impossibilities inherent in the situation. And in the past few hours I'd created a complication that wasn't going to be resolved easily, if at all.

After he'd flown me to Waipuna, I retrieved the Datsun from in front of Crystal Blue Inspiration and drove south to Lihue, where I did some simple research at the county clerk's office and the public library. What I found strengthened my suspicions about Tanner's promise to Elson Wellbright. But in order to verify them, I'd have to tell Russ what I'd done.

I walked to the end of the beach, sat down on a smooth shelf of lava rock. The sea here was a turquoise I'd previously thought existed only in travel brochures. Aside from the white-haired couple and a few surfers beyond the reef, there wasn't a soul in sight. A good place to think undisturbed, only my thoughts wouldn't proceed logically. Images from the past twenty-four hours kept intruding.

I pictured Hy's face, pained and drawn in the candlelight on the lanai at Malihini House last night. I felt the phantom touch of Tanner's fingers as they twined through mine on the same lanai this morning.

He'd warned me to let the subject of his bargain with Elson Wellbright be, but I wasn't one to ignore such a thing, not when it might be essential to my investigation. Still, at the clerk's office and at the library I'd felt like a burglar breaking into a very private part of Russ's life. Soon I'd have to admit my intrusion, and that could end it between us.

Well, good. I'd wrap up this investigation, go back home, get on with my life. Repair my fractured relationship with Hy. We'd forget all this had happened, buy our new airplane, build our house. And someday we'd sit on the bluff above Bootleggers Cove looking at the sea as peacefully as the couple down the beach.

And if Russ took it into his head to hate me for prying, let him.

*So why don't you get your butt off this rock and go talk with him?*

Give me a few minutes, okay?

*Do it now. Hustle!*

This island isn't conducive to hustling.

*No, what it's conducive to is impulsive behavior and warped judgment.*

So my judgment's a little bent. I'm working on straightening it.

*Face it, McCone, the only thing you're working on is a method for justifying having sex with a handsome* hapa-haole *helicopter pilot.*

Didn't I wish my feelings were that uncomplicated!

By the time I did get my butt off the rock and back to Waipuna, Tanner was out on a charter and not expected back for a couple of hours. Rather than wait around, I drove toward Malihini House and into yet another Well-bright family contretemps.

Peter and Matthew stood in the road at the foot of Pali House's driveway, toe-to-toe in argument. If anyone had come along at excess speed, there was an odds-even chance that the surviving family members would be holding a triple funeral this week. Both men's faces were red and contorted, and when I slowed down beside them, they glared at me as if I were a meddling tourist.

Matthew snapped, "Drive on! This is none of your business."

Peter said, "Don't you dare speak to her that way!"

I asked, "What the hell's the matter, that you can't talk about it off the pavement?"

Matthew growled, Peter opened his mouth to reply, and a red convertible full of teenagers roared around the curve from the west and nearly took them both out.

I said, "Get in the car. Now!"

They complied, looking sheepish.

I drove to Malihini House, parked by the garage, and told them, "Out."

Peter headed for the house, mumbling something about a drink. Matthew remained by the car, kicking at pebbles like a kid in a school yard. I went as far as the lanai, glanced back, and said, "You'll be more comfortable up here."

He shot me a venomous look but eventually followed.

Peter came out of the house with the makings for gin and tonics. I shook my head, remembering the night before, and went inside for a soft drink. When I came back I said, "Now, will one of you please tell me what's going on?"

Matthew snatched a glass from his brother's hand and drank, ignoring me. To Peter he said, "You'll regret this."

"I'm beginning to regret everything, including being born."

I tapped my fingers on the tabletop, the little patience I had left almost gone.

Peter said, "It's Jill. According to my brother, she's gone missing again. Truth is, she's been out of his sight for less than four hours. She's probably shopping or at the movies or visiting a friend."

"She didn't take her car," Matthew said, "so she can't be shopping or at a movie. And she doesn't have any friends."

"Because you won't permit her to."

"I can't have her gallivanting around God-knows-where. She's mentally unstable."

"Emotionally fragile."

"She needs watching over, and I'm going to do that if it means putting her under house arrest."

Peter said to me, "House arrest, because she likes to take walks by herself."

"Jill wanders all over the north shore. It's dangerous."

"She's lived here her whole life. She knows every inch of the territory."

"Still, there're hazards. Cliffs. And the surf is treacherous."

"She doesn't go up on the cliffs or swim in the ocean."

"How d'you know? Besides, there're drifters. Drug addicts. Wild dogs—"

"Feral chickens, too."

"You know, Peter, you always were a wiseass."

"And you always were a pain in the ass."

"Well, fuck you!"

"Ditto."

I said, "If I may interrupt this high-toned debate—"

"Fuck you too!" Matthew slammed his glass onto the table and headed for the steps, muttering to himself. Peter and I watched as he strode along the driveway, arms pumping jerkily, like a cartoon soldier.

He said, "If you ask me, Matt's the one who's unstable."

"Does he mean that literally, about locking Jill up?"

"God knows what he'll do, given the state he's worked himself into. I walked down to Pali House earlier to see how the arrangements for Mother's service are coming— it's supposed to be tomorrow—and he popped out of the bushes by the road, which he'd apparently been scouring for Jill. When I suggested he might want to take it easy, he started ranting at me."

"You don't suppose Jill really might be a danger to herself?"

"No. It's true she hasn't been too well wrapped since she lost the baby, but it's nothing a competent psychiatrist couldn't help her work through. Matt's discouraged that. He claims people should be able to handle their own problems. And Jill goes along with whatever he says."

"Well, if she gets any worse, maybe you can talk some sense into him. By the way, I saw Glenna's note to you on the cottage door. I take it she's not back from Oahu yet?"

"No. I suspect she's decided to stay over. We had an argument last night about my father's journal. I haven't read it—I've got a thing about other people's privacy—and she thinks I should. Thinks I should try to get it published as a companion book to the one on the legends. But she tells me it's pretty painful personal stuff, and there's no way I'm going to allow that."

"Things aren't going well for the two of you, are they?"

"Let's just say that I've used her as a buffer between my family and me, and it hasn't been fair to either of us."

## 8:02 P.M.

The day's light was fading as I scrambled across the lava field toward the ruins of Elson Wellbright's forest. Matthew had stopped by Malihini House fifteen minutes ago to apologize for his earlier behavior and to ask that I join in the search for Jillian, whose long absence was now being taken seriously by everyone. I was feeling edgy and out of sorts and, since I hadn't been able to reach Tanner, I readily agreed and set off toward the deadfall. It was the one place Matthew insisted Jillian would never go. Given the understanding of his wife that he demonstrated, it seemed likely she might be there.

Sun-bleached trunks and limbs lay scattered among the black boulders; above them the land rose steeply. Exposed roots protruded from the slope, and beyond was a tangle of fallen trees. Second-growth plants sent tentative branches toward the sky, but they were dwarfed and choked by the heavy mass. I thought of Jillian's drunken ravings about Hurricane Iniki. How apt were the words "the forest turned to Pick-up Sticks."

I climbed the slope, clutching at roots and pausing at the top to take out the small flashlight I'd stuck in my back pocket. I shone it around through the deepening shadow. Nothing but the helter-skelter pattern created by the downed trees. There was no movement, no sound, yet it was not a place of peace. My emotional sensors were registering strangeness, unpleasantness. I stood still for a moment, trying and failing to analyze the feelings. Then I climbed over one of the smaller trunks and made my way on a haphazard course toward the distant road.

A cracking and rustling in the brush behind me. I turned, saw no one. "Who's there?" I called.

The sounds stopped.

Not one of the dogs. It would have bounded over to me.

"Jillian? Is that you?"

Silence.

"It's Sharon. Everybody's looking for you. Everybody's worried."

A slight noise.

I held a branch aside and began inching in the direction the sound had come from.

Another rustle, and something thumped painfully into my right shoulder. I yelled, threw my hand up, and cradled the spot. Something else caromed off a nearby tree trunk, fell at my feet. A rock the size of a golf ball. I dropped down behind the trunk, and just as I did, I heard another rock whiz over my head.

Jesus! If that last one had hit me on the temple, it might've killed me. Given me a concussion at the very least.

I crouched behind the trunk, breathing raggedly. No more rocks flew; the forest was quiet once more. I waited a good ten minutes before I made a slow and steady retreat to the beach. It was deserted, but I ran for the house anyway.

The rock thrower hadn't been Jillian; of that I was reasonably certain. Who, then? And why? I wasn't about to wander around in the dark trying to find out.

## 9:41 P.M.

I found Russ Tanner in his usual place—third stool from the end of the Shack's outdoor bar. He sat alone, hunched over a beer, a dejected set to his shoulders. When I touched his arm he turned, brightening. "Hey, pretty lady, buy you a drink?"

"*Mahalo,* I'd like that. White wine, please."

He nodded and signaled the bartender.

I said, "You looked sad when I came in."

"I am. You were right about the body: it was Tommy. Rob asked me to fly his dental records to Oahu. HPD made a positive I.D."

"How're Rob and Sunny and the others taking it?"

"Hard. Lots of guilt, where-did-we-fail-him. Hell, they can't blame themselves because he wouldn't stay off the drugs. Think I told you he'd been messin' with them since he was eight."

"Drugs? He didn't drown?"

"Nope. Autopsy said he OD'd."

"On what?"

"Heroin. He was a user. I didn't ask Rob for any more details. He's hurtin' enough."

I thought for a moment. "Russ, did you tell the police or Rob about what I saw at the cane lands?"

"Uh-uh. Just said I heard a rumor that the dead guy might be Tommy. Figured I'd go into it if the cops made an I.D., but then when Rob told me it was an overdose, well, what does it matter? Those kids didn't kill him."

Unless they deliberately gave him bad drugs or forced him to shoot up. But that wasn't a suspicion I wanted to plant in Tanner's mind. "Appreciate you taking care of this and keeping me out of it. I owe you."

"No, you don't. I'd walk—or fly—a lot of extra miles for you."

We sat in silence for a few minutes, both leaning our

forearms on the bar, not quite touching. If only we could stay this way, friends instead of lovers. But there was heat between us, and I was acutely aware of the contours of his body, knew he felt the same about me. He took a sip of beer, set the mug down, and rested his arm against mine. I didn't move away.

*Dangerous, but maybe I want to throw myself into a crisis, resolve this emotional push-pull one way or the other.*

Finally he said, "The thing that bothers me, why did those kids toss Tommy in the sea? I can understand them not wantin' to get caught with a dead body on their hands, but why make him shark food?"

"Maybe I didn't describe what happened very well. I was uncomfortable telling you about it. They took his body to sacred ground, to a *heiau*. One man, Buzzy Malakaua, chanted in Hawaiian. Then Amy Laurentz said something, too." I paused, trying to recall her exact phrasing. "Three words in Hawaiian, and then something about being suspended between fire love and fire terror."

"*Ahi wela maka'u.* It's kind of where you and I are at. Fire can mean either danger or the life force. You're attracted to it, you fear it. You run toward it, you run away from it."

The comparison made me uneasy, mainly because it was so accurate. I said, "I think they were holding a funeral service for Tommy."

Russ nodded. "According to your description, they threw him off at a spot where the spirits typically leave the island for the underworld."

Again he was speaking as if myth were fact. It served to remind me of our fundamental differences.

"Russ, Peter told me something disturbing the other day. He said that after the shot was fired at the dry cave, he thought he saw his father standing under the ironwoods across the road, smoking a cigarette. There's no possibility Elson Wellbright could be on the island, is there?"

"God, no. Somebody would've recognized him. Don't tell me old Pete's crackin' up?"

"No, he saw someone, but . . . Does Eli Hathaway really look that much like Elson?"

"Made up, he's a dead ringer." Tanner grinned, seeing where this was going. "And he also smokes."

I nodded. "After the take of his scene, he came out of the cave lighting a cigarette. Then he walked off toward the road. I should've put it together as soon as Peter told me what he thought he'd seen, but in the commotion after the sniping I forgot about Eli, only dredged up the mental image while I was driving here this evening."

"Well, that's one mystery solved."

I bit my lip. "I think I may have solved another. After I left you this morning I went to Lihue, to the county clerk's office and to the public library. I wanted to confirm some suspicions Elson's journal had raised."

"We're back to that again, eh?"

"I want to run a probable series of events by you."

"Sure, why not?" But his body was tense now. He sipped beer, created a little distance between us.

"In October of 1985, at a time when, as he put it, Elson craved warmth and brightness in his life, he met a woman. It wasn't a suitable match. He was in his sixties and married. She was much younger, a college student. But the next spring she became pregnant. In order to provide for her and the child, Elson turned to the man who had introduced them. That man married her and, in exchange, Elson settled a substantial sum of money on him."

Tanner sat very still, breathing shallowly and staring straight ahead. His hands gripped his glass.

"The marriage only lasted four years before the man divorced the woman and got custody of the child. In early 1990 the child's mother died of a drug overdose, which made Elson realize he should make long-term provisions for the child's future. He changed his will—"

"Why the hell're you tiptoeing around this?" Tanner's voice crackled with anger.

"I guess I want to hear you admit it."

He swiveled toward me, face set, eyes hard. "You want to hear me admit it? Like it's something I should be ashamed of? Well, I'm not. But, yes, Elson was Casey's father. I married Liza Santos and accepted the money from Elson and started my charter service. I also divorced her. And when she died and Elson got worried about the future, I encouraged him to make the new will, which he was glad to do because he trusted me and knew I'd use the inheritance to raise and educate Casey. So now I've broken a promise to the man who treated me better than anyone on earth. And I'd really like to know what business it is of yours to pry into the dead past!"

I moved back from the heat of his anger. "The past isn't dead, Russ."

He stared at me for a moment longer, but then his face and eyes softened. "Of course it isn't. Especially when you know the whole story." He pushed back from the bar and stood, holding out his hand. "Come on. I can't do this here. We'll go to my place where it's private, and I'll tell you all of it."

When I preceded Russ into his house, I heard the mutter of voices on the scanner. Comforting sounds to any pilot, because they mean home or another destination, coffee or emergency help—all within talking distance. The interior of the house was hot and damp; Russ went to open some windows while I stood in the darkness listening to the nighttime air traffic. When he came back I misjudged the distance between us and bumped into him. He put his hands on my shoulders and pulled me close.

"Sorry about the way I reacted back there. I know you're just doing your job."

I looked up, saw the indicator light on the scanner reflected in his eyes. Moved on tiptoe and reached for him as he bent to kiss me.

*This is insane, McCone! You're throwing your life away.*

I don't care!

"Six-six-kilo, can you give me an exact location?"

"Looks like the Wellbright property. That deadfall west of the Mori house. Fires all over it."

Tanner raised his head. "Christ!"

"Six-six-kilo, hold your position."

"Six-six-kilo, wilco."

Tanner and I simultaneously let go of each other, and I

rocked back on my heels. An odd mixture of relief and confusion washed over me—anger, too—at being interrupted. I shook my head. "Fire?"

"That deadfall's a disaster waiting to happen!" Already he was pulling me toward the door.

We ran down the steps from the lanai, and he headed for the chopper. "Russ," I called, "you're not legal!"

"That was my first beer today, and I didn't finish half of it. Besides, what we were doing in there kinda burned off the alcohol. Give me a hand, will you, while I do a quick preflight."

The scattered lights along the crescent-shaped shoreline were faint, but to the west orange flames danced and leaped in the blackness.

Tanner said, "It's the deadfall, all right."

I leaned forward, counted at least eight separate blazes. "This must've been deliberately set. Sparks from an unattended campfire wouldn't jump in relatively even spacing like that. Those fires're intended to burn the whole tract."

He nodded, his face grim. "Arson."

Now flashing red lights sped along the road. A fire truck, coming from Hanalei. I pointed the lights out to Russ, and he said, "Hang on, I'm gonna take it down for a closer look."

The chopper swept to the side and descended off shore by the deadfall. The fires were burning briskly, showers of sparks swirling in the wind. I could smell smoke: acrid, with a faint chemical tinge.

Tanner began an ascent. "If this wind kicks up any more, Stephanie and Ben's place could catch. Or those properties to the west. We'll set down at Malihini House, see if there's anything we can do to help."

As he turned the chopper I gripped the edge of the seat, peering down. One patch of flames flared as if something had exploded, and another sprang up closer to the shoreline. Yet another moved with demonic purpose toward the road where the fire truck was stopped. More flashing lights appeared in the distance. Through the trees bordering the deadfall I spotted the blue roof of Lani House, and then the aquamarine shimmer of a lighted swimming pool. Figures milled around it. They seemed small and helpless in the face of nature's rage.

As we ran from the chopper and through the trees past La'i Cottage, a third fire engine streaked along the road, siren wailing and flashers smearing the palis blood red. The cottage was dark, but the Mori house and yard were garishly illuminated. Peter and Ben were using a compressor to wet down the roof with water from the pool; Stephanie and Matthew stood at the edge of the lawn, watching streams from the fire hoses arc through the air. Great hissing clouds of steam rose from the deadfall, but the fires still burned.

Matthew turned when he heard Tanner and me. His hair stood up in spiky points, his face was streaked with sweat, and he was wiping his hands compulsively on his shirtfront. In spite of the heat, Stephanie had thrown a sweater over her shoulders, and her fingers worked at its sleeves, wringing them. When she saw Russ, she burst into tears and ran to him.

"Oh, Russ, everything's going to burn," she said between sobs. "Why do these horrible things keep happening to us?"

He put his arms around her and made soothing noises, but kept worried eyes on the deadfall.

Matthew exclaimed, "It's all her fault!"

"Whose?" Tanner asked.

Matthew didn't reply, just clawed at his hair and ran his hand over his chin.

I went over to him. "Whose fault is it, Matthew?"

"Nobody's. I don't know what the fuck I'm talking about."

"Have you found Jillian?"

He shook his head.

Russ guided Stephanie over to us, one arm around her shoulders. "When did the fire start?" he asked her.

"Ben and I noticed it maybe fifteen minutes ago. We were sitting on the lanai talking about what we'd say at Mother's service and . . . For a while I thought I smelled gasoline. And there was a lot of cracking in the deadfall, but I didn't think anything of it. The dogs're always messing around in there. Then we both smelled smoke and ran over and looked through the trees, and we saw fire everywhere, from the beach all the way back to the road. Thank God we bought the compressor in case something like this happened and—" She broke off. "I'm babbling, aren't I?"

Tanner said, "That's okay, honey, you're entitled."

"Jill's been missing all day," she added in a small voice, "and I'm worried about her. She was missing the day of Iniki, too."

"She was okay then, she'll be okay now."

I glanced at Matthew. He stood, shoulders slumped, arms slack at his sides, not listening.

"You say you thought you smelled gas?" Tanner asked Stephanie.

"I did; Ben didn't, but he smokes, so his sense of smell isn't very good. Besides, it was kind of intermittent, like when the wind shifted."

Russ looked at me, and I nodded. Definitely arson.

For a moment we were all silent, watching the streams of water that seemed mere trickles compared to the intensity of the blaze. The night had been dead calm and humid, but now a strong wind began to gust from the east.

Stephanie said, "Oh, God, what if the fire spreads to the neighbors'?"

"It won't. They're getting it under control." But Russ sounded worried.

A stronger gust swept past us. A shower of sparks rose from the deadfall and danced through the air. Palm fronds rattled and the ironwoods bent and swayed. There was a cracking sound as one of their branches sheared off; something crashed against the side of the house. Matthew started and whirled, peering over there.

By the pool, Peter was still working the compressor, but Ben had stopped wetting down the roof. He stood with the hose dangling, staring helplessly at the wind-tossed trees. In spite of the outdoor lighting the night became very black. Stephanie put her hand to her lips, pale under her tan. Russ stood with his face to the sky, as if he were communing with one of the ancient spirits. And

Matthew said in an awed voice, "It reminds me of when Iniki started."

Alarmed, I looked up too. Dark clouds had blown in, swiftly blotting out the moon and stars. Was this the way hurricanes began? But this wasn't the season, and there hadn't been any warnings on the radio. Before Iniki, the worst in the island's recorded history, the residents had had many hours to prepare.

Suddenly rain began to fall on my upturned face. Huge drops that blew slantwise and splatted on the roof and the pool's flagstone apron. Stephanie closed her eyes, moved her lips as if in prayer. Russ grinned and squeezed her shoulders. Peter gave a jubilant shout and clapped Ben on the shoulder so hard it threw him off balance. And Matthew said in a shaky voice, "Why the hell are we standing here?" Then we all broke and ran for the shelter of the lanai.

Once huddled there, everyone was silent, looking out at the driving rain. Finally Stephanie laughed—a shrill sound edged by hysteria. She said, "I never thought I'd be glad to experience something like that again!"

"Like what?" Peter asked.

"Oh, right, you weren't here. It reminded me—all of us—of when Iniki hit."

"I thought that was in the afternoon."

"It was. One-thirty. The same kind of weather. Oppressive."

Ben said, "The calm was deceptive. We were up at Pali House, sitting in the patio. When the first winds started, we actually welcomed them, because they eased the heat."

Matthew added, "Welcomed them because we'd been dreading the hurricane's arrival since around eight the night before. First civil defense sirens went off at five-thirty that morning. When it did hit, it was a relief because at least something was *happening*. And it did get dark."

Stephanie asked Russ, "Where were you?"

"With my daughter, my mother, and some other relatives, trying to get to one of the shelters." His voice was heavy with emotion. "We never made it. The road was blocked by downed trees, so I ended up pulling my van into one of the dry caves. Other people who couldn't get through were in there. Man, was it scary when the eye passed over!"

Matthew shuddered. "Why are we reliving this?" he demanded. "Why can't we just be happy this rain is putting the fire out?"

And it was. Steam still rose from the deadfall, but the flames were no longer visible. A fireman emerged from the trees and came toward us. Ben and Russ went to talk with him.

Matthew was in bad shape, shaking and twitching. I said to Stephanie, "Why don't you and Matt go see if Jill's turned up at home? I'll check La'i Cottage and Mal-ihini House, meet you later at Pali House."

She flashed me a grateful look and went over to Matthew. Took his arm and said, "Matt, sweetie? Let's go see if Jill's come home."

He turned to her slowly, his face so expressionless that it seemed as unformed as a baby's. "Jill," he said. "She'll be at home by now."

"Yes. And I don't want to walk alone in the dark."

He nodded and took her hand. Together they began moving toward the road.

The fireman was leaving, and Ben and Russ came back to the lanai, their faces grim. Ben said, "They're pretty sure it was arson. One of the patches that didn't catch was soaked with gasoline."

Peter and I exchanged glances. "More of the same?" he asked.

"Why, now that you've called off the filming?"

"Maybe it was never about the filming."

"Maybe."

Russ put his hand on my neck, massaging it and staring out at the rain. It was letting up now, as if it had been sent for the exact purpose it had served. I looked up at him, saw the calm set of his features, and knew if I voiced the thought, he'd say that was what had happened.

One positive thing had come from the fire: it had saved me from taking an irrevocable step over a line that I still wasn't sure I wanted to cross. I wasn't a woman given to casual affairs and infidelity; neither was I one to lead a man to expect more than I could deliver. I'd play no more of these minor-league sexual games with Russ. When—or if—I decided to play, it would be in the majors.

I moved away from him. "I'll get started looking for Jillian."

Soft light glowed behind the shutters of La'i Cottage. I stopped under the dripping branches of an ironwood, frowning. I could've sworn the cottage was dark when Tanner and I passed it earlier. Perhaps Glenna had returned from Oahu?

The door was partway open, a sliver of light falling along the lanai. I went across the grass and mounted the steps. Sound came from inside—a woman crying.

I pushed the door open, stepped inside. At first the cottage seemed empty. Then I saw her, crouched by a native canoe that had been made into a coffee table.

Jillian.

Her hair was wet and matted, her face streaked with dirt and tears, her pale yellow dress torn and filthy. She looked up at me and said, "I can't find it."

My first impulse was to go to her, hold her, but besides the pain in her eyes there was fear. I held back, asked gently, "Find what, Jill?"

She hesitated, shaking her head as if she'd lost her train of thought. The fear in her eyes faded, and bewilderment replaced it. She was shivering.

I grabbed an afghan off a rocker and moved toward her slowly, as I would have approached an injured animal. "Find what?" I repeated.

"The suitcase. It was right here under the table."

"What suitcase? Whose?"

"Hers."

Glenna's? Her things were at Malihini House.

Jillian waved her arms violently. "It was right here!"

I moved closer. "Jill, why don't we get you up off the floor, and—"

"It was *here*! I've got to hide it. And later I'll send it . . . D'you know anything about overseas postage?"

Oh, God, she'd totally flipped out! I had to calm her, take her back to Pali House. "I don't, but I can find out."

"Will you? For me? And her? I can't trust Matt. Or Mother." She laughed harshly. "Certainly not Mother."

Was "Mother" Celia? And who was "her"?

I took two more slow steps and knelt beside Jillian, wrapping the afghan around her.

And smelled gasoline.

It was in her hair and on her dress. Faint, but unmistakable.

*Jillian* had set the fire?

"Somebody ought to have it," she said.

My mind was on overload. I wrapped the afghan more securely around her shoulders, said mechanically, "Have what?"

"The suitcase!"

Back to square one, and I had a feeling that if I questioned her further we'd follow the same elliptical path we'd taken before. "Look," I said, "I'll find it. I promise. And then I'll ask about the postage. Everything's going to be all right."

"That's what Matt says, but I don't believe him. It was small. Tan. With a combination lock, the kind with three teensy dials. D'you really promise to find it?"

"Really."

"Good. I'm responsible, you see. Tomorrow we'll take it to the post office at Waimea. They don't know me there. Most places they know me. I'm a Wellbright."

"I understand." I grasped her forearms, shocked at how thin they were, and began easing her to her feet.

"I'm the only one who cares. She's been nice to me."

Glenna hadn't been particularly nice to her, that I'd noticed. Who on earth was she talking about?

"It's good that you care, Jill. Now let's go home."

"Did you get caught in the storm? It came on so suddenly. That's the way they start, you know. You have to keep in mind the safe places, so you can take shelter."

"This way, Jill."

"I had no idea it was coming. I was upset, so I went out walking all day long. I walked partway up the trail, then back to the forest. I walked . . . Did you see the harvest moon? So strange."

"Watch that you don't trip."

"Yes, I have to be careful. I'm going to have a baby, you know. I hope it's a boy. I don't want a girl, not one with Ridley blood. There's something wrong with them."

"Walk over here so you're not in the road."

"Am I talking too much? I'm always saying things I shouldn't. I make bad things happen. Did you get caught in the storm? I didn't. I knew just where to go. . . ."

Matthew opened the door of Pali House as soon as I knocked. While I'd been locating his wife, he'd changed clothes—showered, too, judging from the comb tracks in his wet hair. When he saw Jillian, his face went slack with relief.

"Where'd you find her?"

"La'i Cottage. We'll talk about that later. Right now she needs attention."

"Give me a few minutes." He took her arm and led her from the foyer.

I went into the adjoining living room and sat down in a big leather chair. I felt drained by the events of the evening, barely capable of marshaling a coherent thought. Closing my eyes and breathing deeply, I tried to empty my mind. I couldn't quite accomplish that, but in a little while I felt better.

Matthew returned, went to the credenza, where a bar service was set out, and fixed himself a tall Scotch and water. Belatedly he offered me a drink, but I shook my head.

"She'll be okay after a good night's sleep," he told me. "Thanks for bringing her home."

I doubted Jillian would ever be okay unless he got her the psychiatric help she needed, but now wasn't the time to address that issue. "You're welcome," I said. "Where's Stephanie?"

"I sent her home. She's exhausted."

Weren't we all? "Matthew, I need to ask you a few questions. Are you aware that Jillian's pregnant?"

"That can't be! We don't—" He covered his embarrassment by sipping his drink.

"Well, she told me she is, and that she's hoping for a boy. She doesn't want a Ridley girl, says there's something wrong with them. Wasn't Ridley your mother's maiden name?" I'd seen it in the background check Mick had run on Celia.

" . . . Yes."

"What d'you suppose Jillian meant by that?"

"Damned if I know." Too quick a response. He understood what his wife had been talking about. "You say you found her at La'i Cottage. What was she doing there?"

"Looking for a suitcase."

"A suitcase?"

"A small tan one with a combination lock. You have any idea what that was about?"

"Well, I've got a briefcase that matches the description, but I don't know what she'd want with it or why she'd look for it at the cottage."

"She seemed to want to mail it to someone. She asked me if I knew anything about overseas postage. And she wanted to take it to the post office at Waimea, where nobody knows her."

"God, what is *wrong* with her?" He swallowed a third of his drink, eyes moving rapidly in thought.

"There's something else," I said. "The fire department believes the deadfall was doused with gasoline before it was set on fire. Arson. And I think your wife is the one who did it."

"Impossible!"

"Her hair and clothing smelled like gasoline when I found her. Didn't you notice?"

"No." He set his drink down and stood up. "Let me check on something."

He was back in five minutes, his face ashen. "I checked the supplies in the garage. We keep a good amount of gasoline on hand for the gardeners' tools and in case we need to use the auxiliary generator. Almost all of it's gone."

"Could Jillian have gotten at it while you were out looking for her today?"

He took his drink to the credenza and free-poured Scotch, nearly filling the glass. "Well, Jill's sly and has been known to slip in and out of places without anybody being aware of her."

"But is she strong enough to cart heavy containers all the way to the deadfall?"

"She's stronger than she looks—all that hiking. And the gas was stored in plastic containers. If she was planning this beforehand, she could've removed small amounts without anybody noticing."

"You have any idea why she'd want to set fire to that tract of land?"

He didn't reply.

I repeated the question.

He shook his head, but I could see understanding dawn in his eyes as he made connections. "Look, did you say anything about this to anybody else?"

"No. I brought Jillian directly here."

"I'd like you to keep it to yourself till she's lucid and I can question her."

"That's fair."

Matthew moved to the window overlooking the patio, stood with his back to me. The outdoor spotlights prevented me from observing his reflection in the glass. After a moment he said, "Thank you again for finding Jill, Sharon. It's been a very long day, and Mother's funeral is tomorrow afternoon. I'd like to be alone now."

\*    \*    \*

The chopper was still on the lawn in front of Malihini House, and Tanner must have been at Stephanie and Ben's. I went up the hill, peered over at the garage to see if Peter's Volvo was parked there. It wasn't, but if Glenna had returned she might've parked at the cottage and walked over to the Moris' to see what was going on. The house here was dark, but I made a quick check for her anyway. All the rooms were empty.

Back outside, I stood at the top of the slope for a moment, listening to a heavy vehicle move along the road. The last fire truck departing. When its sound had died away and the night was quiet, I went downhill and through the rain-wet papaya trees to the cottage. No Volvo. Glenna must've decided to stay overnight on Oahu.

On the other side of the vegetation that screened it from the cottage, the Mori house was still illuminated inside and out. For a few seconds I considered going over there, but decided against it; I wasn't up to making explanations about Jillian right now, and the talk that Tanner had promised me could wait.

The cottage was dark, as I'd left it. I went inside, turned on a small table lamp. Its glow lit up the center of the room, but didn't touch the clotted shadows around the periphery. I stood still, taking a physical and emotional reading.

Temperature: warm. Humidity: high. Smell: damp wood, some mildew, much dust and age. Age in the book bindings, the artifacts, the structure itself. Age in the emotions that were trapped here, too. I could feel nothing of Peter and Glenna, in spite of their recent presence. But

I could feel Elson Wellbright as if he were in the next room.

A cerebral man, yes. But a passionate man as well. Unhappy, longing for things that had passed him by. And what else?

Afraid.

I closed my eyes, breathed deeply, listened to the sound of the nearby sea. Other, more practical, investigators might scoff at this intuitive technique, but it had always served me well.

As surely as minute traces of years-old blood on fabric can be revealed under certain types of light, so can emotions trapped in a dwelling place be revealed to one who is receptive. I was receiving them now: hope, passion, anger, fear.

No, not anger—rage. And not fear—terror.

"Sharon?"

I started. Opened my eyes and saw Peter standing in the doorway.

"Are you okay?" he asked.

"Yes. I was just . . ." Now, how the hell could I explain what I'd been doing without convincing him that his investigator had totally lost it?

He came all the way inside. "You feel it too."

Surprised, I nodded.

"It gives me nightmares. I haven't had a decent night's sleep since I moved in here. Glen hasn't, either." Then he looked around. "Speaking of Glen, is she back yet?"

"She wasn't when I checked Malihini House a few minutes ago."

"Damn! Guess she's really angry with me."

"Maybe she's just coming to terms with the situation in private. The fire's completely out now?"

"Yes. We've decided the land has to be cleared. If Matt wants a monument to our father, let him replant it as it was before Iniki."

I thought of the lehua trees Elson had planted in 1969, in tribute to Mona Davenport. Some things could never be replaced. "Peter, you mentioned the feeling in this cottage."

"I think my father was very unhappy here."

"Mona Davenport described him as contented. He certainly sounded so in his journal."

"Maybe I made a mistake in not reading it. I had very little contact with him after I left the Islands."

"From what I read into the journal, he left here because of another woman, someone he'd met in his travels."

"Good for him. He deserved some happiness."

"She may have been from Santa Fe, New Mexico. At least, that's where they planned to go. My operative's checks didn't turn up any traces of them there, though."

"Well, I suppose he could've taken another name. When you've got money, it's easy to buy a new identity."

"Why would he feel he had to go to such lengths, though? And why move so far away? Why not just divorce your mother and move to one of the other islands?"

"Maybe the woman was as attached to New Mexico as he was to Hawaii, and he was in love and willing to make concessions. Besides, this is a small island, a small state. Even smaller when you're a member of a prominent family. My father probably wanted to make a fresh start someplace where people wouldn't constantly be pointing to him and rehashing his scandalous first marriage. He and Mother were not saints." He glanced at his watch. "Nearly midnight. I'll walk over to Malihini House with you, see if Glen's back yet."

I nodded, glad that Peter, in his concern for Glenna, hadn't thought to ask about his sister-in-law. I'd keep my promise to Matthew until he'd had time to talk with Jillian.

# APRIL 7

•

Kauai

**12:02 A.M.**

As Peter and I walked toward Malihini House, I heard the helicopter's engine start up, followed by the flap of rotors. Dammit, Tanner was leaving without the discussion he'd promised me!

Peter said, "Russ is flying Matt and Jill to Oahu."

"What!"

"Apparently she's had some kind of breakdown, serious enough to make him decide to check her into a hospital over there. A decision I heartily applaud."

And a decision Matthew must have made hastily after I left him. "Why's he going at this hour? Wouldn't it be easier to get her admitted in the morning?"

"It may take Matt a long time to make up his mind, but then he moves full steam ahead. Probably afraid that if he doesn't he'll change it again."

Or maybe he was in a hurry because he was afraid Jillian would be charged with arson. Even though I'd promised to say nothing about her being responsible for the fire, there was always the chance that someone had seen her transporting the gasoline cans to the deadfall, or that the cans would be recovered and traced to Pali House. Matthew had chosen to put a shield of influence and money around his wife.

When we reached the lawn, the chopper had cleared the trees and headed out to sea. I watched it, wondering if Tanner would return here tonight. Wondering if I wanted him to.

Peter looked up at the garage. "Glen's still not here. Tomorrow morning I'll call my friend who owns the equipment-rental house, ask him if he spoke with her and what her plans were."

"Let me know what you hear."

He said good night and left me.

I went up the slope to the lanai and collapsed in a chair. The sky was clear again, the Milky Way scattered across it like shaved ice. Odd to think of coldness on this warm night, but after the feelings I'd experienced at La'i Cottage I felt chilled at the bone.

My thoughts drifted to Hy, and I wondered where he was tonight. Usually I had some sense of him, no matter how far apart we were, but now I felt as if I were calling a cell phone that had been turned off. I tried to picture him in a hotel room in Honolulu, but couldn't. An airport? An airliner? Yes. He'd left, or was leaving, the Islands. He was working at shutting me out, in order to give me the latitude I needed to deal with the investigation and with Tanner. Working at it single-mindedly, but not with total success.

"Give it up, Ripinsky," I said softly. "We haven't lost each other yet."

## 11:35 A.M.

When Peter came by, I was sitting on the lanai with my coffee. Weariness born of the previous day's events and a restless night after Hy left had caught up with me, and I'd slept for nearly ten hours. While I was feeling refreshed and ready to tackle the investigation, Peter looked as though he'd spent the same ten hours wrestling with nightmares.

"I spoke with my friend," he said. "Glen dropped the camera off before noon yesterday. She told him she planned to do some shopping and spend the night in Waikiki. She had a return reservation on the first Hawaiian Air flight this morning."

"So you were right about her needing to get away for a while. She should be back soon."

He shook his head. "First flight's at five-thirty, gets in at six-oh-five. Even if she overslept and caught a later one, she'd be here by now."

"Maybe she made a stop on the way back from Lihue."

"Where? None of the shops're open that early, and she doesn't know many people. I've already called the ones she does, like Russ, Sue, and Eli, and they haven't seen her. I'm worried."

He might have cause for alarm after all. "Okay," I said, "are you sure she was flying Hawaiian Air?"

"My friend seemed sure."

"Then the first thing we need to know is whether she was on any of their flights."

"Will they give out that information?"

"Probably not to me, but somebody in RKI's Honolulu

office will have an airline contact." I got up and went into the house, Peter following. On the scratch pad beside the phone were several numbers scribbled in Hy's hand, one of them the office on Oahu. I hadn't wanted to call there yesterday, but now my sixth sense told me Hy was on his way home. I punched out the number, identified myself, and asked to speak with one of the specialists.

"Ms. McCone, this is Jerry Tamura. I was planning to call you later. Before he left for the mainland yesterday Mr. Ripinsky gave me a local address and phone number to trace for you. I was working something else, so I didn't get to it till this morning, but I have some information."

So that was what had happened to the scraps of paper I'd found at the sugar mill. As hurt as he'd been at the time, Hy had taken them with the intention of doing me a favor.

"Thanks for checking. What've you got?"

"The address is a house near Sand Island Access Road. It's owned by the Sunshine Corporation, which buys up and leases cheap properties all over the island. I'm working on finding out who's occupying it. The phone number is unlisted, but I've got a call in to a contact at Hawaiian Tel who'll get me the name and address of the subscriber."

"I really appreciate this, Mr. Tamura. But I'm afraid I'm going to have to ask for something else."

"No problem. Mr. Ripinsky asked that we assist you in any way possible."

"This shouldn't be too difficult. A woman named Glenna Stanleigh had a reservation on Hawaiian Air's five-thirty flight this morning. I need to know if she was on it, or any later flight."

"If you want to hold, I'll get on to my contact at the airline."

"*Mahalo.*" To Peter's anxious look, I said, "He's checking."

In a few minutes Tamura came back on the line. "Glenna Stanleigh was on the seven-thirty flight, arriving Lihue at eight-oh-five."

I thanked him again and ended our conversation. "Well," I said, "she arrived here at a little after eight."

"Now I'm *really* worried."

"Let me check one more thing. What's the license-plate number of your car?"

He wrote it on the pad while I looked up the number for Lihue Airport security. When a man answered, I identified myself as an operative of RKI and asked them to check the parking lot for Peter's Volvo. He called back in a little while, said it wasn't there.

"Where the hell did she go?" Peter asked.

I shook my head, very concerned now. It was a drive of no more than an hour and fifteen minutes from the airport to the Wellbright property; even if Glenna had made multiple stops, she should have been here by now. "It might be a good idea for you to go back to the cottage, in case she tries to call," I told Peter. "She may have had car trouble or some other problem. What time is your mother's service?"

"Two o'clock, at the church in Waipuna."

"Maybe Glenna will turn up there."

"Maybe." But he sounded about as optimistic as I felt.

*    *    *

After Peter left, I went down the hall on the opposite side of the house to the room where Glenna slept when she wasn't with him. It was a slim chance, but I hoped she might have left something behind that would give me an indication of her present whereabouts. The door was closed, and I hesitated briefly before opening it.

I'm not big on prying into other people's personal space, but in my work it's a necessary evil. All the same, I had to work harder at it now, in the aftermath of the intrusions that had nearly wrecked my life two months before. After a moment I pushed the door open and stepped inside.

Chaos reigned there, just as it did in Glenna's office at the pier. The bed was unmade; linens were rumpled and pushed to its foot, indicating that her nights here were as restless as those spent at La'i Cottage. Clothing was draped over every conceivable surface, including the head of a two-foot-tall Japanese statue. Half-empty cups and glasses stood on the nightstands, growing mold. I began searching, ending up on my hands and knees going through piles of books and papers on the floor by the bed. One of the stacks toppled, and I had to reach under the bed for it.

My hand encountered something that felt like a suitcase. I lifted the dust ruffle, looked under, and saw a briefcase—tan, with a combination lock. It had seen hard and frequent use; the leather was scratched and scarred. I dragged it out, noticed fading gilt letters above the latch: A.J.C.

Not Glenna's, but it looked like the one Jillian had described to me. What was it doing here?

The latch wasn't locked. I looked inside, saw an unlabeled manila folder. It contained only three things: a browning cream vellum envelope, a boarding-pass stub, and a China Airlines ticket. The used portion of the ticket showed that Ms. A. Carew had flown from Taipei to Honolulu on September 6, 1992; the unused portion was for a flight from Honolulu to JFK on September 11.

The day of Hurricane Iniki.

The boarding-pass stub was on Aloha Airlines, from Honolulu to Lihue on September 6. There was no return ticket. I opened the vellum envelope and slipped out a sheet of folded stationery. It contained three words in a backward-slanting hand: "Please forgive us."

Forgive who? For what?

Maybe Peter could tell me. The case must've come from his cottage, since Jillian had been looking for it there.

I put the folder back inside, closed the case, and headed for the cottage, but when I got there I found it deserted. Dammit, where was he? I'd suggested he stay there in case Glenna called. Maybe she had, asking him to meet her somewhere. Or maybe he was responding to another family emergency.

I went back to Malihini House, changed into a skirt and blouse that were suitable to wear to a funeral. Then I went to see if one of the gardeners could give me a ride into Waipuna, where the Datsun was still parked outside the Shack.

*     *     *

The woman at the helicopter tour office next to the grocery told me Russ was out on a flight but would be back to attend the service. To pass the time I went into the deli section of the store, ordered a pastrami sandwich topped with a ferocious assortment of condiments, and took it to a bench in the shopping plaza across the street. Children were playing on the swings and jungle gym while their mothers watched them from nearby picnic tables. Small-town life was going on at its pleasant and unhurried rhythm, and it seemed to me that I was the only one out of sync with it. I tore into the sandwich, realized I was gobbling out of frustration, and made myself eat more slowly.

When I finished, I balled up the wrapper, tossed it into a trash basket, and sat down again, watching the kids. One of them reminded me of Casey at the age she would have been when her mother died. Casey, the child Elson Wellbright had given up to Tanner. I recalled a passage from his journal, written on the day the public records showed she was born: "This is the saddest day of my life. I've gained, but lost. Irrevocably."

Why had Wellbright felt he had to give up all claim to his daughter? Why hadn't Russ told Casey her real father's identity? Was he waiting till she was older, or would he keep the secret forever?

Well, he'd promised to explain, and Russ was a man who kept his promises.

"Ms. McCone?"

I looked up, saw Donna Malakaua standing next to me. "Hello. How are you?"

"Today I'm better. Buzzy called me last night." Her round face beamed with pride.

"Oh? Where is he?"

"Honolulu. He got himself a job driving for some rich guy. And Amy, she workin' for him too. Buzzy says they gonna be on easy street soon."

How many times had she heard that before? And yet she continued to believe. "Did he give you his address or phone number?"

"Said he would, soon as they got settled. Right now they stayin' in some house the guy owns. He got a big place, back of Diamond Head. You gotta have megabucks to stay there."

"Well, it sounds as if the two of them have got a good thing going. If . . . When he gives you the address or phone number, will you let me have it?"

"Sure. You still stayin' at the Wellbright place?"

"Yes."

She shook her head. "Poor people, the mother goin' like that. I see they gettin' ready for the funeral over at the church. She musta been *pupule* to do what she did. 'Course, she was a Ridley, and those girls always were nuts."

I sat up straighter. "Oh? Why?"

"Well, the oldest killed herself—something to do with a busted marriage. The next one went schizo, died in a nuthouse on the mainland. Guess old Celia was the best of the lot, but look what happened to her. The brothers turned out okay, though." Donna pivoted, shading her eyes with her hand. "Look, there's the limo with the family. Pretty soon they be givin' old Celia her big send-off."

*    *    *

The small church was nearly full when I stepped inside. A mahogany casket covered with a blanket of plumeria stood on a trestle in front of a simple altar flanked by floral arrangements. The air was fragrant with their perfume. Stephanie, Ben, and Peter sat in the first row of pews, but Matthew apparently had been detained in Honolulu. Russ, Casey, and Mona Davenport were seated directly behind the family. I scanned the assemblage for Glenna, but didn't spot her.

Russ looked around, saw me, and motioned for me to join them. I hurried down the aisle, slid in next to him, nodding to his daughter and Mrs. Davenport. Casey smiled, but Mona returned my nod stiffly and looked away. Probably afraid that somehow I'd managed to ferret out her secrets.

Russ said in a low voice, "Sorry we didn't get to talk last night. I guess you heard I had to fly Matt and Jill to Oahu."

"He didn't come back with you?"

"Nope. He said he'd catch a commercial flight back to Kauai today. Too bad he's going to miss the service."

Peter had turned when he heard my voice. Now he whispered, "No word from Glen." The anxiety in his eyes told me he cared more for her than he'd previously admitted.

"Don't worry. We'll find her."

A murmur at the rear of the church drew my attention away from him. I glanced back there, saw a rumpled and breathless Matthew striding down the aisle. He slid in next to Peter. "Sorry I'm late."

"Doesn't matter, you made it."

A door to the side of the alter opened, and a white-haired man in minister's robes stepped out. Time for Celia's big send-off.

The minister said the usual things: devoted wife, loving mother, steadfast friend, servant of the community.

The children said the usual things: she nurtured, she loved, her death will leave a terrible void in our lives.

The friends said the usual things: always willing to lend a sympathetic ear, there when you needed her, a tireless volunteer.

No one said that Celia Wellbright had been inattentive to her children, had drunk too much, had been flagrantly unfaithful to her husband, had played the imperious queen of her own small dynasty.

No one dared to suggest there had been something wrong with this last of the Ridley girls.

That's the hypocrisy of funerals: don't speak ill of the dead, no matter what.

No matter if they deserve to be spoken ill of. No matter if they've hurt people and alienated their own families. Better to lie, because it eases everyone else's survivors' guilt.

I sensed that the family and friends of Celia Wellbright would suffer a long time in their various and separate ways for the damage she'd done during her time on earth.

As the mourners gathered at the graveside, Russ took my arm and said, "I don't put much stock in burials, and I'm sure you feel the same. Let's go talk."

"As long as it's not about us." I let him lead me around the church to a stone bench set under an arbor draped with fragrant yellow flowers. We sat silent for a moment, and then he said, "What a crock!"

"The service, you mean."

"Yeah. A saint she wasn't, but they made out like she's sittin' up there at the right hand of Mother Teresa."

"I noticed you didn't speak."

"If I'd been asked to, they'd've gotten an earful. Hey, what's this about Sweet Pea goin' missing?"

"She went to Honolulu yesterday, flew back early this morning, but never turned up at the estate."

"Christ, that's all Pete needs on top of Celia dying, the deadfall burning, and Jill cracking up."

"Speaking of Jillian, how did she seem on the flight to Oahu?"

"Pretty well sedated. I don't think she said a word the whole way."

"Matthew tell you where he was taking her?"

"Nope. I'm just the hired help to the lord of Pali House."

"Hired help whom he must heartily resent on account of his father's will. You want to tell me about that now?"

"I do. In a way it's a relief to be able to speak out after all these years. Only other person who knows what happened is Mona, and we've never talked about it. You were right on the money about most of the story, but you've only got the bare facts. It's the rest that matters. I'll start back before it all happened.

"Liza Santos was the little sister of my best friend. He got killed in a surfing accident right after high school.

Liza was havin' a rough time growing up; her family life was kinda ugly, and she got in trouble with the boys, too. But she was smart and pretty, like Casey, so I tried to look out for her like a big brother. After a while she turned her life around, like the good ones do, and got a full scholarship to the University of Hawaii."

"She was studying there when she met Elson?"

"Right. Worst thing I ever did was take her to Pali House."

"He seduced her."

Russ winced. "That's kind of a harsh word. He was lonely and felt that his life was over. And Liza was no innocent. Plus she needed affection and caring of a kind I couldn't give her. Elson was a gentle man, the father figure she'd never known. I thought that was all there was to it, didn't figure out what was goin' on till way too late."

"When you found out she was pregnant."

He nodded. "Elson was a nice man, but he wasn't strong. Certainly not strong enough to risk the flak he'd take if he divorced Celia and married her. And Liza didn't have it together enough to cut it as a single mother. Elson was scared, both for her and for the kid, so he came to me, asked me to marry her, be a father to the kid, protect them. And he gave me the money to start the charter service, not only because he wanted me to be able to support them properly but also because he knew it was my dream."

"But your marriage failed."

"Was a given. Liza really loved Elson, or maybe she just thought she did, but what's the difference? Point is, she didn't love me, and she didn't want to be a mom, and she hated living in what she called a shitty little house with a husband who was gone a lot of the time. She started doing grass and coke and hangin' with the wrong people. By the time I figured it out, she was hooked on heroin." He laughed harshly. "Seems like I was always a little slow figurin', when it came to Liza."

"Don't beat yourself up over that, Russ. You were doing what you could, what you had to."

"Maybe. It wasn't enough, though. At the end of four years Liza ran off with another druggie and I filed for divorce and custody. A year later she OD'd."

"Sad."

"Yeah, it was."

"Did anybody besides you and Mona know Elson was Casey's father?"

"Matt has always suspected. Liza told me he saw the two of them together in Elson's forest once, and he followed her a couple of times to meetings with his father. I suppose when I took Casey to Pali House the other day, it clicked. You saw the way he backed down about contesting the will."

"I also saw the way you reminded him who Casey's mother was."

He grinned wryly. "Guilty as charged. When you've spent your life knucklin' under to the likes of Matt Wellbright—"

"I hear you. Is there any way the family can contest that bequest?"

"It's pretty airtight. And as backup I've got an affidavit from Elson sayin' he's the father."

"Smart of you."

"No, smart of Elson."

"So that's it?"

"No, there's more. The important thing is why Elson thought Liza and the kid needed protectin'."

"And what's that?"

"Celia. She had a history of violence. Nothing major, but she was full of pent-up anger. Elson told me it came on early in the marriage. Jealousy, suspectin' him for no reason. Later there was stuff with the kids. Shouting, slapping."

"Child abuse."

"That's what we call it now. Back then people weren't as aware. And she and Elson'd get into it, only she was the one got physical first. Mona saw her beat horses at the ranch at Haena. She was legendary for gettin' drunk at parties and lettin' fly at anybody. Was Mona who told Elson Liza and the kid needed protectin'."

I thought about what he'd just said, meshing it with what Donna Malakaua had said about the Ridley girls. "Russ, were you close to Elson at the time he left Kauai?"

"Not as close as once. My marryin' Liza put a strain on things. And later I had to deal with Casey's reaction to her mom's death. Anyway, I didn't see much of Elson anymore."

"Were you aware he'd met someone and was going away with her to start a new life on the mainland?"

"I suspected he'd met somebody in his travels not long after I married Liza, but I couldn't get anything out of him. He was real private about it. Protectin' himself from Celia, I guess."

Protecting the woman, too. In his journals he'd only referred to her as "my Special One."

I asked, "D'you think Mona knew of his plans?"

"Probably. Why don't you ask her?"

"From the way she acted in the church, I don't think she'll talk with me. Could you try to persuade her?"

"Sure."

The mourners were leaving the grave site now, walking to cars parked on the shoulder of the road. I stood. "Thank you for trusting me, Russ."

"You're very trustable, pretty lady." He got to his feet too. I knew he wanted to touch me, and I badly wanted to touch him, but we both held back. "Where're you off to now?" he asked.

"Malihini House, to see if Glenna's surfaced. I'm really concerned about her."

"Well, if she's not there and you want to get a search started, give me a call. I'll drop by Pali House to pay my respects, but after that you can catch me at home."

Glenna wasn't at the house, but the light on the answering machine was blinking, and I pressed the play button, hoping for a message from her.

Instead it was Jerry Tamura at RKI's Honolulu office. Quickly I called him back.

"Ms. McCone," he said, "I have the rest of the information you need. The house on Kahai Street near Sand Island Access Road is leased to a Garvin Ridley. The subscriber on the unlisted number is also Garvin Ridley, and his address is on the Gold Coast, back of Diamond Head." I wrote it down as he repeated it twice.

Garvin Ridley. Same name as Celia's father. Of course, he'd be long dead by now, but hadn't Donna Malakaua said something about brothers? Perhaps this was Garvin Ridley Jr.

I said to Tamura, "Can you do a background check on Ridley for me?"

"I've already started. When do you need it?"

I stopped to think. This was a lead I should follow up, but was it right to go off to Oahu with Glenna missing?

Yes. It was too early to bring the police in on her disappearance and, when the time came, Peter's local status and influence would produce quick action. I couldn't go out and scour the island for her; I didn't know the territory and, if Peter wanted that done, he could enlist Russ and his chopper. And I had nothing else to do here.

"Mr. Tamura, is it possible for you to continue with this check now?"

"Certainly."

"Then I'll come over there as soon as I can get a flight."

Russ would have been happy to take me to Oahu, but this was one time when it was better to fly solo.

# APRIL 7

•

## Honolulu

**7:10 P.M.**

I rented a car at Honolulu Airport and took the freeway east toward downtown. I'd visited the city frequently over the past twenty years, and each time I was struck by its continuing metamorphosis. This evening there seemed to be even more spires reaching toward the cloud-streaked sky, even more glass gleaming in the sun's fading light. Yet when I exited for Bishop Street, the sidewalks seemed curiously deserted. Maybe Honolulu had finally reached the saturation point as far as development was concerned and, if so, what did that bode for the state's future?

A key card was waiting for me with the guard at the garage entrance of the Bishop Street high-rise where RKI had its offices. I parked in one of their assigned spots and took the elevator to the twenty-third floor, where Jerry Tamura had said he'd meet me when I'd phoned him after buying my ticket at Lihue Airport. A second guard in an RKI blazer greeted me there, examined my identification, and buzzed me in. After giving me a visitor's badge, she called Tamura.

Cautious people, RKI, even here in the land of the aloha spirit. And with good reason.

After a couple of minutes Tamura emerged through an inside door: a slender, attractive man in a bright green-and-yellow flowered shirt, whose flashing smile and merry eyes—if I knew the firm's operatives—concealed many unamusing secrets. No one who worked for RKI was exactly what he or she seemed, including the partners. My first dealings with Gage Renshaw and Dan Kessell—before Hy took them up on their offer of a one-third interest—had been edgy and distrustful, and I still didn't feel comfortable with them or their practices, which often strayed too far from the letter of the law. But I had to concede that Hy had brought more accountability to the organization. He was their best negotiator and highly skilled at getting clients out of tricky places and situations. Renshaw and Kessell hadn't willingly altered their stripes, but they didn't want to risk losing him.

Besides, I also had to concede that their specialists were good at accessing information that even Mick couldn't get hold of. Sometimes when I used their services I thought I must have tossed out my ethics along the way, but other times I thought I'd grown up enough to accept the fact that there are situations and people who won't be saved if the letter of the law is followed.

Tamura greeted me, offered coffee, then took me to a comfortable meeting room where a maroon folder labeled with my name was set out on the table. As we sat down, he motioned to it. "The information you asked for is in there, but I'll recap it for you. I don't think you're going to like what you hear."

"Oh? It's incomplete?"

"It's reasonably complete, but it raises one hell of a lot of questions. The background check on Garvin Ridley led me to two dead men: Garvin Ridley Sr., a cattle rancher on the Big Island, died in 1967; his son, Garvin Ridley Jr., died in 1990."

"So who's living in the house on Diamond Head Road? Who's leasing the one on Kahai Street?"

"The Diamond Head Road house is occupied by two males, one in employee status. Name of the employee isn't available, but the owner's calling himself Ridley. He purchased the house for cash in 1995. The Kahai Street house appears to be vacant; no phone. Was leased in the Ridley name a couple of months ago. I couldn't find anybody at the management company or realty who remembers anything more about either transaction. Do you want me to do more checking?"

"No, at least not for now. I'll take it from here. How're RKI's relations with the HPD?"

"Great. This is one of those rare large cities where the department fosters close ties with the private investigative community. A lot of us, myself included, are former cops; a lot of the cops do consulting on the side for security firms. Happens in a place where tourism's your main industry."

"So there'll be no problem with me working under your umbrella?"

"None whatsoever. I took the liberty of checking with

Major Harry Medina in the Investigative Bureau. He said anything you need, give him a call. Here's his card."

"*Mahalo.* I appreciate everything you've done for me." I tucked the card into the folder.

"One other thing," Tamura said. "Are you planning to be in town awhile?"

"I don't know. Overnight, anyway."

"Well, our hospitality suite's available, if you care to use it."

I considered. Most of RKI's offices had such a suite on the premises, for visiting operatives or clients who had reason to fear for their safety. The accommodations were usually luxurious, but the security measures could be oppressive. Still, I didn't want to waste time finding a place to stay.

"Thanks, Mr. Tamura," I said. "I'll take you up on your offer."

## 9:12 P.M.

My rental car was the cheapest Dollar had to offer, but still it stood out like a limo in the run-down industrial triangle wedged between the Nimitz Highway and Sand Island Access Road. After two wrong turns and a blunder into a dead-end alley, I found Kahai Street, a narrow three-block stretch with cars parked on either side of the broken pavement.

The buildings there were mainly of the corrugated iron variety—warehouses, auto body and paint shops, light manufacturing—but between them shabby houses and duplexes squatted, most set behind high chain-link fences plastered with No Trespassing and Beware of Dog signs. I parked well to one side, between a burned-out car propped up on blocks and a herd of grocery carts crammed with debris. Slouched down, I studied the house that was leased by the bogus Garvin Ridley.

It slumped between a warehouse and a tire store: bilious green, one small story perched on stilts above a collection of junk and rusted appliances. A torn and discarded mattress leaned against its fence, whose gate was chained and padlocked, and faint light leaked around its shutters. A sagging laundry line was strung between the rickety porch and a listing wooden post.

The night was still, hot, and humid. Jets rumbled above as they approached and departed the international airport. In between, other sounds echoed up and down the narrow corridor: dogs barking, TVs muttering and shrieking, a man and woman quarreling. Glass broke somewhere and in the distance a police siren wailed. I swatted at insects and tried not to breathe too deeply of the smells emanating from a nearby Dumpster. Thought of the fragrant, balmy atmosphere at the Wellbright estate and wondered what this place could possibly have to do with that family.

Half an hour passed without anything happening. Darkness fell. The lights continued to glow in the green house, but not too many of the other dwellings on the block were illuminated. Only two people passed my car, a stooped old woman with a tiny dog on a lead and a ragged man picking through the garbage cans. The sound

of a motorcycle and a flash of lights coming around the
far corner roused me from a partial stupor.

The bike came on slowly, avoiding the worst of the
potholes, and stopped by the green house's fence. The
rider got off, leaving the engine running. He unlocked
the padlock, unwound the chain, pushed the bike through
the gate. As he reclosed it and jogged up the rickety
flight of steps, I could make out only that he was male
and slender.

The man let himself into the house without knocking,
and after a moment the lights in the front room became
brighter. I eyed the bike hopefully. If I could get close
enough to read its license-plate number . . .

I was about to slip out of the car and go over there
when I heard footsteps—the scavenger returning along
the other side of the street. I slouched lower, waiting for
him to pass, and when he finally did, the door of the
green house opened. The slender man loped down the
steps, helmet under his arm, long light brown hair tied
back in a ponytail that bounced with every step. He
wheeled the bike out, secured the gate, and straddled his
machine while putting on the helmet.

The man revved the bike. Decision time: stay or follow?

Follow.

I kept a good distance behind the bike, my lights out,
through a series of turns that took us to the Nimitz Highway. After he'd turned east, I switched on the lights and
continued to follow. He established a leisurely pace over
a couple of canals and along the harbor. Where the Ala
Wai Canal cut inland at the start of Waikiki, traffic be-

came more congested, and snarled on Kalakaua Avenue. High-rise hotels and shopping centers rose on either side, blocking any view of the celebrated and overrated strip of sand, and pedestrians wandered across, oblivious to the honks of irate motorists. The slowdown didn't seem to faze the biker; he moved when the opportunity presented itself, without taking any crazy chances. I, on the other hand, became tense and irritated, afraid I'd lose him.

He took advantage of a limo pulling into a hotel driveway, sped around it and away. I sneaked through the next intersection on the yellow light, but maintained my distance. The garish neon splash was behind us now as we cut through a dark park and returned to the shore, the black outline of Diamond Head looming above. The biker skirted the mountain, heading uphill on a road where homes clung to the edge above a sprawl of lights. I dropped back even farther, saw a flash of red as he braked and turned into a driveway. As I drove past, a black iron gate swung shut in the high white stucco wall.

I kept going to the next intersection and checked the street sign: Diamond Head Road. Well, that figured. A couple more blocks and I made a U-turn and doubled back. The number on the gatepost confirmed that this was the Ridley house.

Neither it nor its lot was very large, and the lower story was screened by the wall and by thick plantings of palms and jacarandas that were illuminated by floodlights. Above them the second story was fronted by a covered gallery, also floodlighted, and in the middle of the red-tiled roof sat an odd cupola arrangement that would afford impressive views from sea to mountains. Small size, huge price tag, here on what Jerry Tamura called the Gold Coast.

This neighborhood was definitely not a good place to conduct a surveillance. Too many security devices, too many automatic connections to the police substation, too many watchful eyes. As I idled in front of the Ridley house, a man walking his dog stopped and stared at the car's license plate. Quickly I moved on.

If I intended to do any more investigating tonight, it had better be on Kahai Street.

The lights were still on in the bilious green house. As I got out of the car I could hear music: island sounds, sad and low. I looked up and down the street while rummaging in my bag for the set of lockpicks with which one of my informants had presented me. Thanks to his lessons in their use, I was as good with a padlock as any sneak thief.

No one was in sight, and none of the nearby buildings showed lights, although sirens howled blocks away. Good, I thought, that would keep the police busy while I accomplished what I had to here. I ran across the uneven pavement to the chain-link fence, crouched in the shadows, and got to work on the lock.

"Four minutes, McCone," I whispered as it snapped open and I removed it and the chain. "You're slipping."

I set the chain and lock on the ground, opened the gate slowly. It was well oiled and silent. Quickly I crossed the yard and ducked into the darkness under the house, went around the rusted appliances to the rear. There a second stairway rose to a tiny service porch. I tested the first step with my foot till I found a place where it wouldn't creak, mounted it, and repeated the process all the way to the top.

The shutters on the two small windows were open, revealing a dingy kitchen. Its counters were covered with dirty dishes, take-out containers, and an army of empty beer bottles. A fifth of an off-brand vodka and two smeared glasses sat on the old Formica table.

The house wasn't much: the kitchen and the front room, with another room opening off the hallway between, all of them probably on the small side. I went to the door leading in from the service porch and tested the knob. It turned. Careless, in this neighborhood.

If I'd been carrying, I might have chanced slipping inside, but even then it would have been a risky proposition. Instead I'd wait. I moved back from the door and dropped into a crouch at a place where I could see through one of the windows but not be seen. Ten minutes went by before a large figure appeared in the archway to the front room and shambled down the hall.

A man, tall and heavy, clad in shorts and a dirty white T-shirt that barely covered his big belly. He had black hair that hung to his shoulders and a round acne-pitted face that instantly identified him as Donna Malakaua's brother, Buzzy. He looked enough like her to be her twin.

Buzzy paused in the kitchen's entrance, blinking against the harsh light. Then he went to the table, picked up the vodka bottle, and drank directly from it. Set it down and stood there, his eyes coming to rest on the glasses. "Damn you, Amy!" he exclaimed, picking one up and hurling it at the sink, where it smashed loudly against the chipped porcelain.

If others had been in the house, his shout and the crash would have brought them running. But nobody came to see what the commotion was about, and after a moment Buzzy picked up the vodka bottle again and went back to the front room with it dangling from his hand.

Okay, he was alone and drunk, but also angry. Specifically, at Amy. George Kaohi had told me Buzzy was stupid and easily led but not dangerous, but maybe George had never seen him with a mad on. Still, there must be some way I could run a bluff. . . .

I thought about it for a few minutes, came up with a scheme that might work, and decided to risk it. Then I went around to the front of the house and up the steps. Pounded on the door, calling, "Buzzy? Buzzy Malakaua?"

There was a shuffling noise inside. He was standing behind the door, breathing heavily.

"Buzzy, open up!"

"Whaddaya want?"

"Ridley sent me."

Silence. Then the door opened a crack and his moon-shaped face peered out. "Who're you?"

"Don't you know?"

He shook his head.

"Well, shit, isn't that the way it always goes? I come all this way and—" I paused, glancing around. "Look, let's do this inside, okay? I can't stand here talking to you where anybody can listen."

He hesitated, looking confused, then opened the door wider. I pushed past him, taking a quick inventory of the contents of the small room. Lumpy rattan couch and chair, boom box on the floor, no weapons.

"Hey!" he exclaimed. "I didn't say you could come in here!"

"It's Ridley's house, isn't it?"

"Uh, yeah."

"Then you don't have any say. I'm here and I'm staying."

Buzzy shut the door, leaned against it. "You gonna tell me your name?"

"Sharon'll do for now." I went to the chair, sat, and motioned for him to take the other. "Where's Amy?"

"You know Amy?"

" 'Course I do. We go way back."

"You work for Ridley too?"

"Now you got it. Where's Amy?"

"Bitch split. This morning. Ran off with this Tongan she met in a bar over on the access road. Told me they was goin' back to Tonga so they could get in touch with his roots. Only root she wantsta get in touch with is his dick!" He paused, eyes narrowing. "How come you didn't know? I told Chip that when he come by before."

"I haven't seen Chip."

"He didn't go back to the house?"

"Not that I know of."

"Damn! I ask him to talk to Ridley, tell him I'm not happy here. That's what I get for trustin' a fuckin' house-boy."

Chip, the male in employee status at the Ridley house, and most likely the man on the motorcycle.

I asked, "Why aren't you happy here, Buzzy?"

"Well, look at this dump!" He swept his arm out and his fingers encountered the vodka bottle. Grabbing it by the neck, he tipped it up and drank.

"Yeah, it's pretty bad. And you must be lonely here without Amy."

"Bitch! I was takin' real good care a her. Brought her over here after Tommy died, got us on movin' stuff for Ridley. The idea was, if we did good, we was gonna go back to Kauai, take over Tommy's territory."

"I heard about Tommy. Did it happen at that old sugar mill?"

"Yeah. Man, was it scary!"

"You there when he died?"

"Shit, no! The way it was, Tommy'd got us this job makin' trouble for a film company was shootin' a movie on the island. Nothin' big, just little stuff—stealin', eh?"

"Who hired you?"

"Don' know. Postcards tellin' us when and where showed up at Amy's P.O. box, but she didn't even know who from. Tommy didn't tell none a us nothin'. The way he was, he hadda be the boss a everything. By now he's probably in charge a hell. Anyway, then he gets this idea he's gonna make the guy hired us pay bigtime."

"The guy? It was a man?"

"Don' know. Coulda been a woman, I guess."

"So Tommy decided to blackmail this person . . ."

"And he set up a meet at the mill. Sent the rest of us out

to the cane field, told us to come back in fifteen minutes. He figgered the guy'd cave in right away, but if he gave trouble, us showin' up would do the trick. But when we got back the guy was gone and Tommy was stone dead. *Stoned* dead." Buzzy laughed, gulped vodka. "The meet went wrong. Whoever it was gave him a hot shot. Needle was stickin' outta his *neck*, for chrissake. Amy yanked it out. Gross, man."

"I heard you had a funeral for him, threw him off the cliff."

"Amy's idea, dumb bitch. Said we hadda give him a Hawaiian send-off. What right's she got messin' with our traditions, anyways? She's a Jew from New Jersey!"

"So then you brought her here and got the two of you on with Ridley . . ."

"Well, she the one knew him. But I did the negotiatin'."

I glanced pointedly around the room, raising my eyebrows.

"Okay, I know what you're thinkin'. But when Chip said a free house, it sounded like a good deal. I was thinkin' TV and video games and maybe a Jacuzzi, and then I saw this place and, oh, man! We was outta money, though, really needed the work, and Amy told me just to put up with it, do a good job, and we'd end up on top again. Anyway, it was Chip who screwed us, not Ridley. He didn't give us enough walkin'-around money to eat on, and he wouldn't give us no dope or blow, neither. When he come by tonight, he give me a few bucks, about what it'd cost for a burger and fries at Mickey D's. And when I complain he say I should shut up or he'll take away my vodka so I'll be sober when I make my drops tomorrow night."

"Tomorrow night?"

"Yeah. How come you're not workin' on that?"

"Who says I'm not?"

"Well, so you know Ridley's got this huge shipment of pure Mexican H comin' in to this house, wants it out to his dealers pronto?"

"Yeah, I do."

Buzzy sucked on the bottle some more. "Smart, him usin' you. Broads're good for that kinda operation. People don't suspect 'em."

I smiled at him and nodded. He sure didn't suspect this "broad," and in his ignorance, he could be very useful to me. The problem was, I needed to get him to some place where I could control him.

"You didn't ask why Ridley sent me," I said.

"Why what? Oh, yeah."

"Ridley thinks it's better you're out of here when the shipment comes in. And he feels bad about sticking you in a place like this. So he asked me to take you to an apartment he keeps where there *is* TV and video games. A Jacuzzi tub, too. And he asked me to tell you he's sorry."

"He is?"

"Very sorry."

Buzzy grew dreamy-eyed. "Ridley's sorry. TV and video games and the Jacuzzi, eh? What else? A bar?"

I pictured the full bar in the RKI hospitality suite, suspected I'd regret my decision. "Yes, a bar. And we can order pizza or anything else you want—all on Mr. R."

"You part a the deal?"

"No."

He hesitated, shrugged. "Broads're more trouble than they're worth."

"So you want to go now?"

"Hell, yes. Sounds like downtown!"

"It is, Buzzy. It is."

# APRIL 8

•

Honolulu

## 12:32 A.M.

"You know, Buzzy, I've been thinking." I glanced at him, saw he was craning his neck to look at the downtown high-rises. We'd just exited the freeway.

"Uh?"

"The more I think about how you've been treated, the more pissed I get. And I've got a plan."

"Oh, yeah?"

"Tomorrow we'll go see Ridley, tell him you're not going to make your drops unless we renegotiate your deal."

"Renegotiate? You mean like a ballplayer?" He smiled, then frowned. "Nah, I can't do that. Chip, he told me to stay clear a the house while this stuff's goin' down."

"And you're going to listen to a *houseboy*?"

"Well . . ." His thick fingers tapped nervously on the dashboard.

"Think big, Buzzy. Chip's just a servant."

". . . Yeah, right. How come he's tellin' *me* what to do?"

"That's the spirit."

"If we go see Ridley, will you get me in? I mean, he sent you to me, sounds like he trusts you."

"No, Buzzy, you've got to do it. To guys like Chip and Ridley I'm just a broad."

"Yeah, yeah, I get it. And Chip, he screens everybody. What if he won't let me in?"

"Remember: he's a servant."

"Right, right. But what am I gonna say?"

"Leave that to me. I'll tell you and we'll rehearse it."

"Okay, you tell me and— Holy shit! *This* is where we're goin'?"

I pulled the car into the garage entrance of RKI's building. "This is it."

"Christ, it's a fuckin' *palace*!"

## 2:32 A.M.

"I think I've maybe like died and gone to heaven."

"Well, Buzzy, you look alive to me."

He was hunched in front of the big-screen TV in the living room of the hospitality suite, playing a video game called "Attackers from the Planet Svarth." A box containing the remains of an extra-large super combo pizza sat on the coffee table, and a tumblerful of RKI's best Scotch was only inches from his hand. In less than half an hour, he'd informed me, he planned to watch *Sxperts 3* on the Spice channel.

God, your average street criminal is stupid!

Relieved that he was fed, watered—or Scotched—and making no further demands for instructions on how to work the remote control, I picked up the phone and punched in the number for Malihini House. Around eight the previous evening I'd tried reaching Peter at all the Wellbright residences, but received no answer. Now I got the machine again, but it had a new message, in Peter's stressed-out voice: "Glen or Sharon, if either of you is listening to this, call me at my place no matter what the hour."

I broke the connection, dialed again. Peter answered on the first ring, sounding terrible. When I identified myself he said, "God, where *are* you? I thought you'd disappeared too!"

"Honolulu. I tried to reach you earlier. Glenna's not back?"

"No, and no word from her, either. After the funeral we all went out to dinner. Then I decided to drive to Lihue and talk with Wen Yamashita. You remember him, the cop from the shoot—"

"Yes. What did he say?"

"Under the circumstances, he's waiving the customary waiting period for missing persons. They'll start looking for Glen at first light. But, Sharon, I know something awful's happened to her."

"You don't know anything of the sort."

There was a pause; I heard ice clink. Did he intend to sit up the whole night, drinking? "Okay, maybe I'm worrying for no good reason. Maybe she took off because she's mad at me, and they'll find her in some hotel down at Poipu. I'll try to keep a positive attitude."

"And go easy on the booze."

"Don't worry, I'm pacing myself. How come you went to Oahu without telling anybody?"

"I picked up on a lead after the funeral." I glanced at Buzzy, who had just crowed in triumph at taking out another Svarthian.

"Tanner was worried. He wants you to call him, something about Mona Davenport."

"I'll talk to him tomorrow. You too."

"Wait, can't you tell me about the lead?"

"Sorry, I have to hang up now."

Buzzy announced, "Almost showtime. This button on the remote, I press it, and it charges the movie to Ridley's account?"

"Right."

"What's this thing called again?"

"Digital cable."

"It's like awesome."

"Especially if you're not the one paying the bill."

"Fuck the bill." He went to the bar, poured more Scotch, then shrugged and took the bottle with him. "Fuckin' died and gone to heaven. Really."

Where were the master criminals I'd grown up reading about? The Professor Moriartys, the Fu Manchus, the Goldfingers? Pure fiction, every one of them, and a good thing for the world, too. But sometimes when confronted with your ordinary dumb-as-a-post criminal, I felt wistful. . . .

**8:48 A.M.**

I'd caught a nap while Buzzy moaned and drooled over *Sxperts 3*, and when I woke he was passed out on the couch. I took a quick shower, got dressed. Then from the bedroom extension I called Major Harry Medina at the HPD. He said he'd be glad to meet with me as soon as I could get to headquarters. Did I know where they were located? Did I know where Beretania Street was? Get on it, and head toward the state capitol.

On the way out I checked Buzzy to make sure he was still breathing, then told the guard by the elevators that on no account was the client in the hospitality suite to be allowed to leave, as his life was in imminent danger.

Harry Medina met me on the wide front steps of the HPD's imposing beige stone building. He was a ruggedly attractive man, curly-haired and stocky, wearing a blue suit and a wild multicolored tie that hung askew from his unbuttoned shirt collar. As he took me up to his office he gave me a tour guide's commentary on the design of the relatively new headquarters, which incorporated state-of-the-art security features intended to help fend off potential terrorist attacks. The front railings, for instance, were too close together to allow a vehicle to crash through the doors, and the building could be completely and quickly shut down from a central command center.

At first the extreme measures struck me as an indication of a paranoid mind-set on the part of the department, but then I thought of Pearl Harbor. That event could never be erased from the collective consciousness of the Islands, and in these days of world terrorism the fears of law enforcement officers in this most remote of American outposts were fully justified.

Medina showed me to an office that was a study in

happy chaos: sports trophies stood along the tops of the bookcases and filing cabinets; files were stacked on the desk and the floor; several colorful ties were draped over an open locker door. Before he seated me the major proudly pointed out a still photo from the set of the pilot film for *Hawaii Five-O*, in which he and several officers had acted as thugs.

When we were settled with coffee cups in hand, Medina said, "So RKI's covering you while you're working in the Islands. You're staying here in Honolulu?"

"Only temporarily. I came over from Kauai on a lead I picked up there. In the process of following up, I discovered something that may interest you."

He raised a bushy eyebrow.

"You've heard about a new highly potent grade of heroin that's been coming out of Mexico?" Articles about it had appeared in the papers at home.

He nodded. "Very strong stuff, can be smoked or inhaled. Some of what they've seized on the mainland was as pure as 76 percent. And now there're rumors it's about to make its way over here."

"I can give you the local distributor and name the place where he's expecting a shipment tonight."

"You're right—I'm interested."

"I can also give you a guy who's supposed to be making drops for him. He's the kind who'll cut a deal and testify."

Medina looked at me thoughtfully. "You offering just because you're a good citizen, or . . . ?"

"Both. I don't like drugs. But I need something from you in exchange. The guy I mentioned can get me in to see the distributor. I need to ask him some questions about an unrelated matter. But I need backup, in case something goes wrong."

"This case you're working, it's got to do with drugs?"

"Not directly."

"But this distributor's connected."

"Yes."

He waited.

"It's a sensitive case, involving some powerful people. I can't go into it."

He shifted in his chair, ran a hand over his chin as he considered. "You're asking a lot. Even with backup things go wrong. It'll be on the department's head if something happens to a civilian—and a mainlander."

"I could sign a waiver, relieving you of responsibility."

"You could. On the other hand, I could insist you tell me the who and where of this. I'm sure you know it's obstruction to withhold information concerning a major crime."

"A major crime that hasn't come off as yet. And I'm not trying to be obstructive."

"Tell me this: how reliable is your source?"

"Let's say he's too stupid to have made the story up."

"Where is he right now?"

"I have him in a safe place."

Medina thought for a moment, tapping his finger on the edge of the desk. "Okay, Ms. McCone, you don't strike me as a game player. Neither am I. So I'm gonna be straightforward: in order to do what you ask, I'll have to check with my superiors. But in order to check with them, I've gotta have more than what you've told me.

Like names and places. And even then I can't guarantee that they'll give me the go-ahead."

"I realize that."

"I'll do my best to persuade them; that's all I can promise."

"That's fair."

He reached for a legal pad, picked up a pencil. "You want to get started?"

"Okay. The guy who's to make the drops is called Buzzy Malakaua. I've got him stashed in the hospitality suite at RKI."

"You can handle him okay?"

"Yes, he trusts me." After all, I'd delivered the TV, video games, pizza, and bar. To say nothing of the Spice channel.

"And the place where the delivery's to be made?"

I gave him the Kahai Street address.

"And the distributor?"

"Garvin Ridley. At least, that's the name he goes by. He leases the Kahai Street house and lives on Diamond Head Road."

Medina blinked and drove the tip of his pencil into the pad. "Son of a bitch! We've been trying to get something on him for a year now. Guy's elusive as hell."

"That's because he exists only on paper. The real Garvin Ridley died in 1990."

"Yeah, we're aware of that." A slow smile spread over Medina's face. "My ability to persuade my superiors just took a big leap. I'll go talk with them; you wait here."

I glanced at a side table where the major's computer

was set up. "I have another request: d'you think I could take a look at a recent autopsy report while you're gone?"

"Amuse yourself with some light reading?" He frowned at me, then relented when he saw I was dead serious. "Okay, come on over here, and I'll access it."

Tommy Kaohi had died of a hot shot, as Buzzy claimed. Combination of heroin and battery acid. One ingredient fairly easy to acquire if you had the connections; the other a staple of every garage. Puncture to the carotid artery. Fast and effective, but you had to get close to your victim.

Tommy must've been as stupid as Buzzy to let someone he was attempting to blackmail get within range to jab him with a needle. Or maybe he was just arrogant. Arrogance would be my pick. Only a man who was overconfident of his ability to control the situation would have sent four cohorts away while he confronted a potential victim. Maybe he'd done so because he planned to keep the lion's share of the payoff for himself. Either way, it didn't matter. He was dead.

"Our records confirm that two adult males occupy the Diamond Head Road house. That accounts for Ridley and the houseboy. We gotta think of some way to place Ridley at the house before she goes in there."

Lieutenant Jack Colby of the narcotics detail motioned to me as he spoke. Harry Medina had returned with the tall bald man in tow and told me we had a deal. Minutes later we were joined by Colby's partner, Dan Ramos.

"Yeah," Ramos said, "we don't want her twiddling her thumbs in his living room all afternoon."

Medina shrugged. "So you make up an excuse, call him."

"Won't work. Houseboy screens all calls."

"Then think of something he'll be sure to come to the phone for. You talked to him once. What'd you use?"

"Fire marshal. Something about a gas leak. He won't go for it twice."

"No, but there're people you'll *always* take a call from."

"Like who?"

Silence fell. Ramos, chubby and cheerful, wearing what was possibly the ugliest aloha shirt on the planet, picked up a rubber band from a container on Medina's desk and snapped it at the far wall.

I said, "The IRS. Or anybody having to do with taxes."

All three men looked at me, surprised. So far, out of familiarity that comes from working long hard hours together, they'd excluded me from their conversation, talked as if I weren't there. Now they nodded.

Medina said, "Last thing a dealer wants is the IRS breathing down his neck."

"Except a call from the IRS might panic him," I said. "What about the county assessor's office? Less threatening."

"Yeah," Colby said, "that's it."

Ramos let fly with another rubber band. "Okay, here's what your primo phone guy does: I say I need to talk with Mr. Ridley personally. It's about the adjustment of his property tax. No, it's about the *reduction* of his property tax."

Medina removed the rubber band container from his reach. "And the boy tells you Ridley's not taking calls."

"So I reinforce that it's essential I talk personally with Mr. Ridley. I reinforce it several times, if necessary."

Colby said to me, "Ramos is good at this stuff. Before he was a cop he used to sell a lot of life insurance—cold-calling, if you can believe that."

Ramos grinned. "Let's say the boy keeps on resisting; he's well trained. However many times I reinforce, he says no, I can't talk with the boss. Worst-case scenario, right? Wrong. Because then I say, 'Tell Mr. Ridley I'll call him back at two o'clock this afternoon. If he's still unavailable, we'll have to pursue the matter through other channels.' And I hang up."

Medina shook his head. "You call back at two, you'll be talking to his lawyer. These scumbags, they've all got a lawyer or two in their pockets."

"Uh-uh. You notice I said *other* channels, not *legal* channels. And I said tax *reduction*, not tax *increase*. It's still a nonthreatening situation—providing Ridley takes the second call."

"Okay," I said. "In the meantime, where'll I be with Buzzy Malakaua? He trusts me so far, but if he gets suspicious he'll bolt."

"You said he's stashed at RKI's hospitality suite?"

"Right."

"Then when we're done here, you head back, call us before you go to the suite. I make my first call to Ridley then. If he doesn't take it, you stay away from Malakaua, go shopping or something. Be back at . . . let's make it two, and ready to haul Malakaua's ass to the Gold Coast. Now let's take you downstairs and get you outfitted with a signaling device so you can summon backup if you need it. You put it in your pocket, it looks like the thing you control your car alarm with."

I nodded and stood, hoping I wouldn't have to use it.

"We're calling Ridley back at two," Ramos's voice said.

"Great. I'm just aching to shop till I drop."

I cradled the phone and said to RKI's guard, "Everything okay with the client in the suite?"

"He hasn't moved." He indicated one of the TV monitors, which showed Buzzy still passed out on the couch.

"Is there someplace where I can make some calls in private?"

"Third door on the right's a vacant office."

I went in there, sat down at the desk, and called Peter, who sounded on the verge of falling apart. The police hadn't turned up anything on Glenna. Next I called Tanner, who used up a full minute yelling at me for not telling him where I was going. He had good news, though: Mona Davenport had agreed to talk with me.

"I miss you," he added. "When're you coming back?"

"This evening, I hope."

"I could pick you up over there."

"No need. I've already bought my return ticket."

A silence. "Puttin' distance between us, aren't you?"

I had no good answer for that.

My last call was to my office. Ted first, for my messages, which were of no consequence. Then Mick. He still hadn't turned up anything on Elson Wellbright.

"You might as well shelve it for now," I said. "I take it you haven't started that check on Glenna?"

"Not yet."

"Well, get right on it. She's missing, and there may be something in her background that'll help us find her."

"Glenna is missing?"

"I'll tell you about it later. Maybe by then we'll have a happy ending."

## 2:04 P.M.

"I been thinkin' like maybe it's not such a good idea to go see Ridley."

"Why not, Buzzy?"

"Chip told me never to come near the house."

"Chip's just the houseboy, remember?"

"I don' feel so hot."

"You've got a hangover. You'll feel better when you get some air."

"Can't we go back? There's a fuck film at—"

"No more fuck films. Get in the car, Buzzy."

"I'd feel better if I had a drink."

"Later."

"How d'you know Ridley'll be home?"

"Don't worry about that."

"Chip might not let us in."

"Don't you remember what we rehearsed? You just keep repeating that, and he'll give in."

"Says you. Somethin' awful's gonna happen."

"Everything'll be okay."

"No, it won't. Shit happens. Least it always happens to me."

"Let's go over what you're going to say to Chip."

"Why? It won't work. He don' respect me."

"Chip doesn't matter. Ridley must respect you. After all, he hired you."

". . . Sort of."

"What does that mean?"

"Was Chip hired me. I've kind of like never met Ridley."

Christ, now he tells me!

"Buzzy, let's rehearse. Can't hurt to try."

"Okay. Um, let's see. . . . Somethin'-bad's-goin'-down-tonight-I-gotta-talk-to-Mr.-Ridley."

"Could you put a little more feeling into it?"

"Like how?"

". . . Well, imagine that the cops're chasing you and the only way you can escape them is to get inside that house."

"Cops? Oh, Jesus! Okay, okay. Somethin' bad's goin' down tonight. I gotta talk to Mr. Ridley. Somethin' *bad's* goin' down tonight. I *gotta* talk to Mr. Ridley. Somethin' *really bad's* going down tonight! I *gotta* talk to Mr. Ridley *now*!"

"Academy Award, Buzzy."

\*     \*     \*

"I really don' wanna do this." Buzzy's thick, clammy fingers gripped my forearm.

I could feel the fear in his touch. Smell it, too.

For a moment I felt sickened at how I'd tricked this pathetic, stupid man. I pictured the pride on his sister Donna's face when she told me he had a job driving for some rich guy. I pictured the shame that would be there tomorrow. But then I pictured the forever-still face of a college friend whom I'd found dead in bed of a heroin overdose.

"Come on, Buzzy. Get out of the car."

"I thought I told you never to come here," the houseboy said through the intercom in the box beside the gate.

Buzzy recited his lines, his fear making them even more convincing.

"What's going to happen tonight?"

"I *gotta* see Mr. Ridley! Now!"

A lock clicked, and the gate swung open. I gave Buzzy a thumbs-up sign and motioned him inside. It closed and locked behind us, and he looked over his shoulder, panicked. I took his arm and led him along a path bordered by palms and hibiscus and jacaranda toward the white house. When we reached the door it opened as if automatically, and we stepped into a marble-floored foyer.

A man moved from behind the door and shut it: medium height, slender, with light brown hair pulled into a ponytail. The biker who had visited the Kahai Street house last night, now clad in shorts and an orange T-shirt. Around thirty, he had regular features, a relatively unlined face, and jumpy pale blue eyes.

For a moment I thought I was looking at Eli Hathaway, the Wellbright relative who had played Elson in Glenna's film. Then I made the connection. Had to bite back a name as I rewrote the scenario I'd previously scripted.

The man looked from Buzzy to me and back again, frowning. Anger made his lips pull taut. "You didn't say you had somebody with you. Who's this?"

Buzzy was silent, studying his flip-flops.

I said, "We're here to see Mr. Ridley, Drew."

In the silence that followed, Buzzy looked up. "Drew? His name's Chip!"

Andrew Wellbright's face had gone pale. He stared at me, a tic making one of his eyelids flutter.

"Buzzy has some demands to present to Mr. Ridley," I told him. "But perhaps you could offer him a drink first? And you and I might confer privately?"

"My demands. Yeah. I wanna renegotiate!" Buzzy seemed to draw confidence from Drew's confusion.

Drew flashed him a poisonous look, then got himself under control. "Buzzy, that door over there leads to the room where the bar is. Help yourself to anything you'd like."

Buzzy glanced the way Drew pointed, then looked back at me, torn. "But what about—"

I said, "We'll ask Mr. Ridley to join us later. Right now I have business with . . . Chip."

Buzzy nodded and moved eagerly across the foyer.

"Jesus," Drew muttered, "why do all the idiots beat a path to my door?" Then he turned to me, eyes narrowing. "Okay, what the hell is this about?"

I took one of my cards from my purse and handed it to him. "My name's Sharon McCone. I'm a private investigator, affiliated with a local security firm. Your family hired me to trace your father."

He looked down at the card, then up at me, lips twitching nervously.

"Your father is all I'm interested in," I added. "I don't care about you or the business you're conducting here."

"Then what're you doing with him?" He jerked his chin the way Buzzy had gone.

"He was out by your gate, trying to get up the nerve to ring the bell. He says he's unhappy with the way Mr. Ridley has treated him."

"Oh? And what's that he said about tonight?"

"Just an excuse to get you to let him inside."

"I'm surprised he's got the brains to think of it. Why are you here?"

"I need to talk with you."

"I don't have time for that." He glanced distractedly into the living room behind him. "An important call's coming in any minute now. You'll both have to go."

"I can't do that. Your brother Matthew specifically asked that I see you. Now that your mother's died— You do know she's dead?"

"Of course I do! Gone straight to hell where she belongs."

"Then you realize the family has to have your father declared legally dead, so the estate can be probated."

"Doesn't concern me."

"Why not?"

"What did my brother tell you about me?"

"Enough so I have a good fix on what's going on here."

"He would let that out. He doesn't like my line of work, but he'll use me when it suits his purposes."

"For what?"

"The present situation, among others."

Best to let him think I was aware of that situation. "What others?"

He shook his head.

"Does he approve of you using the name Garvin Ridley when you're not being Chip the houseboy?"

"Man, he told you everything! No, he doesn't approve, says it's an insult to the memory of Granddaddy and Uncle Gar."

"I think it's brilliant." A little ego stroking never hurt. "Garvin Ridley's a paper man. You're just his houseboy. Anything comes down, how were you supposed to know what the boss's real business was or where he is? Zero accountability."

"Look, if you've got to talk with me, get on with it. Like I said, I'm waiting on a call, setting up a big deal. But I'm warning you: I can't tell you anything about my father. I was long gone from Kauai when he did his disappearing act."

"Something—anything—you remember from before he vanished might help me."

There was a noise on the terrace at the other side of the living room. Drew started, probably thinking it was the phone, but to me it sounded like a wind chime. This Mexican deal had him severely on edge.

"Look"—he glanced at my card—"Ms. McCone, before I left Kauai I was a mess. Did a lot of coke, was strung out, paranoid, afraid of everything. My father traveled a lot. He wasn't there for me, ever. I don't know a damn thing about him, and I don't give a shit what happened to him."

"But the estate—"

"I don't stand to inherit a cent. That was the deal when the family gave me the money to split."

"They paid you to leave Kauai?"

"They called it staking me to a new start. Fifty thou and a stint in a fancy drug rehab hospital. I got straight, then used the bread to start up my business, create my paper man. I'm on my way to being richer than all of them put together."

In the room where the bar was, music flared up. The Beach Boys.

Drew grimaced. "Jesus, now he's playing my jukebox! If I wasn't short on people to make the drops now that his broad's split, I swear I'd kill him!" He took out his wallet, peeled off some fifties. "Here. Give this to Buzzy, tell him Ridley's sorry for the bad treatment. Then take him back to the place where he's staying. There's a few hundred in it for you if you'll stick around and baby-sit him till tonight."

I took the money. "I'll give it to him, but I can't baby-sit. I've got a responsibility to your family."

"Too bad. You look and talk like you've got a brain. I could use you. By the way, how come Matt didn't mention you'd be coming by when he brought Jill here the other night?"

I'd been about to turn the conversation to the film company and Tommy Kaohi, but what he said derailed me. I feigned a coughing fit to give me time to digest the information. "Well, he was upset about her condition and probably distracted. How is she now?"

"Out cold. When you see Matt, tell him the doc's coming on schedule to give her her shots, and I stay in the room while he's with her, in case she says something."

"What would she say?"

"I don't know. Matt says she's out of control, acting weird, making bizarre accusations against him." He laughed, but without amusement. "Kind of like me, before I left there. I told him he should check her into the hospital where they sent me, but he wouldn't go for it. Which makes me think there might be some truth to her accusations, whatever they are. Matt looks and acts like one of the missionary fathers, but they all had their sneaky side, and he's no different."

I thought back to the night of the fire. Jillian hadn't made any accusations against her husband in my hearing, but he'd been disconcerted by something she'd said to me. "Would it be okay if I looked in on her?"

He glanced back at the living room again.

"I know—your call. But it'll only take a minute, and when I see Matthew—"

"Okay, go ahead, but make it quick. Up those stairs, second door on the right."

Jillian lay on her side under a dark blue comforter in the king-sized bed, her pale hair spread out on the light blue pillow. The air conditioning hummed softly, and she made little snoring sounds. I went over to the bed, saw someone had combed the snarls out of her hair; she looked clean and well cared for, but utterly dead to the world. When I touched her shoulder it provoked no response.

"Jillian," I whispered.

Nothing. She was too deeply sedated to know I was there.

"Jill, what do you know that he doesn't want you to tell anybody?"

A little sigh escaped her parted lips.

Well, there wasn't anything I could do for her now, but I'd tell Jack Colby and Dan Ramos she was here, ask them to get her into a hospital where she'd be safe till this business with her husband was resolved. I patted her shoulder, hoping a reassuring touch would communicate itself at whatever level of consciousness she was currently existing on. Then I went back downstairs and found Drew still in the foyer—very jumpy now, snapping his fingers and glancing at his watch. His call was late.

"You'll get Buzzy out of here?" he asked, motioning toward the room where the Beach Boys were extolling the virtues of California girls.

"Sure."

"*Mahalo*." Then he said, "Say, I just remembered something. Yesterday morning Matt met up with a woman when I dropped him for his seven-thirty flight at the airport. Pretty little babe, long light brown curls. He took her bag; they went into the terminal. D'you know who that was?"

"Glenna Stanleigh, Peter's filmmaker friend."

"Oh. I thought maybe she was the reason Jill's making accusations."

I didn't reply immediately, because I was trying to take in this new information. Matthew had flown back to Kauai with Glenna. Why hadn't he mentioned it to anyone?

## 7:10 P.M.

The whole time I was making my official statement at the HPD, I was alternately troubled by the specter of Buzzy's terrified and betrayed face when I turned him over to Ramos and Colby, and the image of Glenna and Matthew entering the terminal at Honolulu International together. I was anxious to get back to Kauai and question him, but when I finished and asked Colby if I could leave, he told me not yet.

"Harry Medina wants to talk with you, but he's tied up for a while. You can wait here for him."

"Here" was a small windowless interrogation room. I looked around it in annoyance.

"Sorry, it's the best we can do at the moment. You want anything? A Coke? Some coffee?"

"No, thanks. I'll use the time to make some calls."

First to Peter. The KPD, he told me, had assigned two officers to look for Glenna. They'd covered the hospitals, hotels, public beaches, and campgrounds without finding either her or the Volvo. Tanner and some of his pilot buddies had organized an air search, but with no results.

"This is looking very bad," he said. "Wen Yamashita

told me the first few hours after a person disappears are the most important to finding her alive."

"I've heard that too, but I think the statistic applies more in the case of child abduction. You're going to have to hang in there. By the way, have you seen Matthew?"

"He left a while ago to drive over to Princeville Country Club for a meeting with Michael Blankenship, our attorney. Why?"

"Just wondered if he's heard how Jillian's doing."

I ended the conversation and pressed the automatic dial button for Mick's condo. He wasn't there, but I tracked him down at the office. "Working late, aren't you?"

"Couple of new skip traces, and besides, Lottie's still showing her girlfriend the sights."

"Did you manage to get to the check on Glenna?"

"Yeah. I left you a message at RKI."

"I haven't been back there. You can recap it in a minute, but right now I'd appreciate it if you'd pull the Elson Wellbright file, see if there's any mention of this name: A. Carew, or a variation."

"You know, I think there is. The name's familiar." Keys clicked. "No, no, no." More clicking. "Yeah, here it is. *National Geographic* article on Bali, published in 1989. Photographer's Abigail Carew. Funny, though, I could've sworn I saw the name someplace else. Damn! It was— Oh, sure, the check on Glenna. Her mother's name is Abigail Carew."

For a moment I couldn't believe what I was hearing. Then the full impact of his revelation hit me.

*I loved my mother, but she was never home. She was a*

*photojournalist and traveled a lot, so I was raised by nannies and then shipped off to boarding school in England. When I was at UCLA, Mom ran off with another man. . . .*

A photojournalist: Abigail Carew.

Another man: Elson Wellbright.

So *that* was Glenna's hidden agenda.

"Shar?" Mick said.

"Thanks, you've been a big help. Good luck with those skip traces."

I broke the connection, looked up Mona Davenport's number, called her. When I identified myself she sounded subdued and reluctant to talk.

I said, "I have only a few questions for you, Mrs. Davenport, and then I'll leave you alone. Am I correct in thinking that in September of 1992 Elson Wellbright intended to move to the mainland with a photojournalist named Abigail Carew?"

Silence. Then: "So you found out about her. May I ask how?"

"Please just answer the question. This is urgent."

"Well, yes, he did."

"Tell me about her."

"She was from Australia. Married, with grown children, and out of love with her husband. She and Elson met on assignment in the late eighties, arranged to work as a team whenever possible. He lived for the time they spent together in various places, but after several years both of them wanted a more settled arrangement."

"She came to Kauai that September?"

"Yes. I warned Elson it was unwise, that Celia might

find out, but he badly wanted Abigail to see the island before he left forever. So I kept Celia occupied for most of the visit."

"When did Abigail and Elson leave?"

"The day before Iniki. There was a hurricane east of the Big Island that looked threatening, but Elson had been tracking a smaller storm—Iniki. Knowing our weather system as he did, he was more concerned about it, so they decided to spend the night on Oahu before flying to the mainland the next day."

"They were going to New Mexico?"

"I have no idea."

"He didn't tell you their destination?"

"He said Abigail had business in New York City and planned to deliver his manuscript to the literary agent who had agreed to represent it, but he was going to their new home. She was to join him there in a few days."

"I find it hard to believe you had no address, no way to get in touch with him."

"That was how Elson wanted it. He said cutting all ties was the only way he could disappear completely."

"And they needed to do that? Disappear?"

"Abigail's husband was a very powerful and possessive man. And Elson . . ."

"Yes?"

"Elson had appropriated large amounts from the family's liquid assets. He was afraid Celia would come after him and take legal action."

"I see."

"He wasn't committing a crime, Ms. McCone. What he

took was far less than he'd inherited from his father, and it isn't as if this is a community-property state."

"I realize that."

"Is there anything else?" Her tone was clipped and defensive.

"No, Mrs. Davenport, you've told me what I needed to know."

## 9:41 P.M.

As I watched the neon high-rise glare of Oahu disappear into the distance, I thought about the events of September 1992. Put all the things I'd learned since I'd been in the Islands into a coherent, unshakable order. Then I began thinking about the police search for Glenna, ruling out various possibilities on a logical basis. . . .

# APRIL 8

•

Kauai

## 10:57 P.M.

*Dark here among the cane fields. Only the misted lights of the missile range and the green-white-white wink of the airfield's beacon.*

*No headlights behind me, none ahead. That's good.*

*Park behind the trash dump like before?*
*Drive in and risk being trapped there if he returns?*
*Time. Time is precious.*
*Drive in.*

*Mill looks the same, all tumbled in on itself and silvered by the moonlight. No sound except the sea and the rustling of some night creature in the brush. No car—where would it be stashed? Smell from that refuse is stronger. Or is it . . . ?*

*No, not that.*

*Not that!*

\*   \*   \*

*Funny, the wall wasn't pulled away like this when I searched the place last Friday night. Where's my flashlight? Bottom of my purse, as usual. Got it.*

*And here inside we have the car. Peter's Volvo.*

*And Glenna . . . ?*

She was lying on the backseat, and only the fact that she'd been bound and gagged gave me hope she might be alive. I yanked the door open, put a hand on her neck, feeling for a pulsebeat.

She flinched, pulled away violently.

"Easy, Glenna, it's Sharon." I turned her on her back so she could see me. Her eyes were huge and terrified, but soon the fear leaked from them in a trickle of tears.

"Let's get you out of here." I began working on the knot of the cloth that covered her mouth, a filthy rag that had probably been left behind by the squatters. My thumbnail tore; I cursed but kept working till the knot yielded and I could pull the cloth free.

She tried to speak. At first nothing came out; then in a hoarse whisper she said, "Water?"

I'd seen a half-full bottle of spring water on the backseat of the Datsun. "Hold on, I'll be right back." I hurried out there, found it. Took it back, propped her up against the door, and held it to her mouth. "Only a little at first."

She drank, some of it dribbling over her cracked lips.

I felt around in my purse for my Swiss Army knife and went to work on the ropes that bound her wrists and ankles. When they were free she still couldn't move them.

"Numb," she whispered.

"They will be, for a while." I gave her more water, then

looked over the seat back to see if the keys were in the ignition. They weren't. "D'you know if there's a spare key anywhere on this car?"

She shook her head.

I backed out of the door, inspected the glove box and the ashtrays, felt around for a magnetic container under the bumper. Nothing.

"Let me massage your feet and legs," I said to Glenna. "I'll have you out of here in no time."

"Scared." Her voice was stronger now.

"Don't be. I've got things under control." I gave her more water, then began trying to get her circulation going. After a few minutes I asked, "Any feeling in your feet?"

"Some. Don't think I can walk yet. Got to get out of here, though. He said he'd be back tonight."

"I know you ran into Matthew at Honolulu International. How'd he get you here?"

"Said he wanted to talk, since I'd probably be marrying Peter. Thought I should see the family's other properties. Stupid me, I was flattered, bought into it. What he wanted to do was offer me a lot of money to leave the Islands. He knows who I am, what I'm after."

As soon as she spoke the last words, she looked as if she wanted to take them back. I said, "I know about your mother and Elson Wellbright."

"How?"

"We'll talk about that later. You refused the offer, of course."

"Didn't want money. Wanted to know what happened to my mother. Wanted Peter."

"So Matthew left you here to think it over. He say what time he'd be back?" She shook her head. I let go of her and got out of the car.

"Don't leave!"

"I'm not." I shone my flash around the mill. There was room to pull the Datsun in here, transfer her to it. "Be right back."

"Wait!"

"Quiet, Glenna!" Now I heard a car gearing down on the highway. I slipped outside, saw its headlights turn off into the cane fields. "Christ!"

The car was coming too fast for me to load Glenna into the Datsun, much less drive out of there. I ducked back into the mill, yanked open the driver's door of the Volvo, found the trunk release, pulled it. "Glenna, can you put your arms around my shoulders?"

"Think so."

I got hold of her, pulled her from the backseat. Dragged her to the rear of the car and propped her against the opening. Then I lifted her legs and rolled her into the trunk. Her eyes were huge with fright.

"You'll be okay in here," I said. "Just keep quiet."

I slammed the lid before she could protest and raced out of the mill. The headlights were slicing along the dirt track. I plunged into the brush.

*Okay, what now?*

Call 911.

I yanked the cell phone from my bag and punched in the number. Gave my name and location, said I'd found Glenna Stanleigh and that someone was trying to kill us.

Twenty feet away a dark-colored Buick was pulling up on the Datsun's bumper.

"Keep the line open," the dispatcher told me.

"Can't." I broke the connection.

Matthew got out of the Buick. Stood looking at the Datsun, then stared at the mill.

He wasn't armed, at least not with a gun, but that didn't make him any less dangerous. I suspected he'd thrown the rocks at me when I went into the deadfall in spite of his insistence that Jillian would never hide there. He'd killed Tommy Kaohi with a hot shot—easy enough to lay hands on when your brother's a major distributor. He might have brought another lethal dose with him tonight.

Matthew went to the front of the Datsun, raised the hood, and disabled it, as he had Friday night. Then he turned around and scanned the shadows. I remained still, barely breathing. A mosquito landed on my upper arm. I ignored the sting, concentrated on Matthew.

His stance was alert, every sense primed for danger. He began moving slowly toward the mill.

How long before the police could get here? Not soon enough, if he thought to check the Volvo's trunk. In a crouch I began moving through the brush till I was only a couple of yards away from him.

He stopped, looking around again. I froze. His senses were too keen; I wouldn't be able to take him by surprise, and surprise was my only advantage against a large, strong man.

I'd have to create a diversion. Lead him away from here until the police could arrive from Waimea.

He reached into his shirt pocket and took out an object

that at first looked like a large marking pen. Uncapped it. The moonlight shone off the hypodermic needle as it had shone off Tommy Kaohi's earring during the improvised funeral service.

He stepped into the mill, moved toward the rear of the Volvo.

I raised my arm and let my cell phone fly at his head.

I whirled and ran through the brush, dodging and weaving. Behind me I heard a startled cry, and then Matthew began running after me.

Heart pounding, adrenaline flooding my limbs. Up the rise, past the *heiau*, a quick jog to the right. Across barren moon-bathed ground toward the shelter of the wind-rippled cane on the adjacent acreage.

Thrashing and grunting behind me. He stumbled, fell. Cursed and scrambled. Started running again.

I burrowed deep into the cane. Crouched between the stalks, sucking in warm, damp air. Listened.

Nothing but the pulse of the sea.

A minute. Still nothing.

He had me trapped here. Playing statues, waiting me out. Listening for a telltale breath or rustle.

Well, I could play statues too.

*I know what happened in September of 1992. Enough of it, anyway, and the rest I can surmise. The story's there, in what I've found out about the Wellbrights. In the note in Glenna's mother's briefcase. But mostly it's there in Jillian's disjointed monologue after I found her at La'i Cottage the night she set fire to the deadfall.*

*It was Jillian who had written "Please forgive us" and tucked the note into the case. I should've realized that as soon as I saw it. Hadn't I seen the beginning of the same message written on the sand in her childish back-slanting script? Jillian, still consumed by guilt, still asking for forgiveness.*

*Don't know if she was living in the present or the past when she set fire to the deadfall. Probably the present. She wanted the truth to come out. But when she went to the cottage, drenched by the storm that was so like the beginning of Iniki, she was back on September 11, 1992— the night she took shelter in Elson's cottage and found Abigail Carew's briefcase—*

A cracking sound. A rustle. Silence. Matthew, close by now. I couldn't see him, but I felt his presence.

Moonlight bathed the top leaves of the stalks, but it couldn't penetrate below. If I stayed still, he wouldn't spot me.

Silence again, except for the ripple of cane, the crash of the surf.

*Jillian and Abigail. What happened to each is tied to the other.*

*Abigail came to Kauai on September 6. In spite of Elson's efforts to keep the visit a secret, Jillian, the wanderer, found out. Perhaps the two women struck a rapport. At any rate, I can't see Jillian deliberately giving Elson and Abigail away. But I can see her letting something slip accidentally. And that was when, as she said*

*during her crying jag after the party at Pali House,*
*everything ended.*

*On September 10, before Elson and Abigail could*
*leave the island for Oahu, someone killed them. Most*
*likely shot them during a confrontation, with one of the*
*guns from the cabinet in the cottage—*

Matthew was moving again. Moving with the wind,
thinking it covered the rustling and snapping. Passing me
now, only yards away. Going deeper into the cane, toward
the sea.

I held my breath and suffered the sting of insects. Dust
tickled my nose and I choked back a sneeze. Listened to
more rustling and snapping. More movement of the
stalks, and then he was gone.

A trick, or was he disoriented too? Whichever, I didn't
dare move yet. He might be waiting right out there with
that deadly syringe. . . .

*September 10, 1992. The bodies were in the cottage,*
*they had to be buried, and Elson's forest was safe and*
*convenient. It would take two people, though.*

*Matthew and Jillian. No one else he could trust to help*
*him.*

*While other islanders mobbed the stores for emergency*
*supplies, Matthew and Jillian worked to conceal the*
*crime. Worked into the night, with only the light of the*
*harvest moon to aid them. And in the morning Jillian was*
*driven from Pali House by guilt and revulsion. Went wan-*
*dering in spite of the hurricane alert.*

*In the confused aftermath of Iniki any remaining traces*

*of the crime and cover-up were lost. By the time the family hired detectives to trace Elson, the trail that had never existed was presumed to be cold. Would have remained cold if Jillian hadn't secreted the briefcase away and later mailed it from Waimea to Abigail Carew's home address in Australia. Still, it was nearly six years later, when Glenna arrived on the island, that discovery became a real fear and Jillian's guilt became a real threat. . . .*

I'd been hiding in the cane for what seemed like hours but in total couldn't have been more than five minutes. Time to double back to the mill, be there when the police arrived. I began crawling between the plantings, trying not to bump the stalks. The earth cut into my palms, lacerated my knees, but I gritted my teeth against the pain and kept going.

At the edge of the field I hesitated, facing the barren moonlit area between there and the trees that ringed the *heiau*. A run across it would expose me. . . .

Dammit, I needed a weapon! But I'd stuck to the letter of Hawaii's law, had left Peter's gun at Malihini House. I had my Swiss Army knife, but it wasn't any use at a distance, and not much more in combat with a large man carrying a lethal syringe. My purse held many other objects, though. Could I simulate a weapon with one of them?

I felt through it. Wallet, checkbook, lipstick, sunglasses, small long-handled flashlight—

It was the right color, would gleam like gunmetal in the moonlight. And if I positioned my hands on the bulb end in a certain way, it might resemble a handgun.

I slipped it out, extended it in two hands.

Yes!

Still I hesitated, palms clammy, body cold in spite of the balmy night. I took a deep breath, let my adrenaline surge to a higher level while I listened to the sounds around me.

Whisper of cane, crash of surf. Deceptively quiet, but time was running out.

I told myself I was playing a role. Use the prop well, and it'd come off. I grasped the flashlight in both hands as I would my .357 Magnum and ran across the open space, sweeping it at the shadows. The moon was my spotlight.

Under the trees by the *heiau* I crouched, listening again.

A rudden rustling behind me.

I spun around, went into a shooter's stance, bringing the flashlight up.

Matthew staggered to a stop perhaps a dozen feet away, panting, hair hanging over his forehead, glasses askew. A ray of moonlight rippled through the wind-tossed branches and shone off the needle in his right hand.

"Don't come any closer," I said. "Drop the syringe on the ground and kick it over here."

He held on to it, lowering his hand to his side. With his other he pushed back his hair, straightened his glasses. One lens was webbed with cracks; maybe that would prevent him from seeing this wasn't a gun.

I said, "I know about your father and Abigail Carew. I found Glenna, and she's safe now. And I've called 911; the police are on their way. You're going to drop the syringe. Then we'll go back to the mill and wait for them."

"I can't do that."

"Yes, you can. I'm offering you a way out of a six-year nightmare. All you and Jillian did was improperly dispose of two dead bodies."

Surprise showed in the lines around his mouth.

I added, "I know Celia killed them and asked you to cover up for her."

Long silence. Then: "If that was true, it would make us accessories after the fact."

"She was your *mother*, Matthew. D'you really think your local prosecutor will press charges? Especially after the way you and Jillian have suffered?"

No reply. He was thinking it over, trying to figure if there was any evidence that would link him to Tommy Kaohi's death. "What about the Stanleigh woman? She'll claim I kidnapped her at the airport."

"Did you?"

"No. I brought her here so we could talk in private. She got hysterical, attacked me."

"Well, there you go. And I'll tell you, she's plenty scared. Probably scared enough to accept your offer."

Sirens in the distance now. Matthew ran his tongue over his lips, looking at what he still thought was a gun. Gauging his chances of overpowering me.

"I'm a good shot," I said. "I couldn't miss at close range."

He shifted from foot to foot, glanced at a helicopter that was rapidly approaching offshore. "How'd you find out about Mother?"

"Russ told me about her history of violence. And I saw

the film footage of her right before she went off the cliff. She hadn't visited any of the earlier shoots, so she didn't know how much a made-up Eli Hathaway looked like Elson. Something snapped when she saw him. Her face was enraged, her arms were out to push him. She meant for *him* to go over."

Matthew nodded, his body sagging. He looked down at the syringe as if he was thinking of using it on himself. Then he hurled it away, and it bounced off the top slab of the *heiau*. His mouth twisted in an effort not to cry.

He said, "The day she died, when I told Jill . . . Jill said, 'Celia was trying to kill your father all over again.'"

Now the helicopter was homing in on the cliffs, searchlight sweeping the ground. Matthew raised his head, stared blindly. Looked back at me, eyes panicked. I sensed what he was thinking: no way to back out of this mess, no way to go forward. He was smart enough to know he'd be charged with kidnapping and probably connected with Tommy Kaohi's death.

Suddenly he moved. At first I thought he was going to attack me, tensed and set myself. But he veered away from me, past the *heiau*, his footsteps slapping on the hard-packed ground.

Heading for the sea.

The police chopper's light found and followed him, and by the time I reached the edge of the rise, he was standing on the cliff. I shouted, "Matthew, come back!" but my words were lost in the engine's roar.

He looked sidelong at the breadfruit tree, then up at the helicopter.

"Don't!" I started after him.

Too late. He went up on his toes, arms spread, and launched himself in a graceless dive into the sea.

Another desolate ghost, looking for a way home.

# APRIL 9

•

Kauai

## 6:53 A.M.

Tanner was waiting for me when I came out of the brightly lit police substation at Waimea into the predawn murk. He'd left the chopper amid a gaggle of its official cousins near the parking lot.

"Hey, you okay?"

I nodded wearily, preferring to ignore how horrible I felt.

"Caught the news on the radio, talked to a guy on the force. Pretty radical stuff. Too bad about Matt."

"He took the easy way out of a no-win situation."

"Well, anyway, I thought I should fly down, give you a lift back. Where's Sweet Pea?"

"Inside, with Peter dancing attendance. And I don't think you want to be calling her that anymore. Sweet, she ain't."

"You sound pissed."

"I am." I started toward the chopper.

"Don't you want to wait for them?"

"No. Peter, Ben, and Stephanie drove down together.

The cops aren't finished with them. Won't be for a while. I am, though—with Glenna, anyway."

"You want to tell me about it?"

I leaned against the big red bird, rubbing my forehead, where a headache throbbed. "Yeah, I do. Ms. Sweet Pea has been lying to me the whole time I've been here. Well, maybe not technically, but she sure hasn't been telling me everything. If she had, it might've saved three lives: Tommy Kaohi's, Celia's, and Matthew's."

"My brah filled me in on most of it."

"So you know Glenna's mother was—"

"Yes. And I know what happened to her and Elson."

"Good. I don't think I could go into that one more time. Glenna found her mother's briefcase in the attic at her father's house outside of Melbourne when she returned to Australia to settle his affairs. It was in a mailing carton, addressed to Abigail Carew and postmarked Waimea in November of 1992—two months after she left her husband, and around the time Jillian would've felt strong enough to drive there and send it. Inside were Abigail's airline ticket and passport, Elson's manuscript and journal, and a note of apology that Jillian wrote. The carton had never been opened."

"So Glenna started checking up, found out who Elson was."

"Ironically, with materials on investigative techniques that I'd provided, because she expressed an interest in doing a documentary on my business. Eventually she connected with Peter and manipulated him into backing the film, so she could use it as a cover to come over here, get close to the family, and find out what happened to

Abigail. Her presence stirred things up: Matthew figured out who she was, and he and Celia panicked. Jillian's guilt became more than she could handle."

"Abigail was her mother, Sharon. She had a right to know."

"Sure she did, but I also had a right to know what was going on with my own client. When she realized she was into more than she could handle, did she tell me the whole story? No! Not then, not when we discovered that somebody—Matthew, with Ben's help, it turns out—was monitoring her every move at Malihini House. Not even when one of the lowlifes Matthew hired to scare her off took a shot at her. Not even when Celia died!"

"She explain why not?"

"Oh, sure. Hy was right on about her wanting to grab a piece of the Wellbright fortune by marrying Peter. And she's not even ashamed to admit it. D'you know what she said to me? 'You're so good at your work that I thought you'd figure it out on your own. Then Peter wouldn't know I manipulated him into backing the film, and he and I could be together.' The woman caused three people to die and let several others be endangered because she wanted the good life! Well, the hell with her!"

Tanner was watching me with an expression that was half amusement, half admiration.

"What?" I demanded.

He shook his head, smiling.

"Don't you go holding out on me too, Russell!"

"I was just thinking that when you get mad, you've got more fire in you than Kilauea."

"Damned right I do! Your Pele goddess has got nothing on me!"

He came over, put an arm around my shoulders, pressed my head into the curve of his neck. "You know," he said, "I'm gonna tell Casey who her real father was and what happened to him. She's old enough now for a lesson in how folks who have everything can screw up and waste their lives, even in paradise."

"And a lesson in how not to waste hers. By the way, did you hear anything about a major drug bust on Oahu?"

"Nope."

"Well, there was supposed to be one last night, and the distributor they're nailing is Drew Wellbright."

"No!"

"Yes."

"You have a hand in that?"

"Uh-huh. I'll tell you about it later." I reached into my purse, located the wad of bills Drew had given me for Buzzy, and pressed them into Russ's hand. "You know Donna Malakaua? Crystal Blue Inspiration?"

"Sure."

"Give her this money. Tell her it's for her brother's legal defense fund."

"Don't tell me that moron Buzzy was involved with Drew."

"He and I will be the prosecution's star witnesses."

"That I'd like to see. Might even fly over for the trial."

"You do that." I closed my eyes as I leaned against him.

After a bit he said in too hearty a voice, "So where to now? Malihini House to pick up your gear, then Hotel-november-lima?" The phonetic alphabet designation for Honolulu International.

"Not yet."

"Oh?"

"You know that ledge in Waimea Canyon where you left me off the first time we flew together? I want to go there and watch the sun rise with you."

It was the only place I could think of to say good-bye.

Russ and I sat on the ledge, our feet dangling above the canyon floor, holding hands. Across from us the rugged peaks were backlit by streaks of pink and gold.

We didn't speak, and as the colors grew more intense, I felt my anger with Glenna ebb and flow. Then all of a sudden it was gone, as if the sky had leached the fire from me and claimed it for its own.

Finally he said, "You know, the ancients believed there's a language of the heart that we can understand if we only take the time to listen. That's what you're listening to now."

"Am I? I've been hearing mixed messages the whole time I've been on this island."

"Yeah, but even in the most complex mixes there's one sound that stands out. The message you're getting from Hy is stronger than any I could ever send you. I know it, and so do you."

I squeezed his hand, stared at the now fiery peaks. We were both feeling the same sadness and regret, but mine would fade as I crossed the Pacific toward home and the future. He would remain here among reminders of what might have been.

He said, "I like Hy. Dammit, I admire him. And it's not easy to feel that way about the man who's got the woman I want. But he's an exceptional guy—takes one, to let go and walk away peaceably like he did, when his guts were screaming for him to hang on and act unpeaceable as hell."

"You're an exceptional guy, too, Russ. You prove it every day in the things you do for the people you care about."

"*Mahalo*." He ran his finger across my cheek, kissed my forehead. "Sun's risen, pretty lady. Our time here's done. There's a midday flight from Honolulu to San Francisco. I'll take you over there."

I smiled at him. "*Mahalo*, Russ."

# APRIL 10

•

Touchstone

Hy had heard my approach and was waiting beside our dirt strip when I brought the rented Cessna 150 to a stop on the concrete pad next to the 172 that he apparently still had on loan. While I shut it down and gathered my things, he wedged chocks under the wheels, then came around to help me out.

"About time, McCone," he said.

His matter-of-fact words were the same he'd spoken years before, when I'd also appeared unannounced at the door of his Mono County ranchhouse, some five months after we'd met. Today he didn't even act surprised that I'd guessed he was here.

He shut the plane's door, thumped the wing. "Where'd you find this puddle jumper?"

"You don't recognize it? Old Two-five-whiskey?"

"Christ, it gets more scabrous by the hour! Cheapest thing the FBO had available, right?"

"You got it."

We started across the ice plant–covered ground toward

our stone cottage. The flowers underfoot were in full bloom—magenta, red, orange. Suddenly something caught my eye and I stopped, pivoting. An earthmover.

"Ripinsky! It's started!"

He grinned. "This morning. New contractor bulldozed the old foundation."

"*New* contractor?"

"I fired Virgil. Like I've been saying since we hired him—"

"'What kind of a name is that for a contractor, anyway?'"

He took my hand and led me over to where one day our house would stand. There was no sign of the old fire-blackened foundation.

I asked, "So what's this new guy's name?"

"Florian."

"You went from a Virgil to a *Florian*?"

"Don't worry. He's smart, honest, and his crew shows up on time and sober. At least they did this morning."

"Miracle of miracles." I stared at the bulldozer, my eyes misting. Hy had walked out on me on Kauai with no reassurances that we could put our relationship back together, but still he'd had enough faith in us to hire the new contractor and press forward with our building plans.

"Glad you're home," he said, shyness edging into his voice.

"Me too." Now *I* was sounding shy!

"Heavy-duty stuff, what happened with the Wellbrights."

"It was in the news here?"

"Some of it. The rest I got from Tanner. He tracked me down through our Honolulu office yesterday, said he'd brief me, since you probably wouldn't want to talk about it yet."

". . . He say anything else?"

"You mean personal? No."

I glanced at him, saw his neutral expression. Went over to the bulldozer and kicked its tire to see if maybe I wasn't dreaming the whole situation.

"By the way," Hy added, "he asked me to tell you that Drew's been arrested and Stephanie's moved Jillian to a good private hospital where she'll get the treatment she needs. He also said that it looks like Glenna's going to grab that brass ring she's been reaching for."

"Meaning Peter will marry her. Oh, well, maybe a conniving woman like her is what he needs to help him kick that island into the twenty-first century." I paused. "Aren't you going to ask what went on between Russ and me?"

"No. What matters is you're here."

"Just like that—don't ask, don't tell?"

"It's a policy I've always subscribed to."

Now I frowned. "What does that mean?"

He grinned and shrugged.

"Ripinsky, you never—"

His eyes shone devilishly. "You'll just have to guess at that, now won't you?"

I pursed my lips, considering this new possibility.

"Ah, McCone," he said, "I purely *love* keeping you off balance!"

All right, he'd had his revenge. I glared at him for a moment before I relented. "Well, as far as I'm concerned, you can keep me off balance for the rest of my life."

Then, when I saw his smug grin, I added, "Maybe."

## 5:55 P.M.

The phone receiver began a series of staccato beeps.
I stared as if it were a foreign object, then replaced it
in the cradle. My world had tilted a few minutes ago,
and everything seemed askew.

I went over to the windows and looked down at the
lower deck of the Sea Cliff house where the post-
wedding party was coming to an end. It was a perfect
September day, warm and clear, without a wisp of fog
to spoil the view of the Golden Gate—the start of the
season we San Franciscans consider our summer.
The guests were dressed in brightly colored clothing,
ranging from shorts and Hawaiian shirts to formal attire. Typical eclectic crowd for a California wedding.

And it had been a terrific wedding. My friend and

operative, Rae Kelleher, and my former brother-in
law, country music star Ricky Savage, exchange
vows by the deck rail, the Pacific gleaming in th
background. Then the band struck up the title song o
his new album, *Red*—written and recorded as hi
wedding surprise for Rae—and the serious partyin
got under way. Caterers passed through with gallon
of champagne and mounds of shellfish, caviar, an
hot hors d'ouevres; we ate and drank like pigs i
heaven. The wedding cake—nontraditional choco
late—was decimated minutes after the bride an
groom cut it. Even Ricky's six children by my siste
Charlene, initially subdued by their father's remar
riage, perked up and were soon behaving in the vari
ous modes that had earned them the nickname th
Little Savages.

When it came time for Rae to change from he
wedding gown to going-away clothes, I went insid
with her to perform my final maid-of-honor duty—
namely, to ensure she and Ricky didn't miss thei
honeymoon flight to Paris. The phone was ringin
and she said, "Why don't you get that? I'm ol
enough to dress myself." So I left her and went to th
living-room extension and picked up.

And my world changed.

Now I put a hand to my hair, touched the circlet o
autumn flowers I wore. It was wilted. My dress, a sil
swirl of similar shades, was rumpled, and I was bare
foot because I'd been dancing. On the deck below, th
band had stopped playing and people were starting t
drift inside. Soon they'd be spilling up the stairway t

watch the couple leave, and I'd need to be on hand and smiling as Rae tried to lob her bouquet at me.

"God, how can I?" I whispered.

Behind me I heard footsteps and voices. The room was filling up, but I stood frozen. I *had* to pull myself together, turn around.

*You've been through lots worse, McCone. Just act as if nothing's happened. Pretend you never picked up that receiver; don't wreck Rae and Ricky's moment. Plenty of time to break the news later.*

I squared my shoulders, took my own advice, faced the crowd. They were all talking and laughing, but the sound seemed curiously muted. I spotted Ricky's youngest child, Lisa, a gob of frosting on her cheek. My office manager, Ted Smalley, and his partner, Neal Osborn, looked handsome in vested suits and wild ties. Attorneys Anne-Marie Altman and Hank Zahn held hands with their adopted daughter, Habiba Hamid—proof that some families, no matter how oddly assorted, worked. And there was Hy Ripinsky, my very significant other. . . .

Hy was talking with Ricky's manager, Kurt Gird-wood, and didn't notice me. Quickly I turned away, started walking toward the staircase Rae and Ricky would be coming down. I couldn't let Hy see me; he'd instantly know something was wrong. In the years we'd been together I'd never once been able to conceal my true feelings from him.

A tap on my shoulder. Mick Savage, Ricky's oldest son and best man, and my agency's computer expert. His blond hair was tousled and he had traces of bright red lipstick on his mouth. Charlotte Keim, the source of the lipstick and another of my operatives, clung to his arm.

Mick said, "Wedding came off okay, huh?"

I managed a grin. "Great. And neither of us lost the rings."

"What the hell's taking them so long?" He glanced at his watch, probably anxious to get out of there and back to the condo he and Keim had started sharing two weeks before.

"They're going to *Paris*, darlin'," she said. "Takes time to get gussied up for a trip like that."

"Hell, Dad's probably grabbed Rae for a quickie."

"Let's have a little decorum here," I told him. Not that the remark offended me; knowing the bridal couple, it might very well be accurate. But Mick expected an auntly rebuke and would have found it odd had he not received one.

Then Rae and Ricky came down the staircase. She was stunning in a blue suit, her long red-gold curls loose on her shoulders; his handsome face looked happier and more at peace than I'd ever seen it. He caught my eye, pointed to Rae's bouquet, and winked. I shook my head, made a fending-off gesture.

Raising his hands for quiet as he did on stage, he called, "Okay, folks. It's time for the next lucky couples to learn their fate! Gentlemen first—preferably single ones." As the men moved forward, he turned his back, waved Rae's lacy green garter in the air, and hurled it over his shoulder. It landed in the hands of Jerry Jackson, his drummer.

"Been there, done that!" Jerry yelled. But he pocketed the garter carefully and grinned at his pretty blond woman friend.

"Now it's the ladies' turn," Ricky announced, motioning for us to draw closer. When I didn't move, he looked at me and frowned; he was another man I had trouble deceiving. Quickly I stepped forward, and he shrugged: Sister Sharon, as he sometimes still called me, was simply being weird again. "Throw it, Red, so we can get out of here."

Rae pivoted and heaved the bouquet over her shoulder; she must've been on radar, because it flew straight at me. I sidestepped, and it ended up in Keim's arms.

"No way!" Charlotte exclaimed. "Rae may be the marryin' kind, but not *this* gal!" She tossed the flowers away, and Ricky's college-age daughter, Chris, caught them. She blushed, rolled her eyes, and smiled up at her date, a UC Berkeley wide receiver.

I let out a sigh, glad that this ordeal was nearly over. Catering people appeared with bags of confetti, and then Rae and Ricky ran the gauntlet to a waiting limo. As it drove off, more trays of champagne were circulated, but the party had a definite winding-down feel.

"McCone." Hy came up behind me, put his hands on my shoulders.

"Hey there." I rested my cheek against one of them. "Well, we got off scot-free in the garter-and-bouquet department, in spite of the happy couple's intentions."

"You sure that's a good thing?"

The question surprised me. "Since when have we needed legal sanction—" My voice broke, the strain overwhelming me.

For a moment Hy didn't speak, just tightened his grasp on my shoulders. Then he said softly, "I've been watching you. You've done a good job of fooling everybody but me. What's wrong?"

". . . Let's go down on the deck, and I'll tell you."

The sun had dipped below the Marin County headlands, and the temperature had dropped. The musicians were packing up their gear while the caterers moved about filling plastic bins with plates and silverware and glasses. I went to the rail and leaned there, staring at the slow-moving lights of a departing container ship.

Hy came up beside me. "If you're cold, you can have my jacket."

"I'm okay."

"Temperature-wise, maybe. Now, what's wrong?"

I turned toward him. Drew comfort from his sensitive dark eyes and the concerned lines of his hawknosed, mustached face. Felt, with a painful and unexpected jolt, how empty my life would be should I lose him.

He took my face between his hands, eyes gentle on mine, and waited.

"There was a phone call when Rae and I went inside," I finally said. "From my brother John. I've been keeping the news to myself because I didn't want to upset the kids and Ricky. Even after he and Charlene got divorced, he'd remained close—" I broke off, sucking in my breath.

"Something's happened to Charlene?"

I shook my head.

*If you put it into words, it makes it real.*

"Who, honey?"

*Atypical term of endearment, for Hy.*

"My father. He's . . . he's dead. He had a heart attack this afternoon. In the garage of the San Diego house, all alone, working on some carpentry project."

*There, I've said it. Pa's dead. And in spite of all the death I've seen over the course of my career, I don't know how to deal with this.*

Hy did, for the moment. He put his arms around me, pulled me close, and held me.

## 11:17 P.M.

"Can't sleep, McCone?"

"Uh-uh."

"Sure you don't want me to fly you down there in the morning?"

"No. A commercial flight's faster."

"At least let me come along. I should be there for the funeral."

"Didn't I tell you? There won't be one. Pa didn't believe in them. John's having him cremated, and on Monday the two of us will scatter him at sea."

"Just you and John? What about the others?"

"Charlene's at a conference in London. Patsy can't leave the new restaurant. John couldn't get hold of Joey—his phone's been disconnected."

"Well, if I went down with you, I could rent a plane and fly it while you and John scatter—"

"No, I'll do that. Besides, there's something else I need from you."

"Just ask."

"It's kind of a big thing. Would you mind the agency for me? Whenever I went away before, I put Rae in charge, but now—"

"No problem. I'm between projects, but even if I wasn't, I'm always here for you."

"I know."

*But now I know that "always" is a lie.*
*Now I know that, in the end, death is the only certainty.*

To read more, look for *Listen to the Silence*
by Marcia Muller